Regarding Heart

Also by the Author
Vertical Hold

Regarding Heart

LAUREL BAUER

ROCKINGSTONE BOOKS

For
Deez, Drewski, Beeje, J, AD Esq, RB aka Chowa,
Dex, Roonie, and the Maizette

Contents

CHAPTER ONE

A Stairwell Encounter

One winter evening in 1985, as a thick-falling snow continued to descend over the city of Chicago, Frieda Zale set herself to gather her courage. That she lacked courage was perhaps the last thing one might guess about her. For she had a nose of a certain size, and this was often thought to denote courage when other features rallied 'round to good advantage. So, Frieda did make a generally pleasing impression. Yet there was a hint of some lack. For one thing, her brown hair refused to hold a shape. It verged on downright disarray without conveying anything of the sensuality such disorder can. And consider her habits. She smoked and drank with an intensity bordering on joie de vivre; and now well into her thirty-first year, she still slept alone with the hall light burning and the radio on.

What was Frieda afraid of? Don't ask. Her fears were pervasive and specific. They touched everything that was not Frieda, and, perversely, everything that was Frieda too. Indeed, from this perspective they might hardly be worth remarking on, were one not bound to consider as well where she might be without them. For when Frieda went forth,

Frieda did not go forth undefended. She had a sharp eye, a quick tongue, and an urgent spirit.

Though the evening was already quite late, she was only now preparing to leave her apartment. She put a cigarette between her lips before reaching for her snow boots. Several years earlier, in a gesture of solidarity with a non-smoking suitor, she had made it a point not to light up in the course of completing an action: no smoking, for instance, between pulling on the left and right boot. "En train de," that gentleman had suggested playfully, unaware that among the world's languages, it was French that Frieda feared most. Her Francophobia notwithstanding, he had kept his protestations of affection fierce and frequent, but in the end, he did not win her. Given her age and what were known of her prospects, one might have expected Frieda to extenuate on his behalf; but Frieda Zale was very far from ready for that.

"Oh, what the hell is this?" she demanded aloud, jerking the boot zipper over the innumerable tiny obstacles which threatened its smooth transition. A certain tension marked her approach to even simple tasks. This had been called irritability; but it was, she hoped, seen rightly, something more appealing than that.

Sirens sounded in the distance and she heard them with a sense of relief. Several blocks away the fire engines were rolling out of the station on 55th Street. A snowy, bitter night, especially one with deep drifts and a sharp wind blowing, inevitably brought to certain desolate neighborhoods the ruination of uncontrollable house fires. Without question this was rotten weather. And rotten weather, it must be said, contributed to Frieda's peace of mind.

The hat she now pulled on could not be construed as a winter hat. It was a forest-green chapeau with a tiny feather, an antique, a millinery artifact one might place somewhere between Peter Pan and Thirties Hollywood. In a phrase, it was eternal springtime. Now Frieda gave her little home an appreciative once-over, noting with satisfaction its absolute familiarity, the absence of dark corners. It was a homey scene and, as if to stamp it so, Frieda's cat made herself comfortable in a corner of the once proudly tufted sofa.

But it was a noisy scene as well. Snatches of television dialogue advanced from the bedroom. In the living room, these came up against the music from the kitchen radio, and the issue was joined to unpleasant effect. Yet there was, for Frieda, comfort in the cacophony as well, in the obliteration of silence. Here we may begin to see the tangle of trying oppositions into which Frieda's life seemed ready to formulate itself at the drop of a hat. Note that the comfort itself was hardly unalloyed. For Frieda now must strain to listen through and beyond the noise for the malevolence which (and this, of course, was the point) simple silence would have revealed at once. Frieda did not face such complexity without complaint; she kvetched and grew weary quickly. Indeed, she quailed before the petty complications which plagued her waking hours and which, taken as a whole, she feared made her a likely candidate for a less than happy life.

With one arm in the sleeve of her navy wool coat, Frieda slipped out into the hall between two thoughts. It was for her a momentary, yet supremely desirable, condition. Pushing the door to, Frieda's gaze rested for a final instant on a silver-framed photograph of her parents taken at the party celebrating their 25th anniversary. A month later they were dead. And if that had not been enough, Frieda had had since her youth an obscure, frightening, and very specific expectation that something of the sort would happen to them. Something! She had told no one about this, and most especially she had not told Dr.W. or his successor Dr.T., nor did she have any present intention of telling Dr.O.H. She tried the door. It was locked.

She started down the stairs quickly, her mind racing ahead to secure her passage. It was a mission for which her imagination was in a constant state of readiness, and yet one it performed less well than she might have wished. Circumstance was all when Frieda ventured out. And even then, if everything seemed all right, just then, for the merest split second, she might envision herself falling down a long narrow flight of stairs—and not these particular stairs either—and that would ruin everything. Dr.O.H. had made much of this. In one of the apartments a telephone began to ring.

As she approached the second floor, she pulled up at the sound of a hoarse curse, echoing in the silent stairwell. Had Frieda taken more of an interest in the affairs of the Greenwood Housing Cooperative, she would have been aware that the two-bedroom apartment on the second floor, vacant only a matter of weeks, had been sold to a single man in his middle thirties. She would have learned his name—which was Paul Silverman—and much about his financial assets, as well as his current unemployment. Then, had she been at all inclined to know more, she might even have made his acquaintance, for he had appeared before the Co-op membership for mutual assessment. Had she attended the meeting, she would have seen him standing in the damp, chilly rec room—quite tall and quite handsome, neatly-attired, slightly ill-at-ease but willing; perhaps she might even have been drawn to something noble in his features, or to his manner which seemed calculated to mock any such effect.

In the event, however, she rounded the corner and saw a stranger, a man unremarkable except for a kind of absolute wetness, bent at the door. The telephone, closer now, stopped ringing; "I can't come to the telephone now," a male voice could be heard faintly from within. The man whispered a final fierce imprecation and wrenched the key free from the lock whirling so quickly that drops of water flew from the fringes of his sodden scarf and from the strands of hair at his collar. Frieda, hugging the rail, skittered across the landing, and it is a tribute to the absolute dominance of her essence that she was able to skitter in her rubber-soled boots.

"I like your hat," the man said. There was something pleasing in his voice that made Frieda want to raise her eyes to his, but she did not.

"I like yours too," she replied, not stopping, or directing the words over her shoulder, or even raising her voice.

He was not wearing a hat. The words were hardly out of her mouth before she had reason to regret them. Now what would he think of her, should he, as she suddenly hoped he would, think of her at all. But this, she understood with a simultaneity that took her breath away, was highly unlikely; for the man was surely a burglar. The skin under her arms prickled as fear vied with vanity. A burglar, of course. She hurried through the small vestibule and out the front door.

But he had a key, she remembered, he had a key. So not a burglar. Nevertheless, this bit of objective evidence was met instantly by a surmise, which was met in turn by misinformation, which created an irony she could barely savor, before it had to start all-over again. And so it went, back and forth, back and forth, agitational and inconclusive. Frieda ran through the snow.

"T'ain't a fit night out for man nor beast," she said aloud, and her mediocre Fields impression served to cut off the internal debate. But as soon as she began to wipe the snow from the car windows with broad sweeps of her coat sleeve, the dialogue was taken up again. The maturity issue was raised now, and Frieda gave up without a fight. It was true, she acknowledged, she should have a plastic scraper with a brush on its end. Everyone else did.

Not even wasting the brief moment she sometimes took to wonder whether the car had been wired with explosives, Frieda turned the key in the ignition. Once on her way, she drove with excruciating slowness over the snowy pavement toward the main thoroughfare, windshield wipers flicking at the heavy snow. Had she followed the politics of her city, she would have known that this block in particular would remain unplowed and treacherous for the duration of the winter. She would have known that she had a city alderman for a neighbor. She would have known that the mayor hated his guts.

"'In the meadow we will build a snowman, dah, dah-dah that he is Parson Brown,'" Frieda sang along with the old winter classic on the radio as she turned the car very slowly around the corner onto 55th Street. This broad, near-boulevard of a street had, decades earlier, been renewed into submission, so that its urban characteristics were now solely in the eye of the beholder. Frieda was on the look-out for something more basic than that, however. She drove even more slowly past a row of low town houses, trying to look in through their bright yellow windows, trying with darting glance to isolate each flash of reality, certified as it was by another's life.

"'He'll ask are you married; we'll say No man! Dah, dah-dahdah-dah while you're in town.'" To her astonishment, the burglar in the stairwell, drier but no less chagrined, presented himself at once as an eminently suitable candidate for matrimony.

The Castle was Frieda's destination. Properly known as Castle's University Tavern, the pride of Frank and the late Wilma Castle was located several blocks further down 55th Street hard by the University campus itself. Its exterior was undistinguished in the extreme, yet perhaps all the more inviting for that. Frieda parked her car in front. Here the snow on the sidewalk had already been transformed into some other altogether different substance by the feet of many thirsty scholars. Of course, the Castle welcomed among its customers as well many non-scholars, and scholars-to-be, and also a goodly number of persons whose prospects for the future were either less clear or, in certain cases, non-existent. The Castle was, with regard to society's measuring sticks, adamantly democratic.

Perhaps this accounts in part for its enduring appeal (serving the university community since 1955), for it would be difficult to credit that any intention, commercial or aesthetic, lay behind the dingy inscrutable paint job, the collection of second-hand restaurant furnishings, or the ill-assorted bartenders. In any case, it proved easier to say, upon reflection, what the place was not, than what the place was. It was not, for example, a cheerful place, nor was it a very clean place. And yet, there were those who loved it.

"It's what you would call your je ne sais quoi," Frieda had taunted her erstwhile and Francophile suitor. The air reeked of smoke and beer and just a trace of the malodorous disinfectant Frank Castle applied with a heavy hand. Frieda did not object to the smell; she was a person who needed to know where she was.

Inside, the students milled and gawked, on the whole an unprepossessing lot in the tavern half-light, breasting a winter sea of deflated down and damp shearling. Frieda had been a student once; but, as she was wont to misquote, that wench was in another country. Now she felt not the slightest sense of solidarity with these youths; in fact, they were mere stage dressing for her, background noise. Because Frieda was an habitué of the place, a regular, and while it could not be said that the Castle valued the patronage of any one customer over that of any other, the regulars knew who they were.

As she made her way down the crowded aisle between the bar and the tables, she was conscious as always of how pleasantly diminished was her sense of moving through space here at the Castle. Her hat, however, Frieda was well aware, played a dual role—it must simultaneously deflect and draw attention. This was an ambivalence that made her uneasy, but only in retrospect, only when the hat was not on her head.

Then she would upbraid herself as a sham, pick at her pretensions, mock her weaknesses. The morning after was usually a good time for that—for then anxiety and shame were at a fever pitch, and these, of course, are the spice of life.

A gnome of a man seated at the far end of the bar caught sight of her and raised his short arms over his head. Though there was about this tavern a strange sense of physical restraint, Julius Spitzer nonetheless began to cross and uncross his arms over his head with uncommon vigor. When Frieda acknowledged his greeting with a more modest gesture, Spitzer began to point and to mouth his salutations. His behavior left Frieda totally unembarrassed. Such were the joys of the place.

"Yoolyoos," Frieda greeted him, Germanizing his name for effect, sliding up onto the empty barstool at his side. On the wall to his right hung a framed photograph of the late Wilma Castle, one of many such which dignified the tavern walls. Frank claimed to consult with Wilma on a regular basis; her picture around the place helped, he said, to focus his mind.

"Hallo, Zalechen," Julius Spitzer lit her cigarette and took one from her packet for himself, "if you don't mind." A foreigner in his mid-sixties, Julius Spitzer had been a fixture at the end of the bar since shortly after his arrival in the country twenty years before. His quick brown eyes bespoke a coffee house provenance, but the bulb of a nose and grim dry little mouth clearly belonged in a bar. He had a very round head, a hard head in the manner of Caesar and Brecht, with fine gray hair combed straight back to promote a touch of unlikely elegance.

A raffish hounds-tooth fedora lay on the bar at his elbow; the initials of a well-known novelist were embossed discreetly on its leather sweatband. This novelist lived in the neighborhood, and nearly every day he and Spitzer passed in the street and exchanged a silent greeting. Spitzer treasured this feeling of kinship, not to mention the secret knowledge that the author was a charitable sort who made his hats available for second-hand use. He even imagined that they might someday talk over a matter of literary interest—what, Spitzer wondered, would the illustrious novelist make of Himmelfarb or Feuerbaum had he been entrusted with their stories. For the time being, however, the simple thought of their companionship through common enterprise was inspiration enough.

"Your hat needs cleaning," Frieda broke willfully into her own thoughts of hats and hatless strangers.

This bit of waspish advice did not sit well with him. "It is something to you suddenly?" he asked with more than a hint of pique. He was particular about his clothes and she knew it. His wardrobe, replenished annually at a synagogue Tag Sale, relied heavily on tee-shirts advertising sights he'd never seen, teams he'd never followed, sentiments he'd never cultivated. But the look—the look he thought was very American—carefree, slightly pugnacious, at home with hype. Yet the more his barrel chest proclaimed his sense of belonging—the more a stranger, beneath the cotton-polyester blend, the man himself felt. Spitzer had a continental taste for the dichotomous.

"Sorry, Yoolyoos. Ignore me." She poked at the soft material of her own hat, moving it back and forth on her head to no particular advantage. "Do unto others, etc.," she added pointedly.

"'The rest is commentary,'" a stocky young man with close-cropped reddish-brown hair put in placidly, reaching between them to put his glass of lime seltzer down on the bar. He looked at Frieda with a variety of youthful longing which was only part desire. "Do not unto others, etc. That is the whole of it," he paused significantly, his blue eyes moist behind his glasses, "that's the Torah."

"Spare me, B.T." Frieda had taken to calling him B.T. after he had told her that he was intending to become a Ba'al T'shuvah, a repentant, a returnee to the Jewish faith of his fathers—the most recent of whom had chosen, in fact, to name him Kenneth.

"Call me Issachar," he begged, giving her one of his sweet inward smiles. He took a sip of seltzer keeping his lips to the rim of the glass for some time, taking the opportunity to test himself on the names of the other tribes of Israel. He ticked them off—Rueben, Shimon, Levi, Judah.... At the same time, however, he remained alert for his next opening.

"Is-a-car," Kevin-for-crying-out-loud called from four stools down the bar. As his sobriquet made plain, he was a promiscuous listener.

"I knew an Issachar...," Spitzer brooded, his inbred sensitivity to a slight apparently enhanced by alcohol, "once."

"Yoolyoos sulks," Frieda called out to Joe Finneran who was just approaching, pushing his little wife ahead of him through the crowd. The bartender placed a brandy and soda in front of Frieda.

"So might we all." Finneran took a fistful of paper napkins from the dispenser on the bar and wiped at the melting snow down inside his collar. "So might we all." He ran a nervous hand through his thinning black hair.

His wife gave him a quick look, just a tiny upward flick of the eyes, the merest hint of apprehension. She was a pale, weak-chinned woman often tired after a day's work in the Bursars Office at the University. "Shouldn't we get a table, Finn, honey?"

"If you don't mind," Julius Spitzer said politely, pulling a cigarette from the package Finneran's wife had just taken from her purse.

Mrs. Finneran did mind, but she said nothing more than "There's a table over there, Finn."

"Hie thee, then," Finneran said with sudden animation, handing her a glass of diet soda. He drank his shot of Irish straight down. "Kenneth, lad, do you take an interest in the canine world, specifically the world of the Chow?" He gave the B. T. a knowing look. "Fierce damn dog," he continued obscurely, nearly confidentially, "Gene had one, fine beast, expensive." He hitched up his trousers and headed for the table, feeling better than he had all day, and closer than ever to the great Irish-American playwright.

"'But against any of the children of Israel shall not a dog whet his tongue,'" the B.T. called after him. That this verse should spring to his lips just now was a source of great satisfaction. A year ago, his would have been a more well-worn and wholly secular riposte. A year ago, Kenneth Andrew Blane, just beginning his graduate studies in the department of English Literature, had reached a low point in his life. It was during the critical months when his spirit was numb and nothing ever seemed to happen, that Shlomo had befriended him. "Timtum ha-lev," Shlomo had called his condition knowingly, "dullness of the heart."

The front door of the tavern had opened and closed many times since Frieda's arrival, but just now, as she rose to follow the others to the table, reaching at once for her purse and her cigarettes and her drink, something compelled her eyes away to the front of the long narrow room. The man she saw standing there seemed just as wet and just as agitated as he had been earlier. Paul Silverman looked around the barroom, tugging at his scarf with a vague motion, until suddenly he appeared to catch sight of her. He looked away and looked back again, stunned, but started off through the crowd in her direction. Agitated herself, Frieda fumbled for her glass; brandy and soda splashed on the bar.

"Ach," Julius said, lifting his hat quickly. The bartender came with a rag. Frieda, sensing the stranger's approach, hurried to light a damp cigarette.

"I said, I like your hat," he began abruptly but with a mildness at odds with his agitation. "I was being neighborly. You were not neighborly in return. You were enigmatic." This was almost surely meant to be a compliment.

"I'm happy to hear it," was Frieda's unlikely and unlikeable reply, and her stomach turned over at the sound of her words. She took a sip of the fresh drink, very nearly turning her back on him.

The man's face stiffened; he was all business now. He looked around the room. "I just need a telephone." His voice had grown slightly querulous, but even so Frieda found it quite compelling. She led him to the telephone in the second of the tavern's three barrooms and, for no reason she could name, stood aside and watched him while he made his call. She was not aware of having actually looked at him yet, but she nonetheless understood her first impression to have been fully positive. Indeed, she saw, she found him attractive in all respects. She glanced at one of the snapshots tacked up above the service window connecting the two barrooms— Wilma Castle, wearing an apron, hamburger flipper a blur in the tavern's ill-lit kitchen. Be friendly, Wilma seemed to advise, be warm, be welcoming. It occurred to her suddenly that all was not lost, she might yet make amends for her lack of neighborliness, for her suspicion.

Before the man had the telephone receiver completely back on the hook, Frieda was at his side. "I could buy you a drink," she informed him with considerable urgency.

CHAPTER TWO

Mother and Child

The houses of her neighbors were dark, but at Lois Sills', née Silverman's, home there were lights on behind the olive-green living room drapes. Lois rented the house, a dilapidated ranch two miles past the war Memorial at the crossroads of a small village in southern Maine. She had known the lay of this land well for she had spent several of her girlhood vacations at a summer camp nearby; and although the rural poverty which had shocked her during those idyllic, privileged summers had been largely eradicated by an influx of outlet stores and the tourists who sustain them, she had nonetheless managed to ferret out and settle in a pocket of poverty resistant to that boom.

In the living room two men were arguing about the best time to leave for the drive back to Boston. One of them was a stocky black man in his early forties with a square dark face and large, very round eyes. This was Simon Washington, ex-con and freedom fighter. The other man, younger, taller, with lighter skin and a prominent scar in the center of his high forehead, was his cousin Willis. From her bedroom down the short corridor, Lois could just make out the rise and fall of their voices above the mix of sounds from the television. She had to be up early in the morning—several years ago she had started Freedom's Children, a small alternative-pay-what-you-can-daycare program for the neighborhood—otherwise she would have been out in the other room with them. That was where her heart longed to be—with *them*—with the poor and the Black, the down-trodden, the unfree. Hers was the dream of a better world. And so—when all was said and done—when the hippies and the yippies had all gone home, when the Maoists had taken jobs and the Feminists had left for grad school, when the student politicos and the lost souls had found refuge in the ashrams—it had come down to this, to Simon and his charismatic cousin Willis Washington. We're the revolution now, Lois thought with perfect sincerity, we are the fuckin' revolution.

Lois turned on the radio at her bedside. There was snow in the forecast, blowing in from the Middle West by late afternoon. It was but two days since Rosie had left home, and already Lois missed her keenly. They were very close, Lois and her daughter; more like sisters, they liked to say, mostly to modernize the intensity of the feeling. Rosie's departure had been sudden and surprising. But Lois had not tried to stop her, attempting only to dash her hopes with the observation that Rosie's chances of finding her father were about as good as her own chances of lunching at the White House with Nancy Reagan. Lois trusted, she told her finally, to Rosie's good sense—though it was mother-love alone which could conceive that this young girl was endowed with any such thing.

Did she have any ambition for her daughter, she

wondered now sternly, any need of her own that Rosie get an education, marry, perhaps even return to the material ascendancy of her ancestors. Was it not precisely the rejection of all that—the very things for which she herself had been brought up—that had made her free, had opened her up to the possibility of the revolution?! Why should all that be any more appealing to Rosie than it had been to her. But somehow it is, Lois pressed her hand to her heart in the universal gesture of suffering motherhood; face it—it just fuckin' is.

She moved the radio dial this way and that until she heard a familiar voice. Long a fan of late-night radio, Lois was not at all surprised to hear a familiar voice, in fact, expected to hear one, wanted to hear one. Sleep is at hand, she thought, allowing the sounds to abstract—the voices of the men in the living room, the noise of the television and the radio—turn out the light, she thought, yawning, will the last one out please turn out the light—the light....

Suddenly she heard a voice that was at once more and also less than familiar. She strained to listen through her sleep; but then stretching unconsciously toward the night table for her glasses, she knew she was awake. Unlike the copper-dyed hair, the clear-lens glasses had become a permanent part of her look. The next minute all at once she seemed to know who it was—it was him—it was him—it was him—she leapt from the bed—that fascist pig—that fucking male chauvinist—that narc—that mole—that snitch—in short, he was the only man she had ever truly loved.

Lois rushed out to the living room, tripping on the hem

of her long flannel nightgown and tearing it out. Worse, he was the father of her child. It was him! It was him! The room was empty. The lights were on, the television set was on, there were French fries on the couch, a bottle of gin and a thick envelope on the card table, but the men had gone. She had not heard them leave. Perhaps, then, she tried to calm herself, she had already been asleep; perhaps, then, she had only dreamed the voice on the radio. Dreamed of Randall "Rip" Parks. It wouldn't be the first time. That was likely, she sighed; that was common enough on the edge of sleep.

Lois looked around the sparsely furnished, ill-kept room. Once her stomach had rebelled at the touch of an oily glass, her bowels had frozen at the sight of a bathroom black with grime, her flesh had crawled pressed against a filthy mattress. How long it had taken to rid herself of her addiction to bourgeois luxe. Even today she remembered just what had finally done the trick. It was at the time when all her friends were Welfare Mothers. There had been an apartment—as wretched as the Guatemalan hovels she would come to know—and she had gone there to visit a friend. It was impossible that American people should live in such a place—she had rushed back to her own room and, weeping, ripped the sheet from her bed. Later everyone got together and it was decided that the sheet be inscribed with the words "Amerika Out Of America" and hung on the clothes line in their weedy, littered yard.

She bent over and began to smooth and fold the pile of laundry she had dropped in the corner of the sofa earlier in the evening. Such simple chores had long since lost their charm, but she could still remember well how it had made her feel at first, moving a mass of dripping laundry from washer to drier, careless and carefree, one of the people. There had been a laundress in her parents' home; it was the one thing she had never confided to anyone. Now she picked up and shook out the last sheet only to find a black smudge near its center. She glanced down at the sofa and shrank back from the little gun she saw there, an unlikely response for one who had appeared in the bloom of her youth as a cover girl for one of the liveliest rags on the New Left. There she had been pictured, her face a barely recognizable blur, standing in front of a weeping willow, wearing cut-off jeans and a Daisy Mae blouse, and raising a rifle skyward. But this little piece, this slick, oily, misshapen turd of a gun was something different altogether, and she did not even want to touch it. It was not that Lois had any objection to violence, or even to the use of guns if it came to that. And it would. But this was no political weapon, she thought angrily. And yet, she cautioned herself, Mao's dictum made no such distinctions. As long as it has a barrel. She forced herself to pick it up. Love is a warm gun, she remembered; or was that happiness. She pointed it at the talking head on the television screen.

So, she had not heard the men leave. Perhaps, then, she had already dozed off. She aimed the gun at a spot of ketchup on the rug in front of the sofa. Perhaps she had only dreamed the voice on the radio. That voice. Her heart had yet to quiet. She pressed the gun point-blank against the neck of the gin bottle. Simon would be angry at having to turn the car around to come back for it, and she did not like to make Simon angry. She put the little gun down and dropped the sheet back over it.

Taking the envelope into the bathroom with her she pulled out the money and sat down on the toilet to count it. She put the bills in order and made sure they were all facing the same way. It seemed somehow appropriate to her that she always counted money sitting on the toilet, although she had no recollection at all of certain discussions which had taken place many years earlier and might have had a bearing on such a connection. Filthy Lucre. She had listened eagerly then, but with little comprehension. Indeed, Lois had really never felt at ease around the kind of charged theoretical discussion that had been so much a part of what had gone on in those years. Especially when she made the effort to appear involved, she had most often felt left out, isolated. It seemed likely in retrospect that it was under such circumstances that she and Rip Parks had been drawn to each other, for Rip had chosen to appear distant during these discussions, uncomfortable like her, Lois had assumed. He had characterized himself as a man of action, above "all that pretentious bullshit." Lois would not go quite that far, but it soon became clear that Randall "Rip" Parks was one of the few people in the movement she could feel really close to. Their relationship had gone from there.

In the bedroom, Lois looked around to make sure the shades were down and the curtains closed before walking over to remove a large framed photograph from the wall. It was a formal portrait of one-time Governor Milton Schapp of Pennsylvania, which Lois had received from a friend who had received it from her father who had received it from the governor himself as a token of appreciation. Behind the picture was a crude hole in the plasterboard, punched out by Simon for the purpose. She pulled out a draw-string bag which hung from a nail between the studs, and stuffed the envelope in. Replacing the picture, she smiled at the evil-looking chow who lay at the governor's feet; it was her conceit that this fierce animal would guard their stash as well.

•   •   •

At the Interstate Rest Stop east of Chicago, an extraordinarily thin young man with a pinched face and long hair walked out of the Men's Room and looked out the restaurant's glass doors at the service plaza. The snow continued to fall. This was making travel more difficult. He unfolded a wad of yellow paper and stepped up to the bank of telephones. Again, there was no answer at the other end. Well, she was going to let them in anyway, wasn't she, he told himself. Both of them. Frieda Zale was like that. She was no bitch.

"Going as far as Chicago?" he asked a fellow traveler who stood lost in thought before the candy machine. Receiving a negative reply, he returned, stone-faced, to the companion who awaited his report in the cafeteria.

Rosie Sills did not lift her head from the table. Her face, where visible beneath the tangled hair, was as pale as the crockery and hardly more expressive. Indeed, though there was not among the other patrons here another one named Rosie, every one of them appeared to have a greater claim on that name. In any case, for reasons of her own, the girl had only days before decided to call herself Xenia. This came naturally to her after a semi-underground-childhood spent not quite on-the-run. "It's gotta be at least midnight," she now accused Tom Waggoner, "are we gonna get a ride from here or what?"

Tom lit a cigarette and scanned the room. "You tell me," he mumbled. He had quickly wearied of her habit of inquiring of him things that she could just as well worry about on her own.

"Well, take a seat," she said brusquely, a girl of many moods and many faces, but strangely innocent of contradictions. As a young child she and Lois had moved often from place to place; and the people they had lived among had left her a legacy of random phrasings which were by now second nature. Rosie had many things by second nature, and very little by first nature.

She brought her fist out from the sleeve of the over-size tweed overcoat she was wearing and pushed it under her cheek lifting her head several inches from the table. With her left elbow she nudged the smudged creamer aside. "Well," she said, her voice quickening, "lemme take a look around this place as long as I'm here, and see if maybe by any chance I can recognize my Dad." She laughed a private laugh. "He could be a travelling salesman, ya never know, or a trucker or on vacation or," she flicked her eyes toward a nearby table where a man in a fur-collared coat drummed his fingers on the latch of his attaché case, "or some rich guy. Hi Dad," she raised her voice but received not so much as a glance in reply.

"Oh sure; he's gonna be in here," Tom's narrow lips twitched before settling into a slow smile. He took off his dirty railroad cap and gestured broadly to the large, mostly empty room. His mood had changed suddenly in tandem with hers. This had been happening almost from the moment they had met—as Tom and Xenia—a day and a half ago in a similar establishment just outside Lowell, Massachusetts; and he had begun to be concerned about these unintended mood swings. It gave him a funny feeling, as if somehow she had bewitched him. Xenia was a name for a witch, he thought. "And you know who else?" He shook the cap several times before replacing it.

"Do you mean your dad's in here, too?" She sat up now, smiling, pushing her hair back from her face with both hands. "Your dad, you mean, right?" She looked him in the eye, relishing his compliance. "Is he alone... or...is he...with her?" Clearly, they had already exchanged many confidences.

"That fat slob. Hah!" Tom brought his palm down swiftly and with great force onto the table top. "Splat!" He studied his palm with mock concern. "Hey did she get ya, Dad?" Rosie giggled and hit the table top herself. "Hah! Splat!" She often echoed a move or a sound she liked. Though nearly of an age with Tom, there was, as here, something of the very young child about her.

Tom had left his father's home recently when an overweight woman he barely knew moved in claiming to be his step-mother. She was pregnant, and brought twins with her. "I told him, man, you must be desperate, and then he hits me. So I went, whoa." He studied his nails, "You know who I told you we're staying at in Chicago, Frieda? My Dad sort of went with her a long time ago. I mean and now he's gotta marry this fat slob."

"Well, the thing about my dad is that he's not even married, so that's one good thing." Rosie had perfect faith.

"You said you didn't know shit about him," Tom complained, disappointed. "You said you didn't even know his name."

"Some things are more important than a person's name," Rosie said and had good reason to believe it.

Tom sucked in his cheeks and smacked his lips. "Not when you're out there looking for someone, they ain't."

Rosie sucked in her own cheeks. Suddenly her eyes shifted away from her companion in the direction of the portly man in the fur-collared coat now at the cash register, and held there with a sense of purpose which however did nothing to banish the dullness from them. She pulled a round knitted cap over her auburn curls and, still staring, got up and left the table.

Moments later she was waving to Tom from the door where she stood in conversation with the man who still held his gold money clip in his hand. Once he had agreed to the ride, there was so much Rosie wanted to know from him. It was her habit to put herself in conversation with men of a certain age for the purpose of learning what kind of fathers other daughters had.

"Are you on a business trip?" she asked the man, nodding toward his attaché case.

"Yes, on my way home now. Is your friend ready to go?"

Tom had taken up his knapsack and was walking toward

them slowly; slowly, partly because cultivated languor was at the soul of this boy, and partly to prove his scrupulosity. With his long hair, his skinny frame, his black clothing, he looked, or so he thought, rather dramatic enough to give an average citizen reason to reconsider his offer.

"You look like you work in an office with a secretary," Rosie continued, "what kind of a job do you have?"

The man waved Tom on. "I work in a bank." He held the door open for them.

"Do you ever wish you could steal the money?"

"All the time." He walked ahead of them to his car, which, even under a layer of snow revealed itself as large, foreign and expensive.

Tom nudged Rosie. "Maybe he already did," he muttered.

"Yeah, my mom always says 'take from the rich according to your means,' or something like that."

Once in the car and on their way, Rosie went on with her questioning. "Do you have a den at your house, where you watch TV excetera?" she wanted to know.

The man glanced at her out of the corner of his eye. "I don't watch much television," he said.

"Do you ever, let's say, bring home pizza, or...."

Tom's light snoring could be heard from the back seat. "Why don't you get some sleep too," the man interrupted her, "it's late."

Although the fatherly tone of this suggestion was surely perfunctory, Rosie could not help feeling a surge of hope. "Do you have a daughter," she asked him, "or any other children?"

"Look," he said, suddenly anxious about her line of

questioning, "I'm sorry, but I've got to concentrate now. This surface is slick."

Yeah, Rosie thought, crushed, and so are you. You might be riding in this car with your own daughter and you don't even want to know it. Your own daughter is sitting right here next to you and all you care about is the surface. That's all you care about—the surface, she reiterated with knowing emphasis. Well, now you'll never find out, so fuck you. She turned her face toward the window and remained thus resolute, though her mind was filled with many dark thoughts as they drove through the night. And she did not say another word, not even when the car stopped and he wished her well in whatever she chose to do in life. Still, as she stood on a windy lakeside corner on the South Side of Chicago, Rosie could not help feeling a little like she had just been blessed.

CHAPTER THREE

Yolanda at Home

Locked out of his new apartment, Paul Silverman had arranged to spend the night at his sister's home. He did not, then, take Frieda up on her offer of a conciliatory drink; and while this rankled with her and she attributed to his refusal a thousand cruel motives, the simple fact was that Yolanda had insisted that if he planned to come, he must come at once. This was Yolanda Silverman at her most sisterly— pre-emptory, over-bearing, even, one might say, unsisterly. Nevertheless, she was, Paul understood, only flexing her muscle; for Yolanda was at the top of her game.

The same could not be said of Paul. To everyone's surprise, a time came when life on Wall Street had turned out not to suit him. Certainly, things had gone along well enough at first; after an exemplary career at all the best schools, he had thrown himself enthusiastically into his work. His days were long, challenging and, it seemed to him, filled with significance. Though still young, he soon made a name for himself as a man of craft and subtlety. Indeed, as a genius of sorts, although that word was used rather loosely in that place at that time.

The intricate strategies which he developed, utilizing

a complicated set of technical indicators in conjunction with certain fundamental data, were talked of as plowing new ground, opening new frontiers, exploring new worlds. Meanwhile, they were so refined in conception as to occupy a mere pin-point-of-an-intersection between real world and model—but, crucially, a juncture which had heretofore gone quite undetected. The strategies worked like crazy. Five years running—let the economy do its worst—Paul Silverman contributed mightily to the record profits of an investment firm already so prestigious and powerful as to require no further identification.

There did come a time, however—he could not say exactly when or how—when there began to be signs that all was not well with him. Nevertheless, his work was so intense, his cocktail hour so various, his socializing so constant, that he was barely aware at first that there was something amiss. He ignored the fact, for example, that he had spent an entire evening at the theater ("African Voices") without falling asleep. This was unprecedented. Then, too, he had found an excuse for his purchase of several large paintings by an emerging Nigerian artist, for his spending much of his bonus on them. Actually, it was not until he booked the flight to Nairobi, when what they had planned was New Year's skiing in Aspen, that he had any real inkling, that he began to be slightly afraid.

Then one day, at a delicate moment during a highly complex series of negotiations, his mind began to wander. This, too, was unprecedented. Perhaps, as it was alleged later, he was in fact muttering or mumbling or even humming under his breath. In any case, the others looked over at him expectantly, for he had been able from time to time over the period of these talks to clarify certain arcane details of a strategy he alone truly understood. As he recalled it, he was at that moment innocent of a clear intention of any kind; but something made him open his mouth.

"Bolobo," he was heard to say.

"Boola boola," cried Bill Winch jovially, quick to cover for a fellow Yale man. But there was no coming back.

It was thought at the time, of course, that Paul had succumbed to the Drug of Choice, though there were more than a few who came down on the side of one of the other diseases of the day—stress-out, burn-out, sell-out, and even wig-out were prominently mentioned. But that was not it at all. It was just that his mind had begun to wander. And wander most mysteriously, for every so often an African place name would rise uninvited to his lips. Try as he might, Paul could not get his mind back on track. Worst of all, the technical insights and gossamer webs of strategy he had himself formulated were now as baffling to him as they had heretofore been to his colleagues. He tried everything. He tried another firm—he tried a large corporation—he even tried an oil-patch S&L—try as he might, to none of these excellent job opportunities was he able to bring the right stuff. Suddenly the atmosphere, rarified, thinned out through manipulation of money and ego, seemed to him no longer able to support life. And as his prospects dwindled, he discovered in himself a concomitant and intense desire to learn about the African continent.

So Paul had eventually returned to Chicago, the city of his birth, in an attempt to wipe out the poor impression he and the world had made on each other. This effort did not always make him a pleasant companion. He had earned a lot of money during his time on the Street, and spent a lot too; but enough remained for a modest cooperative apartment on the South Side and, for the time being, a pleasant living to boot.

Now he found himself standing in the vestibule of the three-story brownstone apartment building where his sister Yolanda lived. He took a moment to prepare himself. Ndola, Kitwe, Chingola, the names came to him unbidden. Yolanda had long since set a standard of regard for herself so high that few, not even Paul with his genuine familial affection for her, could hope to match it. This was often a barrier to a comfortable visit. He pressed the button next to a card on which the name Silverman-Silbermann appeared. A child's voice asked him, coldly, what he wanted. This was Letitia, called Letty, who was four, and refused him admittance on the general principle that she was the light of her parents' life and wanted to keep it that way.

Paul stepped outside again. He looked up at the large lit window on the third floor and conceived an alternative plan. Bending over the low wrought-iron fence into the bit of urban front yard, he was gathering snow with both hands, packing a snowball, when suddenly a great force was brought to bear on his back, and he felt, through the damp wool of his overcoat, the pressure of the wrought iron spikes against his chest.

"Fuh." The tail of his coat was lifted up over his back. A sneakered foot was raised, slowly, deliberately as if for a shoeshine, and then jammed against his buttocks.

"Muhfuh." One hand entered the back pocket for his wallet, another entered at the right-front for loose change, and at the same moment a hand reached for the top of his trousers.

"Fuh Muhfuh." They pulled down his pants and they ran.

Paul had not been mugged before. Hopeless, yet driven by a pressing need for continuity, he bent again to the snow and packed the ball carefully. But when he straightened and cocked his arm to throw, the power drained from it all at once, and the snowball fell and splattered on the sidewalk. Only then did he pull up and refasten his trousers.

This time when he pressed the buzzer it was Yolanda who answered. Shivering, he stepped into the tiny elevator and was lifted at a stately pace to the third floor. But still, it could not move slowly enough to satisfy Paul. There were as yet no words with which to greet Yolanda, admire Letitia, keep Ian Silbermann's banter at bay. In any event, he did not know much about this little family which had sprung up largely in his absence. The elevator stopped suddenly.

"What took you so long?" Yolanda had the apartment door open and she had framed herself, wiry black hair, high-necked frilly blouse, voluminous red skirt, to some advantage there. She was a statuesque woman with a broad face of the type often called striking, and broad commanding hips. In her late thirties, with four books out of the way, Yolanda Silverman-Silbermann had made a name for herself. It could not be said with any certainty to what extent her bold dramatic looks had been instrumental in the selling of her books, but her publisher's decision to feature her photograph on the jacket without the benefit of promotional copy made this at least a possibility.

Yolanda was a novelist; and, yes, she could not deny what she had known from childhood, she saw life with a novelist's eye. In this she had no thought to impute to herself a particular view, or even any generality of vision. No, she was all sensibility and glad of it too. Her very first book had been coyly hailed as "an auspicious debutante" and she herself personified as "an unerring ear" and "an infallible eye." The reviewers found especial merit in the familiarity which an abundance of hard detail lent her work—"Silverman-Silbermann gets it just right!" There was no higher praise in a consumer society.

"I asked you particularly to come right over so that you could spend some time with Letitia." Her voice was low-pitched and measured even now when she was irritated with him.

He approached and she embraced him quickly. "I was mugged," Paul said, nearly whispered, into her thick hair.

"Please don't joke, Paul. Letty is such a pleasure; you'll see." She moved ahead of him eagerly through the short hall on the left into the living room. Her heavy, confident gait left Paul feeling oddly more desolate, revealing, as it seemed to, the tendency of the world to go on.

"Yo-Yo," he used her childhood name to compel her attention, and told her what had happened on her own door step only moments before.

"Poor Paul," she said, turning and looking quickly into his eyes to make sure he wasn't joking after all. "Oh poor Paul. Outside this building!"

"They were enormously efficient, well-disciplined, quick…." he began with some passion.

But Yolanda did not stay to listen. These very words were so often associated in her own mind with herself, that she was quite incapable of putting on them anything less than a positive construction. In fact, she was very nearly in danger of losing the thread of their conversation altogether. She lifted her head sharply, as if sniffing the air. "Were they wearing those enormous sneakers?" she asked over her shoulder, walking to the French doors beyond which was the sun porch they had converted into a small den. "God, I'm tired of seeing those damn sneakers." Behind a sheer curtain the light from the television diffused the darkness. Yolanda turned back for a moment. "Letty gets the sanitized version," she told him sternly.

Letty however preferred to remain in the den where she was eating a bowl of peanuts and watching "The Nutcracker Ballet." "It's of particular interest to Letty, of course," Yolanda explained, "since she's studying ballet herself." She opened the door to the den again. "Letty honey, are you sure you don't want to come out and see Uncle Paul." She was sure. Her mother smiled at Paul, as if to acknowledge the rigors of the dancer's discipline, as if to say, what are the demands of consanguinity to this? Instead she said, "Paul, we have a marvelous little locksmith."

"It was like one of those Hindu gods. All the hands." Paul assumed a posture which was of necessity only vaguely reminiscent of the statues in question.

"How awful. Hindu?!" Yolanda accommodated his conversational lead with a hint of reluctance.

"It's possible, of course, that I don't mean Hindu. I know nothing about the religions of the East." It was crucial, Paul realized, that he remedy this lack as soon as possible. He felt a mild anxiety when he pictured the library that his sister's guestroom was likely to house.

"I thought you said they were Black kids." Since his return to Chicago, Yolanda had become aware that there was very little pleasure in conversation with her brother. His mind tended to wander and jump. She had much preferred him as a hot-shot; indeed, before the divorces, they had often discussed energy levels, a shared commitment to detail, a conviction that situations alter cases, while their spouses yammered for attention across the room.

"If you think I ever give any thought at all to what you do and do not know, you're crazy. By the way we're thinking of getting a dog, a dog that will just put the goddam fear of G-d in them. Did I tell you? I don't know the breed; all I know is Virginia Woolf had one. Isn't that perfect for me?!" Yolanda walked back across the polished wood floor. The oak boards had recently been stained dark, nearly black, the better to display a number of small Peruvian rugs. "Ian-dearest," she stooped and spoke into the intercom. "Ian, Ian-love."

The intercom crackled and Yolanda put her palm over the speaker. "What I went through to get this installed you will never know. In the middle of the book, too. It was a major undertaking." She tapped the intercom in irritation.

"Yolanda-my-love, did you want me?" Ian Silbermann's hearty, tailored bonhomie reached them without the aid of the speaker, echoing instead down the long hallway, bouncing off the walls where the corridor jogged, and emerging from the dark with all its quality intact. It was a radio voice. "Give me a minute, will you." Ian, a professor whose special interest was in "communications," understood the imperatives of the art, the sweetness of anticipation.

"Sit down, Paul. You're not yourself. Ian-dearest," Yolanda spoke into the intercom once more, "my brother is finally here."

Paul sat down on a hand-carved rocking chair with modern paisley upholstering. He wondered whether Yolanda would offer him a drink now. He remembered that he had been offered a drink earlier in the evening; the odd intensity of that offer struck him anew, indeed the odd intensity of the woman herself struck him, and struck him not unpleasantly.

"That chair doesn't quite belong there," Yolanda mused. She and Ian were dedicated to a type of interior decoration that transcended completion to realize itself in eternal process. Unaccountably, Paul sprang to his feet. He was definitely feeling jumpy. "How many of them were there?" his sister asked immediately, as if she had some purpose in keeping him off-balance.

He tried to think. "They pulled down my pants," he told her.

"Whose pants, Mommy? Who?" Letty stepped into the living room. The skirt of her pink tutu was crushed and limp and covered with bits of peanut shell. She put her hands on her hips. "What's going on around here?" she demanded.

At her mother's gentle reply, which emphasized the rewards of the coming day as well as the certain benefits of a good night's sleep for ballerinas and other creative persons, the Young-young Person ran from the room and down the darkened hall crying, "Daddy, they don't want me; they don't want me." Letitia was indignant.

Ian Silbermann entered the room with his daughter, cheeks flushed in triumph, on his shoulders. He was just slightly shorter than his wife, a broad, stocky man with a rough face and greying curls. Maileresque, was Yolanda's opinion. "How do you like the intercom, Paul?" They shook hands. "Nifty, eh. You will never know what she went through to get it installed. In the middle of the book, too."

Yolanda, however, had not stayed to hear this affirmation. The Silverman-Silbermanns took the tag-team approach to entertaining; one of them was always out of the room. Their time, they felt, was just too valuable.

"What about something to drink?" Ian offered, absently snapping the elastic on one of Letty's pink ballet slippers.

"Virgin Mary," the child demanded loudly before Paul had a chance to reply. "Me want," she clarified, tugging at her father's big ears. Silbermann shrugged his shoulders, whether to reveal his helplessness in the face of such manifest charm or merely to redistribute his daughter's weight was not immediately evident. "Giddy-up," the girl cried, and Ian left the room with nothing more than Paul's polite silence to go on.

Yolanda entered immediately then, an antique watering can in her hand. "I made a note," she announced not by way of apology for her absence, but more because she felt that people were generally curious about the work habits of writers. "When I jot, I jot; I don't use the typewriter for jotting." She poured water into a hanging plant in the corner over the highly-polished piano—further evidence of her enormous sense of self-possession.

Ian returned with two bottles of beer, trailed by Letty who came in slowly, her eyes nearly crossed on the large glass of tomato juice she held before her. After one small sip of the juice she handed her father the glass. "Well, what should we talk about?" she asked, settling herself in his lap. At his deftly-constructed reply, which included a characterization of himself as a patient man but one who had his limits, Letty put her thumb in her mouth.

Paul looked to Yolanda as if for guidance, but she had left the room.

"So, your key doesn't work," Ian began pleasantly and not at all as if they were locked in a titanic battle of wills with the Young-young Person.

Paul explained that he had been mugged—without saying "mugged" or "Black" or "sneakers" or "wallet." While there was just so much that could be said about a key, now the worlds of politics and sports were fair game, and conversation was easier than it would otherwise have been. Ian had a great reputation among colleagues and students alike as a good listener; the Windy City Award that his radio show had received was generally thought to have been based on this quality. The fact was, however, that Ian rarely listened, in the common sense of the word; rather, the man had a sixth sense for the flow of conversation and a real talent for eye contact.

Letitia was asleep where she sat in her father's lap. Ian set down her glass of tomato juice. "Did I mention we're planning to buy a dog? I've been all over hell looking for some fierce s.o.b. that won't scare the daylights out of Letty." He smiled down at his sleeping daughter.

Yolanda appeared in the archway. Her face was mask-like, grim. "You put her to bed then," she told her husband angrily. "I've had it. It's late. I'm going to bed."

"Yolanda, my love," Ian struggled to keep his voice low out of consideration for Letty, but he did not have that kind of voice.

"I've got to get some sleep."

Already Ian was heaving himself up, straining his well-exercised thighs to keep his daughter comfortable and still in his arms.

"Your bed is made, Paul." Yolanda yawned dramatically, head tilted back, mouth open. She turned away with a wave, and there was nothing left for Paul but to take his beer and follow her down the dark corridor to the guest room.

He closed the door and sat down on the bed. The room had been recently redecorated with an eye, Paul saw, to preserving certain glories of the past: diplomas, crayon drawings, awards, photographs, and dust jackets had all been framed and hung above the wainscoting on the yellow walls.

The door opened and Ian, like a nervous ventriloquist, thrust Letitia back in through the doorway. "Top of the line," he advertised the new mattress they had purchased for the guest room, "you'll sleep like a baby."

"Baby," Letitia echoed distinctly, struggling in his arms. And they were gone again.

In one corner of the room, a hand-crocheted afghan was folded over the back of a well-preserved Depression-era kitchen chair. A bookcase under the window, Paul saw, did not contain a single volume on Hinduism or any Eastern religion for that matter. It would have been nice, he sighed, picking up instead a book on Jews in professional sports that lay on the bedside table. The books which Yolanda selected for her guests were in marked contrast to those which filled her own shelves where the fiction of the day held complete sway. She had not for many years read anything other than the work of her competition.

Before Paul could begin to read however, his eye caught sight of an old and familiar photograph of himself on the bureau. He was a very young boy and sat, listing slightly, on a deep sofa. His sisters, Yolanda and Lois, sat, ladylike, on either side of him. The girls wore identical party dresses and each held a small patent-leather pocketbook on her lap. Now, of course, Yolanda tended to dress with all the style and drama of a fortune teller; and Lois, not quite a fugitive from justice, the Lord knew what she was wearing these days.

CHAPTER FOUR

Late at Night

At the Castle conversation sped along in a number of well-worn ruts, many suggesting the presence of the nearby University. Arcane allusion and quotation were highly valued, as was one-upmanship of the most meaningless kind. Aimless banter seemed, after a round or two, the height of wit, and insights of an indiscriminate kind flowed freely. Word games were in fashion; also spontaneous trivia challenges, and—when the Cubs weren't playing—the "Who's History" quiz on a local TV news show.

The bartender placed a brandy and soda in front of Frieda. "The elixir," he announced flatly, "the libation."

"Coin of the realm," she replied, pulling a handful of change from her pocket.

"The King's English," The B. T. said quickly, wanting to get in on the game in spite of himself.

"'Queen for a Day,'" Spitzer threw in, surprising them. Ordinarily, he had no use for their games.

"'One-eyed Jacks,'" the bartender said in his turn, sweeping the coins from the bar with practiced ease.

"Enough, children, enough!" Spitzer rapped his knuckles on the bar to get their attention. He had, as it turned out, his own agenda. "Allow me to tell you something which happened once on the television program 'Queen for a Day.'" He took such strenuous hold of the B.T.'s arm that the little button at the B.T.'s shirt cuff popped. The B.T. recoiled, nearly pulling Spitzer off his bar stool. "There was a woman on the program once," Spitzer did not loosen his grip and continued nonetheless, righting himself with all the dignity of an over-worked tailor. "Her wish when she became the Queen was for a plastic surgeon. She wished him to remove the number that was branded on her arm. And it was done, the tattoo was removed."

He lifted his hand from the B.T.'s forearm to his own arm, where, beneath the worn corduroy sport coat, his own blue numerals were displayed. "What is your reaction if I may inquire?"

"Pure Hitchcock," the bartender offered in passing.

The B.T. remained silent for a moment. Then he pressed hard on the bridge of his glasses and muttered, "'Bind them for a sign' not brand them for a sign." Tefillin from the devil, the B.T. mused, though he had never seen a Jew bind those leather cubes and straps to arm and forehead, let alone applied them himself. The truth was he had learned the word "tefillin" itself only recently, but he already felt at home with it. It was this odd, engaging familiarity of things Jewish that spurred him on in his quest; even the Hebrew of the Torah itself seemed to come to him as if he were recollecting it, not learning it for the first time. What more could this mystically-minded student of English literature want!

When Julius turned to her, Frieda rubbed her finger up

and down her nose, appearing to ruminate for one final moment before giving him her considered response. "Is this what you would call a Jewish nose?" she asked then. She paused in anticipation, drawing on her cigarette. There may have been more to this question than Frieda intended, indeed must have been more, for she was at that point in the evening when intention was regularly transcended.

"Frieda!" The B.T. reproached her. "You have a great nose. Besides, a nose is not a sign, not a, a...."

"If you didn't notice, Frieda," Spitzer broke in, "we are not now joking. In any case, an American knows nothing of such things," he concluded with seeming irrelevance. Nevertheless, the contempt in his voice seemed to suggest that a great deal was at stake here.

"'Queen for a Day,' Yoolyoos. Fairy tales, not history," replied Frieda who was familiar with his thinking on this and a number of related topics.

"No, never history." He took his hat and stood up to go.

"What's got his nose out of joint?" Joe Finneran, who had just stepped up to the bar, wanted to know of Frieda.

"My nose." She wrinkled it.

"Gee," he exaggerated his wonder, "you'll have to tell me all about it," he took a beat, "when I have less time. Meanwhile check out this schnozz," he snapped a finger against the high bony ridge of his own nose. "They didn't call my dad 'Beak' Finneran for nothing."

This attempt to cut across ethnic lines carried no weight with Spitzer. "We are not comparing noses, Herr Finneran," he said stiffly, that ominous 'Herr' a sure indication that his displeasure ran deep. "We attempt to raise the level, to

develop a little history, psychology, literature, and someone can only think of her own nose. This one, Goldmann
would have called an ego and an ignoramus." He walked
back a few steps to lift a cigarette from Frieda's package.

"Who the Christ is Goldmann?" Finneran said, not
quite under his breath, heading back to his table with a
round of drinks.

"I'll tell you who Goldmann is," Spitzer called after
him, threatening. Spitzer had a great many stories to tell,
and one story that he was not yet quite ready to tell. Bits
and pieces of it had become known, nevertheless; some
Spitzer had let slip; the numbers tattooed on his arm had
implied others. For the most part, however, he remained
for them a hard-drinking prole of a foreigner, a crank with
an overbearing hobbyhorse, an employee of the University's
Buildings & Grounds department. Spitzer, of course, saw
himself quite differently—as an artist in all but name, a
cosmopolite with the dirt of the graveyard under his fingernails, a custodian for a lost world.

"If you don't see the point I'm making," Frieda took the
cigarette from Spitzer's hand before he could light it, "then
don't smoke my cigarettes." She tore away a strip of the cigarette paper and dumped the tobacco into an ashtray.

"I am sorry to say that you have no point," Spitzer said, and
before Frieda could think to reply he had pocketed her pack of
cigarettes and was walking quickly toward the back door.

"You see," the B.T. began to explain to Frieda, for these
squabbles caused him some anxiety. "I think he was talking
about...."

"Who cares!" Frieda interrupted him nervelessly. "I

was talking about what I was talking about, and you were talking about what you were talking about." She signaled the bartender for cigarettes.

"That's it," the B.T. said with unlikely animation. "The tefillin are a sign—that's what I was saying—a sign of God's power and dominion." He lit her cigarette. "With a number branded on your arm from a concentration camp, I was saying, it's the opposite. I think you were saying that a nose is a sign and I was saying that a nose is not a sign." Often the passion and intensity of the B.T.'s burgeoning religious sensibility imbued his speech with an aspect of incoherence not consistent with his total sobriety.

"It's a sign to me," Frieda insisted. "It's a secular sign, so you wouldn't know anything about it."

"Hurry up please it's time," one of the bartenders called wearily, but not wearily enough to obscure his knowing and oddly nostalgic emphasis; he had begun a dissertation on Eliot many years before.

The hour was fast approaching 2:00 a.m.—indeed, the clock on the wall, set ahead by design, already showed that time—the Castle was closing. A second bartender tipped ashtrays and flipped chairs up onto the tables with reckless haste. A third stood at the door shooing the laggards out into the snow. "Vaya con Dios," he muttered after them, "get the fuck out."

No one was anxious to leave. The Finnerans had as yet made no move to depart, and Frieda, with the B.T. on her heels, joined their table. Her status, she considered, permitted this. There remained beside the Finnerans only Kevin-for-crying-out-loud. Several of the regulars who had joined the table at one point or another during the course of the evening had moved on as soon as Finneran began to talk of the natural affinity of revolutionary movements. His views were well known to them. Finneran's interest was not, as one might suppose, truly ideological. What little he understood of the matter was restricted to the rumors he picked up whenever he returned to the streets of his youth, the streets where Beak Finneran ruled the brazen cars as a crossing guard at the local grade school. Whispers of gun running for the IRA was the sum and substance of it. Certainly, no Palestinian, no German Commie, no Khymer Rouge had as much right to arms; to hell with affinity—thus did Finneran dispose of the issue once he got his Irish up. He was no longer the jovial son of the old sod he had been at the start of the evening.

"Hurry up please it's time," the first bartender repeated, and to those who had known him as a promising undergraduate the words had an irony all their own.

Outside, the air was even colder than it had been earlier, and yet it seemed to Frieda to have lost its power to chill. There was no question of her concerning herself with this paradox at the moment—it was just that while the air did feel colder, she noted that she herself felt warmer. She let her coat hang open. This is living, she thought. She was loathe to go home. The snow had stopped. The night sky had taken on a soft, benevolent sheen, the snowy ground itself hinted at innocent amusements, the chances of something dreadful happening seemed to Frieda at the moment greatly reduced. She offered the B.T. a ride as far as her own apartment. He accepted with alacrity.

"Shouldn't you be home repenting," Frieda made a U-turn in the empty street, "instead of out carousing?" She was feeling companionable and, although one never knew with this Ba'al T'shuva when a conversation might turn intolerable, she was in a mood to take her chances.

"It's not only repenting, it's also returning," he put in hurriedly, wishing she had given him just a moment to savor being there in the dark in the car with her.

"Which are you supposed to do first then, repent or return?" It was an ultimately idle question on Frieda's part, yet it did nothing less than throw the B.T. for a loop, for it touched on the very problem that had confounded him from the start of his search.

"I don't know," he answered finally, an unseen blush suffusing his entire body, "I have the impression that it might be more of an attitude. Weltanschauung. I don't know."

Frieda didn't know either. Nor was the word "weltanschauung" in her vocabulary; but this did not make the slightest difference to either of them, and that was the beauty of it. "Weltschmaltz," she began hopefully, thinking to press her advantage.

"Weltschmaltz?!," he began to laugh. "O.K., if you're a chicken.... What about weltpeltz? If you're a mink...." It was some time before the B.T. was able to stop laughing, his efforts to choke off his laughter resulting only in a wild series of snorts—which would hardly prove likely, he thought at once, to enhance his chances with her. "If you're a person," he said finally, "and you are definitely a person," he paused to give that statistical secular entity its spiritual due, "it's schmertz. Pain. Weltschmertz."

"Didn't I say that? Didn't I *say* schmutz. Weltschmutz." Once again the B.T. was overcome with laughter. "Dirt," he gasped, "that's dirt."

"'Ave your fun, Dearie." Frieda brought to bear here all the menace of Dietrich playing a cockney hooker. "But it's not as if the world is a very clean place."

Nor, the B.T. added silently, automatically, especially well-lighted either.

From long habit she drove home so slowly and carefully that the car could barely be said to be moving, but the way was short and they were soon there. One might have thought that after an evening at the Castle, squeezing the car into its space between the two blue Hondas would prove difficult, but Frieda never gave it a thought. She was, of course, incapable at that point of thinking about it in any way that would enhance her chances of accomplishing it successfully. In any case, it was always done before she knew it.

Now she stretched in the seat and pulled the open bottle of beer from her coat pocket. "Ah," she said and lit a cigarette, "Back to repenting...."

"What I don't know is if what I'm doing, is what I would be doing," the B.T. told her with some intensity, "if I were doing it the way it's supposed to be done."

"I know the feeling," Frieda confessed glumly, aware that her companion was more than a few years her junior. "What is anything really like?" She drew on the cigarette.

The B.T. looked at her uncomfortably, searching for a worthy response. He sighed, and he hoped that the weight of that sigh would go some way to mitigate his earlier fit of laughter. "This...," he began uncertainly.

"I mean life," Frieda interrupted him sharply. It was a matter of some urgency for one who like Frieda often had the feeling that what she experienced on a daily basis was not life itself, not the grand highway of story and song, but rather a narrow, winding dirt path which, though it had its own pleasures, was at no point wide enough for two to walk abreast. "Real life," she said, putting out her cigarette. She straightened in her seat and drank off the last of the beer. "Do you see those two people?" She pointed with the bottle toward two figures passing under a street lamp a short distance down the block, and then, throwing her head back, put the bottle to her brow with a fortune-teller's flair. "I predict that they're coming to visit me."

For the B.T., who was both a conventional and not an entirely hospitable young man, this was Frieda at her most appealing. "It's two o'clock in the morning," he reminded her primly.

"In fact, I'm expecting them." She turned toward him with a smile he was able to misinterpret at once, and then turned away again to roll down the window.

"What are you doing?" The B.T. grabbed her arm. "Be careful. You're drunk. You don't know them."

Although she was not truly drunk, this much was clear—had Frieda not spent the preceding hours drinking at the Castle, she would have had to have spent them drinking elsewhere in order to achieve her present level of confidence and relaxed amiability. "I don't know her," she admitted, feeling blissfully hospitable in spite of it. "But I used to know him...and his father." Frieda felt for an instant the nervous excitement that father had once caused in her. "The proverbial single father....the three of us spent a lot of time together." She might have looked back on those evenings with less fondness, however, had she been better able to remember them. "Pssssst!" she whispered loudly as the pair drew even with the car. "Tommy! It's Frieda."

Tired and bedraggled as they were, Tom and Rosie jumped straight up into the air and, upon touching down, assumed a defensive posture. Rosie grabbed hold of the back of Tom's coat. "Get away from us, you bastards," she screamed as Frieda thrust her arm out the window in greeting.

"Sssshhhhhh!" hissed the B.T. getting out of the car. "People are sleeping." He looked up at the nearby buildings.

"Yeah, well, people might be dying too." This girl was a great one for drawing the line. She would make it known at once that she herself was under no illusion as to which of these states should command the greater respect. Indeed, Rosie wished him to think that she was acquainted with a world where dying was the far more common complaint. She pulled her knitted cap off and ran her hand through her matted hair. "Sweat," she said, as if to lend a kind of gritty reality to her claim.

The B.T. took her in. He gave her the benefit of the doubt; Rosie, however, took his silence to mean that he had bought it.

"Hey...Frieda!" Tom had a deep slow voice. "Right. Yeah, I tried to call you before. O.K. Right. This is great." He tried to shake the girl loose. "O.K. Right. So...." He awaited his instructions.

Frieda stepped from the car. Rosie looked her full in the

face. "It's cold," she said, pulling her knit cap back on again, her tone an unpleasant mix of petulance and accusation.

The B.T. came forward for a closer look. Only minutes earlier this would have meant simply making sure that anything touching Frieda's life, touched his own as well; and even now he was as yet quite unaware that he had been admiring the wild tangle of the girl's hair, or that he was suddenly susceptible to the allure of a simple knit cap.

"My Dad says, you know, hello," the boy reported formally. "And this is Xenia." He smiled his slow smile, feeling better with all the cards out on the table.

There were to be no further introductions that evening, however, as Rosie headed for the entrance to the yard without another word, and Frieda, dismissing the B.T. with a wave, moved quickly after her. Upstairs, she wheeled the television cart into the living room for their viewing pleasure. She carried one chair into her bedroom to give them more space. She put out towels. All the while Tom and Rosie sat as if stupefied by their travels, watching her move about the small apartment.

"Hey," offered Tom, "don't bother."

"It's hot in here though," Rosie felt obliged to point out, pulling off a sweatshirt which advertised The Maine Mall.

"Thanks for the bulletin," Frieda said testily, relinquishing with little regret the role of perfect hostess. She lit a cigarette, half-hoping the girl was an anti-smoking zealot.

"Can I bum a couple?" Rosie asked holding out her hand. Frieda passed her the package of cigarettes without comment and the girl shook out the cigarettes which remained.

"Tell her why we came to Chicago," she ordered her companion, "I'm going to pee."

"We?" Frieda mouthed the word at Tom. She shook out a sheet and wrapped it around the sofa cushions for Rosie's bed. Tom replied with a pantomime by which he hoped to dispel the notion that anything at all about his companion could apply to himself as well. He began to busy himself with unrolling his sleeping bag.

"I don't hear you telling her," the girl shouted from the bathroom.

"Xenia's looking for her father. Right now she don't know shit about him, not even his name." He brought his hand to his mouth in a languid gesture of apology.

"I didn't say to talk about my shit, did I!" the girl called out with more good humor now than truculence.

"Her mom is from Chicago," Tom continued his mechanical exposition, "so we figure maybe her father is too." There was something in the way he said this that made it plain he himself believed no such thing.

"Yeah, as soon as we got here, I got that feeling very definitely." Rosie entered the room slowly, thoughtfully. She went to her knapsack and began to empty it. "Look at this," she said matter-of-factly, passing Frieda a much-handled envelope as if she, Frieda, were suddenly an integral part of their small search party. Inside was a birth certificate.

Frieda did the best she could. "You were born in Ohio," she told Rosie, yawning. "Here's your name." The words moved about the page at will and she could read no more. "Xenia, Ohio, it says here."

"We moved around a lot," Rosie answered, taking the

document back from her, "but before that it was definitely Chicago. The pigs, the riots...."

"Pigs," Frieda echoed without comprehension.

"I know all about that stuff from my mom." She studied the birth certificate intently.

"Does it say your father's name?" Tom's interest had been piqued by the production of documentary evidence.

"My father's name is not Randall Parks. I'll never believe that. That can't be his name." Rosie's voice seemed to crack.

Frieda stood up abruptly in the face of her emotion. "I'm going to bed."

"My mom never told me one thing about him; so that probably means he was a capitalist." If the word sounded strangely on her lips, she certainly spoke it with a homely ease. "Randall sounds like sort of like a capitalist name, doesn't it? My grandfather's a capitalist, I know that much."

Frieda stared at her. "I'm going to bed," she repeated. She was as good as her word, and asleep without regaining consciousness. That was just the way she liked it. There was no feeling of security to compare with that which a guest on the living room floor could provide.

CHAPTER FIVE

Getting Acquainted

The B.T., with no more to go on than his initial impression, had developed a pressing interest in Rosie's comings and goings. As these were nothing if not immune to schedule, he had reluctantly come to the conclusion that he would have to lay in wait for her.

"Serendipity was out of the question," he imagined telling her at some tender moment well into the relationship. But still, just the thought of serendipity made the B.T. vaguely uncomfortable this morning, revealing as it did that he had yet to come to terms with the idea that God ran this world on a minute by minute and case by case basis; and serendipity had no place in it "no way, no how," as Shlomo put it emphatically. He and Shlomo had discussed it back and forth last night until the B.T.'s ear was numb against the receiver.

Now, in the last hour of the morning, the B.T. took up a position across the street from the Greenwood Co-operative apartments. Frieda had mentioned that her guest was not an early riser, and this had allowed him to spend the morning reading in his carrel at Regenstein Library. What he had learned there, however, could only contribute to the agitation that the present enterprise inspired in him. While nodding over a work of recent scholarship, it suddenly occurred to him that perhaps he had been born for a different, altogether more Jewish type of learning.

He dismissed the thought, shaking himself awake, and yet, he might have seen it coming. Had not his first taste of rabbinic thinking—just over a year ago now—given him the idea that he was interested in literature because he was a Jew. Had it not become clear to him pretty quickly then that the Jews had in fact invented literary criticism. It had stunned him at first to think it, yet by now it was a full-fledged theory; he was convinced—the impulse was a Jewish impulse. So, perhaps, if it were true that he was in graduate school because he was a Jew, perhaps he ought simply to go ahead and be a Jew because he was a Jew.

As he leaned back against the sun-warmed side of a mini-van to wait, he tried to push a variety of career-related thoughts from his mind. The sun shone full on his face, a near-mild breeze eddied by. The B.T. took a deep, prayerful breath and expelled it slowly. He chose a book from his briefcase and began to read. "Ben Bag Bag said: Turn it and turn it and look in it and grow grey and old in it, and do not stir from it, for there is no better portion for you than this." He read the words haltingly and then covered them with is hand, and tried to recite the rabbinic saying from memory.

What if that were true, he wondered, what if there were no better portion? He brought to mind the bit he had read about Rabbi Ishmael's nephew asking whether he could learn "Greek wisdom" now that he had studied the whole of the Torah. Rabbi Ishmael responded that we are commanded to "meditate in it day and night"'; and he told his nephew, "go and seek out an hour when it is neither day nor night, and then study Greek wisdom." The B.T. shivered with pleasure. I've got to go, he told himself with some agitation, I can't wait here like this. I've got to leave.

But just then he looked up and saw Rosie appear across the way. He knew her at once although he had not seen her in daylight before. After an instant during which he took in how young she was, he noticed that her companion had stepped out beside her. Yet he had but to recall Frieda's assurance that they were simply fellow hitch-hikers, for Tom to turn away without a word, and Rosie start off by herself down the block toward 53rd Street.

As he hurried after her, he noticed especially her hair, as wild as he remembered it, but now a radiant mass of red-brown curls under the bright sun. She half-turned at the sound of running feet behind her, glanced over her shoulder to see a stocky, bespectacled young man carrying a satchel, and continued on her way.

"Excuse me," the B.T. called out, crestfallen that she had not somehow known him as he had known her. He lunged the last few steps toward her. "You're Xenia. I was with Frieda the other night."

She took a step backwards. He had come so close to her that she imagined she was feeling his harshly drawn breath on her face. "Ohhhhh-Kay," she drawled with sardonic intent, looking him straight in the eye and folding her arms across her chest for emphasis.

"I'm just identifying myself." The B.T. looked at her wrists where the over-size coat sleeves had fallen back from them. They were very narrow and very white and he liked them. "If you're walking, I'll walk with you."

"Well, I was walking." She underlined the tense. It seemed almost as if she might be unable to resume that particular activity, so great did her sense of interruption seem to be. She studied him for several instants. He's not cute at all, she thought, focusing on his glasses and his nascent beard. "Are you growing a beard?" she asked. She had that common brand of curiosity, genuine enough, but far too circumscribed and shallow for the times.

"I'm trying to, but it's hard." He gave her a little smile.

It occurred to Rosie that he might look better with a beard, and she was encouraged by this impression. "Let's go," she said impatiently. Lifting the headphones which hung at her neck and adjusting them over her ears, she strode off ahead of him, head thrust forward, hands in her pockets.

Nini's Pizzeria on 53rd Street had recently undergone yet another renovation, lending credence to the rumor that Nini's son, an itinerant house painter and some-time cineaste, had dried out and was back in town. Nini always gave his son's creativity free rein; and most often, after running his trembling fingers up and down the walls for minutes at a time, the son rewarded his father's faith. The pictures which hung along the back wall, perhaps they were stills from "The Bicycle Thief" and "The Rose Tattoo," were removed and Nini's son washed the walls down and repainted them with the same brand of projector-light white. New pictures, stills from "Zabriski Point" and "The Great Caruso," for example, would be hung in their place. Patrons admired the job Nini's son had done, and he was usually able to line up a couple of jobs for the Spring. By then, however, Nini's son was rarely still in town; or if he were, he had gotten out of the business, this time for good.

Frieda had a soft spot in her heart for Nini's son. She had whiled away more than an occasional evening at the Castle in his company. They had, they discovered, a similar taste in movies; in spite of this, of course, they had never gone to a movie together, nor even seen each other outside Castle's University Tavern until Frieda went to work for Nini. When she took the job—the photos on the wall were from "Roman Holiday" and "Mean Streets"—Nini's son had not approved; but, as with so little else in his life, he had learned to live with it. So, Frieda was standing at the service bar watching Nini's son crack an egg into the blender when Paul Silverman, newspaper in hand, arrived for lunch for the third consecutive day.

Certainly, Paul had begun to wonder what was drawing him so persistently to Nini's Pizzeria, and he had been content to settle for its location and good fries as an answer. He was, he intuited, only taking the very first steps of what was likely to be a long journey; at this point he simply needed some place to be. His days were predictable and aimless, his laundry piled up, his walls were already a clutter of news reports from the African continent. Just today he had posted this: "Africa remains a mystery, even for Africans." Paul took some considerable heart in that.

"I'm thinking of quitting my job here," Frieda told him,

setting his water glass down. "Nini's is known for anonymity. Now neither of us is anonymous, and," she paused quite pertly enough until it suddenly became apparent that she intended to say no more.

Paul, of course, could not know that it was his patronage specifically that made quitting her job just now the furthest thing from Frieda's mind; yet some instinct—or perhaps it was only confusion—prompted him to maintain a provocative silence, merely snapping his newspaper into shape by way of interrogation.

Frieda wiped down the Formica table. "We have a Special today," she told him, reaching back to tuck her blouse more securely into the elastic waistband of her baggy black slacks, only to find that it was already sufficiently tucked.

He peered at her over the top of the paper. "Perhaps I can arrange to lunch here only on your days off," he suggested with the sort of mock urbanity which had gone over well in his former life; "if that's at all helpful," he smiled, "anonymity-wise."

"It's Osso Bucco," Frieda said flatly. She would have liked to have been able to flounce away from the table at that point, but the flounce, she understood, was not in her repertoire.

"Burkina Faso," Paul replied at once, motivated by who knows what linguistic demon.

Fear struck Frieda Zale. She understood only too well that her inability to make sense of his words meant no less than the onset of a dread neurological disorder. "It's a veal dish," she told him without letting on that anything was wrong, "it's good."

Then, suddenly, he became aware that here was a woman to whom one could say 'Burkina Faso' and live. "I'll take it," he told her jovially, "I like veal." This is going well, he thought. "I used to eat veal out at least three times a week. Piccata, piccata, piccata." He furrowed his brow. For some reason the very word called back at once a flood of sensations. Where had he been dining the evening someone told him a half-million-dollar bonus was not out of the question? What exquisite morsel had he swallowed then, what wine sipped with characteristic aplomb? "And I don't think I actually know what veal is, exactly."

"Well, I'm not a cook," Frieda corrected whatever notion he might be harboring, only to know at once that for him this deficiency would outweigh all else. Nonetheless, she tried to recoup. "Actually, I can cook a few things. I once made kidneys. It was for a literary event."

"A soiree?" Paul riposted casually.

"Don't say 'soiree,'" Frieda ordered, and turned on her heel. She was jubilant; it was as good as a flounce. It was so good, in fact, that she was able to walk away from him without so much as a thought for the figure she cut; that is, if he had not, as indeed he had not, already returned to his newspaper. In the kitchen she was informed that the Osso Bucco had just run out.

Although the B.T. and Rosie had walked the rest of the way to Nini's Pizzeria in silence, when they reached the restaurant the B.T. sat down across the table from her as though this had been agreed on between them; and Rosie, who hated to spend what little money she had left, did not object. The B.T. took off his jacket. He wore a plaid shirt in which olive green predominated, and over it a cardigan in a greenish shade of brown.

He definitely gets the Worst-Dressed Award, Rosie thought. She watched him as he removed his glasses and wiped them with a white handkerchief he pulled from his jeans. She saw that his eyes, which she had assumed were merely magnified by the lenses, were in fact quite large and very clear and sweet in a way with which she was unfamiliar. This was the way which a look of pure intensity, when it isn't hard and cold, can be sweet and inviting. She pulled her heavy coat off to reveal the red union suit she had slept in. "What do you want to get?"

"Whatever you want." He put his glasses back on and pressed them to the bridge of his nose.

"B.T.," Frieda said, surprised, putting down the menus and greeting Rosie without enthusiasm. They had been unaware of Frieda's approach. As there seemed no inclination on any one's part to follow up, Frieda drew on professional experience. "I'll be back," she told them.

"No more Osso and no more Bucco," she reported to Paul. He did not look up at once, so she took a moment to admire his neatly combed hair; it had a rich glossy look which she associated with wealth and romance. And his profile, his features, resolutely forthright, nothing here of anguish or angst; nothing to reflect what she was pleased to imagine as the condition of the man himself. It was a paradox she found oddly inflammatory. She looked down at herself and saw a speck of tomato sauce on the pocket of her blouse. He'll look up now and notice it, Frieda thought.

"Occupational hazard," Paul told her as he looked up,

lifted the paper wide between them and folded it back upon itself.

"I am very familiar with them," Frieda said grimly, facing into the sea of newsprint.

"You're not alone." He gave the paper a final shake and set it back down in front of him. "OSHA used to check in on me on a regular basis." To his surprise, he smiled one of his old charming smiles. How ripe, how sensuous, how downright sexy it had once felt to smile that smile, infused as it had been with the magnificent burden of his will. But how should he understand that same smile now, shining forth, as he thought, from a different man entirely. He looked at the woman. She appeared unmoved.

Yet nothing was further from the truth. Could it really be, Frieda was wondering, just slightly weak in the knees, that she was not alone? Not alone! She stifled a sigh. Uninformed as to who or what OSHA might be, but seeing no way in which such knowledge would help to nurture their relationship, she decided to shift ground.

"Speaking of OSHA," she drew her order pad out, "we've just run out of Osso Bucco."

"This is harder than I thought it would be." He took up the menu again.

"Have you ever noticed that life tends to be like that." Frieda expressed this rather bleak assessment with a cheerful professional neutrality; nonetheless, Paul raised his eyes to her at once, sharply, hopefully. And his look held her. "Have you decided?" she asked him quickly then, to obscure the impression she had that a larger issue had just been broached.

He placed his order and Frieda nearly ran to the kitchen so anxious did she suddenly find herself to have him eat and be on his way. And yet, strong as the desire had seemed in that instant, it was short-lived. No sooner did she imagine her relief at having him gone, then she began to plan how and when it might happen that she would see him again. How lucky she felt in consequence to know that he was still there in the restaurant; that he was at that moment dependent on her for his sustenance; indeed, that it might still prove to be the case that she was not, in fact, alone.

A subtle change had come over Rosie as soon as she heard Frieda call the B.T. by name. Initials as appellation had always been for her something particularly fine, something both macho and lacking in pretense. Something, in fact, that she was looking for in a man. "B.T.," she virtually murmured, "what does that stand for?"

"Issachar. Call me Issachar." He looked at her earnestly, but very much aware that with her the demand had at once become negotiable. "The Jews did not change their names while they were living in Egypt," he could not help adding. To his astonishment, Rosie seemed to draw herself to attention. Was it his imagination or was her doughy pallor actually giving way to a quality more porcelaneous right before his eyes?

"Why didn't they?" she wanted to know. The subject of names was very close to Rosie's heart. Her own name had been a source of fascination to her since childhood and she had questioned her mother often on the circumstances of her naming. The answers had not been reassuring. Rosa Luxemburg, Lois had told her, and something about a revolution and a canal.

The B.T. was elated. "Because they were faithful to the God of their Fathers." Say no more for the present, he cautioned himself, feeling the flood of words building. He picked up the menu.

"I'm dying for a cigarette," Rosie called out to Frieda. "You need to sit at a table with an ashtray," Frieda pointed out in the flat, nearly satiric drone she sometimes used on the job. "We don't put ashtrays out on all the tables."

"You don't have to smoke," the B.T. joined in pleasantly. It was his first false move.

"Yes, I do!" Rosie responded without so much as a glance at him. Never tell me I don't have to smoke, she railed silently. "Do you have one, Frieda?"

"Think of this." The B.T. was not getting the point. "It could be the first of all the cigarettes you'll never smoke." He looked up at Frieda without really seeing her.

Stung by the implicit challenge to her own habit, and by what she intuited of his altered allegiance, Frieda sided at once with her fellow smoker." I'll get you one."

"Thanks!" Rosie responded to this display of solidarity with rarely expressed gratitude. She pushed her chair back from the table and stood up. "Never tell me I don't have to smoke," she told the B.T. before moving to sit at a table across the aisle. "Only my father can tell me I don't have to smoke."

"'Turn it and turn it....'" he quoted at her back, already reaching into the briefcase for his book.

CHAPTER SIX

The Politics of Pure Wool

I am an American, thought Lois with unwitting aptness as her car sped toward Chicago—and this is America. She had been feeling nostalgic on and off all day as she travelled the highways through Ohio, Michigan, and now, in the late-afternoon sun, across northern Indiana. Driving alone like this through an unpeopled landscape, she was nearly able to believe again in the world of her childhood, in an unseen citizenry that was healthy, wealthy and wise, in a land that was clean and beautiful and free. It amazed her now that she had ever learned the truth, had ever come to see through to the corruption and injustice that had been revealed to her at the heart of her country.

When the realization had come, it had been a wrecking ball of a shock, or, truly, the demolition charge that brought down Pruit-Igo. It had seemed to her at the time that nothing could remain standing; but she was to learn, often to her discomfort, that most of what had made her who she was had remained intact. The shock of it—no one could have been less prepared, less informed, or more blinded by conventional wisdom and confident self-absorption. And yet, something must have been stirring beneath the natural ebullience that marked her childhood, behind the pep-rally smile of her teenage years; something that produced a growing impatience with the bourgeois concerns and homey intolerance she had been raised on; something that welcomed the temper of the times, and drove her into the arms of a succession of campus radicals and rent strike orga-nizers. Finally, inevitably, there came the revelation of her beloved and loving father as a plutocrat without a human face, a man politically-incorrect since birth. Her education complete, Lois left college in the middle of her second year.

Then Chicago, the summer of '68, the sight of the armed power of the state—so much violence inhering in its mere presence—had in no way cowed or unmanned her. Rather had violence itself been given a boost; horrible imag-inings preoccupied her mind, held her sympathy in thrall, as if in self-defense. Children set afire, severed ears, slave auctions and lynchings, Indians massacred and Jews tossed into ovens—she felt ready to jump out of her own skin! And, at the same time, she had never felt so much herself, so exalted, so at one with *them*. Sky-high.

Yet still unprepared for the anger, for the raw screams of her heart's grievances, heretofore innocent—as far as she knew—of even the impulse, she had thrown a beer bottle at a policeman's head. And the sight of his blood had thrilled her. Bring home the war. Now. It was never like the first time again—not even the smoke bomb she had delivered and set herself—never again so straight-forward, so deliri-ous, so much of an answer.

Now, after all these years, it remained inconceivable to her that with things the way they were—with decay and deprivation, decadence and deep shit everywhere she looked—it was simply inconceivable to her that the time was not ripe. "What has changed?" she would ask; "Just what the fuck has changed?" she would demand as her former comrades rejoined the bourgeoisie. She, who had gone underground not because she had to, but because it had seemed the thing to do, the fashion of the time, could find no compelling reason to surface. America could not reclaim her.

As to Simon and Willis, as far as she was concerned their commitment was surely a given of their color. Not to mention their status—at least Simon's. An ex-con and autodidact Simon was as made for the part as they come. While Willis Washington, a soft-spoken college boy, was still somehow able to share in his older cousin's lustre. The men were good friends to her; Simon always brought her bagels and the newest in hip hop. Best of all, they were serious men; she liked that in them—their hate would not be appeased. What she could not know was that hate was all of it. That would have depressed and confused her, for Lois believed with Che that "the true revolutionary is guided by great feelings of love."

Lois believed it, Lois felt it, but she often wondered exactly what it meant. Love was the hardest part, of that much she was sure. So often what seemed to be love turned out to be something different altogether. In any case, love had been a lot easier to come by twenty years ago. She remembered the love she had felt for Harmon Smith, the Black fourth grader she had tutored in a campus-community tutoring project. Harmon's schoolwork had improved.

Harmon told her what a good teacher she was. It had been easy to love Harmon Smith. But even then, Lois recalled now with rare candor, it had been harder to love Harmon's restless young mother or Harmon's unidentified young father or even Harmon's beleaguered young grandmother, all strangely less loveable than Harmon himself. Nevertheless, Lois had been up to all of it because she understood that they were victims no less than Harmon himself. Power to the People—that was the answer to restlessness, to youth, to lack of opportunity, to oppression. Revolution. Now.

Yet in the face of all the rhetoric and of her steely hopes, Lois was stuck and in her heart of hearts she knew it. And she also knew that stuck was not the right place to be. Stuck would not do the trick. Great feelings of love trapped her, seemed to immobilize her by their enormity as time had passed; and great feelings cried out for great action. Lately she had come to think that it would take a better generation than her own to bring the remedy to the people. In the meantime, the conviction that an underground existed would bring hope and encouragement, would have a powerful effect on hearts and minds. As for Lois herself, correct action would characterize her daily life, and outrages against the people would be totted up and eventually avenged. An action now would signal an ongoing revolutionary presence, would counteract the propaganda the pigs had put out that the Movement was dead. "You wish," Lois muttered through gritted teeth.

A hundred miles east of Chicago she parked her car at the Interstate Rest Stop. Had she been trailing Rosie with a pack of hounds she could hardly have done better. As she entered the vestibule, she saw but did not look at Simon Washington who was leaning against the glass souvenir case and appeared to be wholly occupied brushing donut sugar from the front of his shiny blue parka. She walked directly into the Restroom and when she emerged after several minutes Simon was still at his post, now pretending to admire the trucker caps and the belt buckles stamped Diamond Reo and Peterbilt. Lois walked by him into the restaurant and took a table near the glass doors the better to see and be seen from the vestibule.

Several more minutes passed and Lois began to wonder nervously whether something was wrong. Simon had not budged from his spot. Instead, he had removed his dark glasses and was glaring at her now with undisguised irritation. What is it, what is it? Lois asked herself anxiously, what had she forgotten? She studied Simon hoping to catch a hint, knowing how far he was from helping her out. She began to perspire. Then she had it. He was waiting for the high sign: all is well, exchange cars as planned. But what was the high sign? She felt around in her coat pockets for a clue, but found only a packet of Kleenex which she had half-withdrawn before a wave of anxious heat broke over her and helped her to remember. Hurriedly she pulled her coat off and folded it over the back of an empty chair. Then with great deliberation she shook out the long wool scarf and laid it over the coat just so. Simon did not so much as blink an eye in her direction, but put on his rabbit-fur ear muffs at once and walked outside.

From a stool at the counter, Paul Silverman watched his sister in the mirror. When she entered the restaurant, he had seen simply a slight woman weighted down unreasonably by a leather shoulder bag, a pale woman in a dark overcoat with a long hand knit scarf dangling. Then he noticed the scuffed cowboy boots and he knew her, recognized the ancient black-watch-plaid coat and understood that he had dismissed her just as she hungered to be dismissed --one of The People. He must tell her that.

It had been some time since she had last suggested that they meet. Then she had been pleased to hear that he was no longer a member of the investment firm so prestigious as to require no further identification. They had discussed this and other matters (Lois pressing on him, from that same leather shoulder bag, article upon article of political analysis) in the small motel room where he awaited the results of yet another job interview. He recalled the Third World Perspective Map and their awful argument about whether or not "the Zionist Entity" should appear on it. Nevertheless, perhaps because they had played together well as children, Paul was always happy when she wanted to see him. He waited impatiently now for her to give the signal they had agreed upon.

Finally, Lois reached over and took the packet of Kleenex from the pocket of her coat. Slowly she drew out a tissue, slowly she brought it to her nose, slowly and noisily she blew into it. At once Paul left his seat at the counter to join her. He squeezed her shoulder hard before sitting down. There were tears in his eyes.

"Is everything O.K.?" he whispered anxiously. "Is anything wrong? I mean," he looked around the room and wondered what he was looking for, "are *things* all right?"

"*Things*," she echoed his emphasis, "*Things*," she became

incredulous, "*things* are fine, of course. The rich are not getting richer and the poor are not getting poorer. The free market and the stock market are at work for the greater good. Americans of all races, religions and creeds are getting good jobs and a good education...."

Paul interrupted her, unperturbed. "But I meant...."

Then there were tears in her own eyes as she told him about Rosie. "I think she's probably in Chicago. She knows about Chicago. She's looking for her father The Pig."

Paul looked into her light eyes and saw the shock of the betrayal burning there as brightly as ever. What must that have been like, he had wondered over and over, for her to have given herself in all her steely purity, her heady idealism, her youthful righteousness—to an agent provocateur from the FBI. He literally grew cold at the thought. "Should we get coffee?" He rubbed his hands. "Your father sends his love." There was something about growing up in the shadow of Harry Silverman that had brought the two of them, many years before, to the conversational habit of disavowing his paternity.

"If I had wanted your father to know, I would have told him myself. I talked to your father on the phone last week. I told him Rosie is turning out to be the All-American Consumer." In fact, this was Lois's way of thanking her father for the assistance he had provided her from time to time over the years. The penchant for shopping, which in her mother she had regularly reviled as status frenzy, conspicuous consumption, narcissism, and worse, in her daughter she understood as victimization by the system. "I didn't want Rosie to grow up thinking that everyone drives a golf cart and has a powder room by the front door," she pointed out, answering a question that had never been raised between them.

"If you're coming to Chicago, I have a second bedroom," his voice trailed off.

Lois looked up at the waitress and smiled the intense, moist smile she reserved for those in the service sector. "How ya doin' today?" She had long since perfected a rough and ready form of address for her work with the public. She aimed for an offhand, authentic kind of familiarity, an I'm-on-the-street-if-you're-on-the-street style of chat, and she had got it down pretty well. Nonetheless, Paul flinched to hear her; were people deaf to that stagey obliteration of clarity and class?

The waitress who had been standing by for more moments than she liked, waiting to take the order, directed her attention to Paul. "You folks want coffee?"

"Actually, I'm trying to give up coffee," Lois told her confidentially, determined to acknowledge the other's humanity as best she could. "Do you drink much coffee yourself," she glanced at the name tag fixed to the woman's pink blouse, "Brenda?" She straightened in her chair and looked up with an expectant smile.

"So that's one coffee then." Brenda maintained, and left them.

Lois, who until this moment had seen in Brenda, as she would in any such Brenda, a tough, savvy, generous representative of the people, was intensely disappointed. "Did you notice how she refused to engage me? Who am I... Nancy Reagan or what?" Her pale, oval face was suddenly over-shadowed by the memory of the ongoing struggle.

"What time is it?" Her watch had been the very first

bourgeois constraint to go. She had not been so burdened in many years, and the impact of this simple refusal had been great. More than once, time had seemed, perversely perhaps, to be on her side. Take Greenwich Village, for example, in the spring of 1970. She had come down from 116th Street to meet someone, who was staying with someone, who was living at the home of someone whose parents were, as a result of their class and white skin privilege, travelling abroad. She had stopped on the corner of West 11th Street, just down the block from the place, to ask the time, and figure out how to get into the back garden behind the townhouse. There had been an enormous explosion then—the townhouse had blown.

Paul checked his watch. "Are you in a rush? Because if Rosie is in Chicago...," he began tentatively, keenly aware that he had not seen his niece for many years, and then only once. Harry Silverman would not approve; he was all about family.

"I'm not here because of Rosie, Paul," Lois corrected him sternly, although she realized at once she might just as well have let him think so. "I just thought why shouldn't you and I see each other as long as I was driving by." The waitress returned with Paul's coffee. "Hot turkey sandwich," Lois ordered, staring into Brenda's eyes as if she might compel in the waitress a recognition of her own recognition. This bold, unburnished stare had become habitual with her—it meant honesty, sincerity, and genuine openness—it meant no bourgeois bullshit here.

Paul looked down at the table. He wanted to ask her where she was driving and why. Instead he said, "Yolanda gave me something for you."

"Who else did you tell you were going to see me? Fuckin' Richard J. Daley or who?"

"It's an article about mothers and daughters. There's a picture of Yolanda and Letty drinking cappuccino. She wanted me to show you." Paul drew the folded newspaper clipping out of his shirt pocket and gave it to her, wondering the meanwhile if it were really possible that Lois believed the elder Daley to be alive and Mayor of Chicago.

""'It's absolutely my favorite thing in the world to do,' exults novelist Yolanda Silverman-Silbermann of these afternoon teas with her four-year-old daughter Letitia,'" Lois quoted without expression. "This is bad news, Paul," she said evenly, "Afternoon tea. Is Yolanda one of these Princess Di people now? Monarchy. This is just what America needs—one more little princess."

"Well," Paul began, but he was unable to address her outburst. Perhaps what had surprised him most when he had first become aware of the color of Lois's political leanings—he recalled well that fateful family Seder—was that she had political leanings at all. He knew of no prior interest on her part in the events of the day, in the faces and places in the news, let alone behind it. Nor was she a student of history.

Lois read from the text of the article, ""'Novelist and mother,' mused Ms. Silverman-Silbermann, 'to me that means simply that I'm a creator and nurturer twice over. Sometimes the enormity of that starts to overwhelm me, sometimes I'll get just a glimpse of how truly demanding those two roles are.' She chuckled at the thought.'" Lois closed her eyes and rested her forehead on her upturned palm. "Tell me honestly if you think she has any idea of what an ass she's being."

"Oh, well," Paul never knew just the right way to talk about one sister to the other. "You don't need to worry about Yolanda. She seems to like her life," he paused, "and your father likes her life too," he concluded, implying an alliance with the sister in his presence.

Lois bent to the turkey sandwich and brought several dripping forks full to her mouth in rapid succession. "What time is it?" she managed to ask again, mouth full; and this from a woman who was fond of warning, "I know what time it is, and you don't."

Paul pulled back the cuff of his shirt to show her his watch. "Have you ever wondered what it would be like literally not to know that there are units of time? In Africa…."

"Paul, that watch is bad news. You know that, don't you."

He glanced at the watch which had been crafted from an antique American gold coin. It had been advertised as the thinnest and most expensive watch in America. "Oh," he said vaguely, "I'm just wearing it to tell time." And indeed he could no longer remember what it had been—ambition, vanity, excess—that had prompted the extravagance of the purchase.

Lois pushed the last bit of soggy bread through the last patch of congealed gravy. Her plate was clean. She dipped the fingers first of one hand and then the other into her water-glass and wiped them dry with her unused napkin. "Ah," she said, sighing, satisfied politically as well, for she had eaten without the compulsion of leisure or the encumbrance of manners.

"What time is it?" she asked her brother again. "I have to go. Do you know what Rosie looks like? Do you think you'd know her? Just in case...."

"I doubt it. She was just a little girl when I saw her." Paul remembered his only meeting with his niece. It had not gone well. No more so had his last visit with Letitia, and the prospects for forming a bond with either niece over the long term, he thought, disheartened, did not seem very hopeful.

"You've only seen her once, Paul?" Lois was genuinely astonished. "Your father would not approve." She searched for her wallet in the capacious shoulder bag. "Rosie likes everyone and everyone likes Rosie. She's one of those people," she told him proudly, handing over a snapshot of a teenage girl, her face mostly shaded by the brim of a man's hat. "Do you see the resemblance?"

"She looks tough here." Paul stared at the picture and put it in his pocket.

"I brought her up to be tough. You and I were not brought up to be tough. It's a tough world." Lois got up and pulled on her heavy coat. "We were brought up to wear coats from Marshall Field's, to believe in the superiority of pure wool," she wound the scarf around her neck, "to patronize the saleslady, to eat the chicken salad sandwich on the eighth floor, to...."

"I was brought up to be tough," Paul interrupted finally.

"You were brought up to make money," she handed him the check. "Is a vulture tough? Is a bird of prey tough? Is a parasite tough?" She started for the door.

"Bobo Dioulasso," Paul muttered after her, leaving more of a tip than he had intended for Brenda the waitress.

Of course, a vulture is tough, he said to himself; a vulture is a tough old bird. In the past he would have succumbed to his irritation with Lois, to the contempt he had for her irrationality, her sophomoric indignation. He would have stormed out after her, he would have raged, he would have snapped his suspenders and stamped his expensive brogues. That he did none of this certainly revealed one dimension of the break that had occurred.

He caught up with her just outside the door. "Where are you headed?" he asked as casually as he could, putting an arm around her shoulder.

She reached up and pressed his hand. "Oh, Wyoming, you know, North Dakota." Her casualness matched his exactly. "Tell your father I'm fine."

As he drove back toward Chicago, Paul relived the visit from start to finish, wondering, as he always did, who his sister was and what she was doing. It was discouraging to realize that he did not even know for sure whether Lois was driving east or west, north or south. He berated himself for not having the wits to follow her at least long enough to ascertain the direction she was driving. This raised immediately the general subject of his competence, of what he was fit for, of his future, topics of sufficient breadth and depth to occupy him the rest of the way back to the city.

CHAPTER SEVEN

Castle Society

Frieda did not regret her nightly dependence upon the Castle's pleasures for she was persuaded that these went beyond drink. On the other hand, however, it had not entirely escaped her attention that the charms of aimless conversation, unasked-for-confidences, and high-hilarity diminished considerably when removed from that comfortable, intoxicating context.

She chewed on her swizzle stick. "Ten...," she began, "ten.... "

"Dum-da-da-da-da-dah, dum-da-dadadada," Spitzer supplied a quiz show theme. He knew his television inside-out, his English teacher, as he put it quite precisely.

"Ten Little Indians," Frieda said finally.

"That's a book," the bartender accused, eyes on the pitcher of beer he was drawing. "No books."

"I'm not using it as a book," Frieda told him confidently, "I'm using it as a epigraph."

"Well, it's not an epigraph." He pulled a bag of potato chips from the wall rack. Beside the rack hung a needle-point work displaying a row of beer bottles. Although the work was unsigned, it was widely credited to Wilma Castle herself who was known to have shared her husband's pride in the tavern's extensive beer menu. "'Mistah Kurtz—he dead,' the erstwhile Eliot man said, "that's an epigraph."

"An epigram then, an epitaph…."

"Sorry."

The B.T. gave her a sympathetic look. He might yet find a way, he hoped, to make himself useful to her.

"Oh, for Christ sake, it's something," Frieda said impatiently. "I know that much. It counts."

"Ten," the B.T. kibitzed in a whisper, "what about The Ten Commandments."

"Oh, I see," Frieda paused to light a cigarette and allow him to feel the weight of her sarcasm, "The Ten Commandments. That cliché!"

"Well, not hardly. The movie," the B.T. answered, believing that the colloquialism carried a weight which the simple negative, popularized by the laws in question, did not.

"Well then, so is 'Ten Little Indians.' Look it up." Was Frieda bluffing?

The bartender reached for one of the crack-backed reference books wedged on a shelf between a plaster statuette—the youthful Wilma as it was supposed—and a row of Frank Castle's bowling trophies. "Good guess," he told her suavely. "Nine to Five, the movie," he said in his turn.

"Eight Angry Men," said Finneran.

"What the hell is 'Eight Angry Men' supposed to be?" the bartender wanted to know. "Why not 'Two Flew Over the Cuckoo Nest,' or…." He moved down the bar.

"Seven-Eleven," Kevin-For-Crying-Out-Loud shouted after him.

"Two Thousand," Finneran called out nonsensically, belligerently. "The fuckin' Year 2000."

"Turn of the century," Kevin-for-crying-out-loud extrapolated, unaware, perhaps, of the fact that there was unlikely to be any such gracious arc for that hyperbolic bitch of an age.

Julius Spitzer was not about to let an opportunity pass. He leaned forward suddenly to address Finneran. "You speak of the future. Did I ever tell you Himmelfarb's story? That was a man with an eye for the future. He had business plans. Did I tell you?"

"Good Christ," Finneran swore, nursing a new grievance into existence, wondering, no doubt, who Himmelfarb was to him or he to Himmelfarb.

Spitzer turned to Frieda. "I have spent twenty years in a graveyard to know their stories, and this Ihrlander tells me only 'good Christ.' Pfui."

On the stool next to Finneran, little Mrs. Finneran, whose hair seemed to be thinning on a daily basis, closed her eyes for a moment. Then she said, just as if her husband were not already well in his cups and quite unlikely to be amenable to the suggestion, "Finn, it's late, hon, let's go."

"'The hopes and fears of all the years,'" Finneran muttered, without a glance in her direction. He rubbed his palms energetically along the tops of his thighs.

"'The hopes and fears of all the years," Frieda echoed dreamily. She drank the last of her brandy and soda. How finely balanced between these two states was her life, and how pleasantly did the balance shift in favor of the former during a typical evening at the Castle.

"The Pope has fears after all these years," Finneran asserted with sudden vigor, straightening up, chest thrust out. He caught the bartender's eye and gestured with his empty beer bottle at his companions and himself.

"Il Papa," Finneran continued, "the Pontiff, the Primate, the Pole, the Prince of the Church, the Holy Father. He's had it, he's outta there. I predict," he gulped at the fresh bottle of beer, "women priests, married priests, gay priests, atheist priests, the whole ball of wax."

"Joe, you are so full of it," Finneran's wife pointed out with prim asperity. The Church of Rome was the only subject any one had ever heard her call him to account for.

"And you're a Polack," Finneran responded flatly. "So that makes two of you. Go bake a golbaki."

Spitzer raised his beer stein toward Finneran. He was one to appreciate a free beer freely given. "Himmelfarb— his wife converted on him. In the end she went to a convent. You see!" Julius was triumphant; a story teller must find common ground at once. "Poor Himmelfarb," he added, sighing.

Frieda swiveled her bar stool toward Spitzer, leaving the Finnerans to it. "Which one was Himmelfarb?" she asked him, mostly for the sake of establishing their privacy; her own mind had all this while been fixed quite determinedly on Paul Silverman who, virtually since their stairwell meeting, had become the focus of all of her hopes and many of her fears too. She looked at her watch, unreasonably convinced that as he had appeared at The Castle the evening before, he was certain to show up this evening as well. She had been given by Julius to understand, that on those evenings that Paul did not appear at the Castle, her behavior underwent considerable deterioration. It was early yet, she saw, and so she continued to sip at her brandy and soda without undue agitation.

"If you don't mind," said Julius taking a cigarette from her pack on the bar. "So, you don't remember anymore which is our Herr Himmelfarb," he raised his head and looked down his nose at her. "Well, I will tell you again with pleasure." Spitzer felt with each telling he was refining his talent, preparing himself for greater things. He lit the cigarette and at once broke into a sly smile. "Oh ho," he said with a meaningful glance at the front door of the bar.

Frieda understood at once what he meant, and it was all she could do to keep herself from looking in that direction. She lit a cigarette. The sweater I'm wearing, she noted automatically, is an unattractive shade of green, and my lips are cracked and dry. She heard the Finnerans hail him, heard the tears in Mrs. Finneran's voice. Then she felt his hand on her shoulder and a sensation, a kind of weakness, spread instantly throughout her body. I'm blushing, she thought, and finished off her drink before turning to face him.

"I thought you'd be here," he said by way of compliment.

"I've been known to be here." By saying which she meant to indicate that if he intended to compliment her, he must do better than that.

"Bujumbura," he offered weakly, wondering if he would one day know just exactly what she wanted of him. He turned to greet Julius.

"What about Boskovice?" Spitzer countered with a challenge of his own. He resented the attention Paul lavished on the cities of Africa. "What about Brno, Bratislava, Bialystok and Belz?"

"It's Kinshasa now. Harare. Maputo. It's the new New World. It's all happening now. All at once. Chaos. Systems, methods, strategies. History working in the present tense. Listen to this." He opened the newspaper he was carrying and read to them. "'When we suddenly got power, we were very young. None of us had ever run a country before.'" Lately Paul had begun to wonder how he could appropriate to himself some of this newness, how he could make himself over in the light of a new order of things.

"You are wrong, my friend. Too much has happened already. You must reckon with the past. I say, reckon." Spitzer was proud of the usage, but his eyes were hard. He picked his hat up from the bar and put it down again. "Especially a Jew."

"Belz, what about Belz?" the B.T. broke in, having returned from the telephone. This interest in Belz should not be construed as a lack of interest in Lubavitch, Vishnitz, or Ger. Indeed, he had recently been giving thought to all these great centers of Chassidism. "The rebbe of Belz had a private secretary whose name was Pelz. I'm serious."

"Kenneth, lad, ye know whereof ye speak." Finneran peeled a wet bill from the bar in front of him. "Give us a little beltz over here on the side," he called to the bartender.

"Kenneth?" It was Rosie's voice, scornful and amazed at once. "What do you mean, 'Kenneth'?" It was almost as bad as Randall, she thought.

The B.T. wheeled around. "What? What are you doing here?" He was unaccountably dismayed. "I was just calling you."

In fact, Rosie had come to the tavern hoping to see him there. Increasingly she was finding reasons to prefer his company to that of young Tom Waggoner. After all, the B.T. had pledged himself to her cause. Then, too, he was an older man, a serious man, and Rosie, like her mother, took to serious men. Best of all, however, he was putty in her hands.

"I.D., please." The bartender stretched his arm across the bar in Rosie's direction. Rosie glanced vaguely over her shoulder toward the front door where one of the bartenders stood with flashlight in hand to check proof-of-age documents; but the Eliot man, who had seen her enter from the back, was having none of it. "Don't waste my time. 'Goonight. Ta ta. Goonight. goonight.'"

"Well, don't waste my time then." Rosie was sullen but unshaken.

"No card? Out you go," the bartender said. "Sorry," he told the B T. in whose intense blue gaze this man who knew people could not help but discern some interest in Rosie's fate, "but she's got to go."

This was all the encouragement the B.T. needed. He gave Rosie a gentle tap between her shoulder blades and to his surprise and satisfaction she headed at once for the door. With a happy heart he hastened after her.

"Back to Herr Himmelfarb," Frieda told Julius Spitzer, perversely, purposefully excluding Paul Silverman from the conversation. "So, his wife's in the convent and then what?" She felt the need to prove that there yet remained a topic unrelated to Silverman himself that was of some interest to her.

A musical flourish from the television suspended in the corner of the room behind Frieda signaled that segment of the local nightly news program for which many patrons had been waiting. The anchorwoman looked directly into the camera while her co-anchor turned his head in her direction simulating rapt attention.

"Well Glen," she read, "tonight's 'Who's History' segment spotlights a Sixties Radical and Chicago Native whose initials are L.S." A blurry blow-up of a news photo appeared on the screen. "Remember her, Glen?"

"You bet I do, Glenda. I covered that story for, pardon me, another network. She's history," his laugh was harsh, "and it's a good thing, I might add."

"Be that as it may," Glenda reproached him for this breach of journalistic etiquette, "we're going to invite our viewers to...."

"Lois Silverman," came the shout from several old-timers in the crush milling about within hearing distance of the set, "It's Lois Silverman." At The Castle "Who's History" was an audience-participation ritual.

"This they call history?!" Julius Spitzer picked his hat up from the bar.

"Paul," Frieda spoke his name aloud for the first time. It was heartfelt; it was spontaneous; it was thrilling. "Silverman?" she questioned, swinging around to face him. But he was gone. Gone, without so much as a word. What had she done? Or was she of so little account to him that he came and went independent of her presence or her will? She turned back to find Julius working his way into his overcoat. She put her hand on his arm. "Don't leave me now."

She pushed both their glasses forward to signify another round. "Well?"

Spitzer sat down again, but he did not remove his coat. "Is it possible perhaps to be a little more charming? Is it possible to smile, to take an interest, to put even some lipstick?"

"I *was* smiling." But actually, as Frieda was aware, she had not been smiling. The exhilaration she felt in Paul's presence was tempered as always by her sobering perception of his own lack thereof. "I've been voted Miss Congeniality," she told Julius wearily, "and I want to get a job working with people."

"The Infant of Prague," Finneran said to the bartender, banging his fist on the bar for emphasis.

"The Defenestration of Prague," the bartender replied calmly.

"How Much Is That Doggie in the Window?" Finneran was so pleased with himself that he squeezed Mrs. Finneran's arm once above the elbow.

"When Hector was a Pup." The bartender said after a moment, arching an eyebrow for emphasis.

Finneran cracked his knuckles. "'Til Heck freezes over," he said, raising himself up on the barstool, fist lifted in triumph.

Julius took the last cigarette in Frieda's package. "If you don't mind," he told her.

And Frieda didn't mind. She moved down the bar to sit with Kevin-For-Crying-Out-Loud and found him to be a far more stimulating conversationalist than she had remembered. Then, half-way through the next drink, Frieda was pleased to find little Mrs. Finneran to be a most companionable sort of woman as well. Indeed, these conversations seemed to do so much for her sagging spirits that she went directly to the telephone in the back of the room and called information. Though confident she had the phone number firmly recollected in her mind, Frieda nonetheless woke a middle-aged machinist somewhere on the far Southside of the city from a very deep sleep. While she took his vituperation very much to heart, she was nonetheless able to remain under the impression that she knew what she was doing.

This can never be a harmless delusion; and tonight would prove no exception. For tonight, as she climbed the stairs to her apartment, she felt the urge, in spite of the lateness of the hour, to ring the doorbell on the second floor and find out for herself what had become of Paul Silverman. Having fallen asleep with some difficulty, Paul felt justified now in posing a crude and general challenge to her sanity before closing the door in her face. Again, Frieda took this very much to heart, but remained unaware, as always, that how she felt at the moment was nothing, really nothing, compared to how she would feel in the morning, when the memory of this reckless deed would oppress her with terror and remorse.

• • •

Julius Spitzer had a great many stories to tell, and one story that he did not tell, his own story. He was presently working to recast it in a lighter, more ironic vein:

"Each year we had at the road circuit near my city the

Grand Prix of the CSR, and this event drew to us the best foreign motor car and motorcycle racers. There in the bar of the International Hotel on Husova street I met the West German driver I will call Karl. Shortly after midnight Karl proposed that he be allowed to smuggle me across the border in an axle container he had adapted for this purpose. How did I make sense of his offer? He was a racing car driver, a young man committed to risk and already beyond the thrill of racing. Also, of course a German, and I a Jew.

"Karl spent the following night with me in my stone cottage beside the old Jewish cemetery wall. He seemed almost afraid to take breath there, and I remembered that the air must have a smell, with the dogs and the food and the damp clothing. Nevertheless, he was polite about it, and after we opened the vodka, he questioned me about my life. I was frank enough, but I did not tell him what had brought me back to that cemetery where I was caretaker; and he did not inquire.

"It was the stories—the stories of those who had died *before*—those who had died in bed or at the Russian front, from a heart attack on the floor of the Bourse, an avalanche in the Tyrol, or bringing bread home from the bakery. Who would visit them? Who would recount their deeds? Hours and years I sat in the underbrush by their half-buried markers—who lay here and who there known to me alone—a traveler in time and space—and listened to their stories.

"Karl accompanied me on my rounds as I said good-bye first to those few stones I had cleaned and tended, the plots I had kept trim, according to the wishes and payment of American relatives. Then we made our way up and down the overgrown paths where the weeds and grass were knee-high and untrammeled. The silence was absolute for Karl was not an insensitive fellow, and I could place myself one last time in silent communion, the stones barely visible under the ivy and the bramble, amid the bushes, or among the low-hanging densely-leaved branches.

"When I walked out through the gate for the last time, I carried nothing with me except the page I had torn from the supplement to the cemetery's log; this appendix listed the citizens who had been deported from our city. It was the page with my own name on it, and I had placed it inside my shirt for safe-keeping. A Jew, a citizen of the world, must have his papers in order when he travels.

The border crossing was uneventful. Soon enough I was out of the axle container and sitting next to Karl on the front seat, driving top speed toward Vienna. There, on my own, I met Boris (who called himself Asher), a skinny fellow in an imitation leather vest and a Star of David on a chain around his neck. Boris had other papers. Boris had the way to make such a trip possible.

"I changed my plane in Frankfort. From the case open on his lap I learned that the burly American sitting beside me was returning from the Book Fair.

"'You enjoyed the Book Fair?' I asked when the stewardess had set down the plastic meal trays.

"He responded with a glance only, and took up the cold utensils to cut his steak into several large pieces. These he sped to his mouth, his fork gripped like a hammer, his knife lying on his thigh. Moments later he had scooped the last spoonful of yellow pudding into his mouth; he began to study my untouched tray. I offered it to him, and by this crude device our relationship was altered. He purchased from the stewardess four small bottles of wine and placed two in front of me.

"In return I told him the best story I knew from Himmelfarb—Himmelfarb, who died when I was still a boy but whom I came to know quite well in later years. Katzman listened with pretended patience while I sketched in Himmelfarb's background, but I felt his attention wander when I went on to his wardrobe (he was something of a dandy) and then spent myself on his ivory-backed clothes brush. I could not blame him. After all, I was still a novice. Too soon he pulled a many-paged document from under his tray and began to read it. He was a young man, yet under the skin of his broad smooth-shaven cheek there was a demon that twitched and twitched. Later, as the plane prepared to land, he gave me his business card. "Nice to talk to a landsman," he said in parting. As the years have gone by—as the touch of irony which I had lost long ago came back to me in this new language—I have often thought of Mr. Mike Katzman, literary agent. Could I hold his attention now?"

CHAPTER EIGHT

Action, At Last

Lois rolled down the car window and turned her face up to the heavens. The stars shone country-fresh over southern Michigan. How many years was it, she wondered, since her last visit—it had been winter then too—the War Council in Flint. They had driven out from Chicago just weeks after the pigs shot Fred, grieving, frustrated, choking on their anger, ready for anything. Be a crazy mother-fucker; shove a fork into Honky America; the spectre of Manson hovered. Did anyone ever notice the stars in those days, with the movement itself a giant canopy, sparkling so feverishly, still holding so much of heaven in trust. All else was dim by comparison, boring, lifeless, fragmented, impotent, and smallfish.

From where she sat, beginning to feel very cold now, in a modest little car Willis Washington had taken from a lot at O'Hare Airport, Lois could see nothing but sky, open fields and woods. The car was parked just outside an intersection, if that junction of two snow-covered, unmarked, unpaved byways in the middle of nowhere could be so-called. The object of Lois's interest lay perhaps half a mile off, along the road to the right, where the silver light on the snow turned black as it reached the thick stand of trees growing down to the St. Joe river. She rolled the window shut again.

How had Lois come to be there on a Sunday evening in prime time, a docu-drama in the making, waiting for the gunfire, for the get-away, for justice at last? Things had fallen into place. When things were right, when things were ripe, they fell into place. No planning could approach it. This was an article of faith with Lois, this went hand-in-hand with revolution. This was a slap in Harry Silverman's face, a man who made no move without a plan.

For some time, she had known, Simon and Willis had not been feeling as well as they liked. Months of unrelieved rage had begun to precipitate a confusion of identity. They were men, they reminded her from time to time, as often as not leaving the verb unconjugated. Proud men, they said, dignified men, yes, but men, too, who ached for action. For several nights the three of them sat up late in Lois's living room reviewing the possibilities. But it had gone nowhere. An explosive device was ruled out almost from the start. It was old hat, Lois felt, she had had her fill of that in the 'seventies. Willis put a new spin on it, then, by pushing the idea of a car-bomb, but here Simon was adamant; too foreign, he thought. Willis had taken issue with that, citing examples from the American underworld, but Simon was unmoved.

A kidnapping had been Lois's suggestion. It would get them a lot of media, she pointed out, especially if they took, say, Lee Iacocca. This, too, seemed to smack too much of foreign politics for Simon's taste. Simon was an American through and through: he loved his car, he loved his gun, and he loved a simple objective. Willis had another kind of problem. Too boring, he argued, too stressful, too much sitting around and waiting. As for Lois, she had had for a split second an odd little vision—America's premier CEO, gray-faced and preoccupied, in a grimy room somewhere, with Lois herself, a comfort, on his navy-blue lap—and this had caused her to draw back just a bit from her initial enthusiasm. She had turned her gaze inward.

Finally, exasperated, Willis had thrust his head forward, attempting to cow his cousin with a look. "Hijack a plane, man," he challenged, knowing very well of Simon's fear of flying.

Then, the following evening, Lois had received a visitor. Ernie Blyda was a friend of a friend, and she had known him, but not very well, in the old days. He was a feisty little white guy who used to sport a pork-pie hat, more of an aesthetician than an activist, a self-promoter who sold grass to the second-best blues harp in town. The Blues had been Ernie's passion. His conversation in those days had revolved endlessly around the question of whether or not the white man was equipped to play the blues.

Though what Lois knew of the Blues at the time was only the mainstream rock and roll of her youth, she was, as it turned out, predisposed to the blues, primed for the wail, hungry for the uncontested reality, and they would chew the matter over whenever they met. For if Ernie felt sorely the burden of being raised a pharmacist's son, Lois was no less quick to note the drawbacks of having Harry Silverman for a father. How colorless and repressed, how hidebound and materialistic, how anal and mental and lead-footed had their upbringings been when they compared themselves

with the soulful, sorrowful, sensual, musical Black Man—
that was an authentic human being if either of them had
ever seen one.

Disabled by a fierce beating he had received in the late
summer of 1964, Ernie considered that he had paid his dues
to the Blues. Snooping around a small Mississippi town in
search of Little Lonnie Griffith, the penultimate blind Delta
bluesmen, he had been mistaken for a civil rights worker
and left for dead. Instead, the beating had left him partially paralyzed and partially radicalized; but as years went
by the former proved itself the more lasting effect. Beside
tending and extending his collection of records and tapes,
Ernie now travelled the Northeast in a specially converted
van to deliver the homemade preserves, smoked fish, and
other delicacies his wife and her friends prepared at home
in Pittsfield. He would stop over wherever he found friends
of friends and revive his spirits with old stories and music,
always leaving behind some little gift—most often apple
butter—and occasionally passing along a bit of information
or gossip as well.

What he had told Lois that night was that he had heard
from someone, who knew someone, that someone had
found (he might have said, 'stumbled on') the group taking credit for the shootings of both Minton Tyler and Lou
Stern. Tyler, erstwhile Black Panther, had become a professional bowler, playing in the money for the first time, and
Stern was a small-town Jew who had won a state lottery.
"LWMA," Ernie Blyda revealed, "They call themselves The
Last White Men in America."

"Assassination," Lois told Simon and Willis several days

later. "We can play that game. Political assassination. I mean that's as American as apple pie."

"Cherry; Rap say cherry pie." Simon, a bit of a pedant, corrected her quote. But this emendation aside, he and Willis liked the idea. Little wonder, for murder was abroad in the land. Not generic killing—let's be fair—it's really mainly shooting that people like. They like it because they can learn how by doing it, because it's convenient, because they see it on television, because it's an answer. Certainly, Americans are a generous people, a compassionate people, a G-d-fearing people, and a freedom-loving people. But the bottom line has always been, Americans are a can-do people. And, say what you will, murder is can-do.

Lois sat in the car and waited. The silence was complete. She worked to occupy her mind by examining her conscience, raising the age-old riddle concerning the Correct Check-out Line. Say there are two check-out lines of equal length, and say the customers' carts in each line contain an equal number of grocery items, and then say that one counter is manned by a Black cashier and the other by a White cashier. "B," she drew the letter in the condensation on the windshield, "W." Which checkout line does one choose. There it was, once again the correct answer was illusive, and that discouraged her, particularly as it was an issue she had been looking at since the late 'sixties. She wondered how Willis or Simon would handle it. Why had she never brought it up with them? Even after all these years Lois had not lost her taste for self-criticism, although she did sometimes long for the days when it had truly been a group activity. Now we're getting somewhere, Lois thought, feeling a little better for having acknowledged within herself yet one more vestige of racist America.

And, in truth, she did feel very much in need of having her spirits raised, for just now, at the very moment the action was going down, she was filled with an unusual sense of hopelessness. The very silence oppressed her. When would America wake up? These men must understand that when it came to shooting people they didn't like, there was little to choose between themselves and the Revolution. Yes, this had seemed like a good idea at the time—but now it occurred to her—was it really anything other than what Harry Silverman would have advised them to do. Fight fire with fire, his words came to her, and her heart sank at that ineffably bourgeois prescription. But then, just when she needed it most, she suddenly saw the bright side of the thing. It was pure politics. It set a tone. It made a statement. It sent a warning. It was a wake-up call. It.... Lois smiled grimly remembering that Harry Silverman had been a great one for wake-up calls.

If she had had Rosie's cassette player with her, she would give herself a wake-up call right now—that last rap tape Simon had brought her. She had played it for Ernie Blyda the other evening, and been puzzled, even angry, to find him so completely unmoved. She tried to put it in context for him—a rally at the local community college in support of the new Rap Civ curriculum – hip hop as Civilization. Ernie, in spite of a life time commitment to the Blues, resisted any such totalizing agenda. Nevertheless, the uplift of that occasion had stayed with her, its afterglow had put heart into the ongoing struggle.

Then, finally, Lois heard gunfire, a lot of gunfire, more gunfire than she would have thought necessary. Staring into the intersection, as tense now as a father-to-be, head thrust forward but body straining back as if she could pull Simon and Willis down the road to her, Lois started the car. The gunfire stopped. Then a dim human shape entered the intersection. It carried a flashlight. Something had gone wrong. A flashlight! It stopped. He stopped! Lois hunched and dropped to the seat, her cheek striking the little gun Simon had left her. What had gone wrong? She could hear nothing above the car's engine. But there was blood on her cheek, and suddenly—the sound of breaking glass above her.

"They're all dead." A man's voice ordered her from the car. She recognized it at once. And in that selfsame moment, she grabbed for the automatic shift lever and ripped it toward her into low gear. She kicked her foot forward thrusting wildly at the pedal, jamming on the gas. The car jumped ahead. She heard the man curse as he tried to pull his arm back. It was him. His gun struck her on the shoulder as she righted herself and drove the hell out of there.

Simon Washington and his cousin Willis, and the two white men they found in the old house that night shot each other to death. Just like that. Of course, it was a political act and there was a certain satisfaction for all four of them in knowing that. What had gone wrong? Lois drove through the bright night for an hour or so heading straight across the state line for the airport at South Bend, Indiana. In spite of her philosophical objection, Willis had made a plan after all; and now her shoulders ached, so grim was her resolve to follow through with it. It had been made with such love, so carefully, so cleverly, so professionally. Nothing in the world seemed important to her in the light of this need to follow through. She tried to keep her mind clear, but she could not silence an insistent inner wailing.

"This is bad," her own voice informed her over and over without pausing, "oh this is bad, this is bad." There was a helpless quality to the wail that looked to nothing less than the comfort of the nursery. Then she began to cry, suddenly overwhelmed by the piteous difficulty of just being Lois in 20th century America. How often had Willis tried to educate her. On the street, had he not explained again and again, on the street, "bad" meant good. It made perfect sense, too, she sobbed, take the language of the slave-master and turn it on its head, rob his judgment of its weight, reject his white-skin values, his Western values, his male values. And now Willis was gone.

CHAPTER NINE

Never Kid a Kidder

The drapes in Frieda's living room now remained drawn regardless of the hour. Rosie Sills, who lusted for sleep with all the urgency of the sorely pressed, slept away great portions of each day. This suited Frieda who desired to keep her under wraps in any case, and unknown to certain un-neighborly members of the Co-operative's board. The activity of Rosie's waking hours was circumscribed by a fine mixture of lassitude and faith, believing, as she did, that having gotten herself to Chicago, she had done her part. While little or no progress had been made in the search for her father, she was now satisfied to let Fate take its turn. Tom Waggoner, on the other hand, bewitched though he was, had begun to chafe under the enforced passivity and the close quarters.

Though leaving had been a part of Tom's plan from the first, he had kept his own counsel. There was much to choose, therefore, as the day he had set for his departure approached, between Rosie's sense of betrayal, Frieda's anxiety, and his own feeling of anticipation. Surely it was Rosie's good fortune that her hostess found herself so in need of protection, that in the face of much that was unappealing in this young houseguest, Frieda had a strong incentive for continued hospitality.

Given Rosie's lethargy, Tom decided he could do her no better turn before leaving than to find her a job. She would need to pay her way while she waited. He took her employment history; beyond several summers in the canoe rental line of work, this consisted mainly of the good opinions of others. She was, it had been said, good with young children, for example; and her mother often told her that she had a good imagination. While Rosie did not see this last as the compliment it was meant to be, Lois, who considered her own mind—the mind of the revolutionary soldier—to be of necessity focused and literal, thought it only right that the next generation be possessed of a diversified imagination.

Attracted perhaps by the red crayon scribble, Tom chanced upon a promising leaflet among the myriad announcements and advertisements which covered the vertical surfaces around the campus: "If You Can Read This You Can Make Money!" Rosie would be paid by the hour for reading to a blind woman. Rosie was dubious; she temporized by paraphrasing at length from Lois's rant on the unfairness of reading test scores. Nevertheless, and much to her surprise, the way Tom explained it, this seemed the perfect job for her.

On the appointed day Rosie arrived less than ten minutes late, fully equipped and well-rehearsed, but nervous nonetheless, for her first day of work. The door was opened by a tall robust woman in red slacks and a low-cut, embroidered peasant blouse who stuck out her hand and waved it about with apparent impatience before Rosie could grab hold to give it a weak shake. The woman's vaguely foreign appearance was perhaps emphasized by the scarf she wore pulled tight across her hair and tied at the nape of her neck. As she introduced herself, her dark glasses seemed to focus on someone standing just to Rosie's right; and for Rosie, who was a skinny pale girl, this was only the least of the reasons she was glad that this vivid Valkyrie of a woman was unable to see.

Rosie trailed behind her down an unlit corridor, automatically trying to tame her anxious gait to her employer's heavy, shuffling steps. The room they entered was unlit as well; it had a raffish air—fringed lampshade, jigsaw puzzle under glass, a brandy snifter on the window sill—none of which made the slightest impression on Rosie, who a kind of apprehensive excitement was keeping tautly single-minded. In any case, Rosie was partial to what she had never had—a pink, more plainly bourgeois style of decor.

The woman found her way easily amid a jumble of furniture. When she had settled in an awkward half-recline along a fat pillowed, chintz-covered loveseat, she directed Rosie to the wing chair and ordered her to turn on the lamp which stood behind it. Rosie bent instead to the shopping bag she had carried in and removed the book Tom had selected from a number of choices the woman had provided on the telephone.

"Turn on the light, I said." The woman made several small jerky movements with her head, and in this rather studied movement she seemed to resemble no one so much as the popular blind singer of the day.

Without looking up, Rosie reached again into the bag

and withdrew a tape cassette player which she placed on the little marble-topped end table. "O.K.," she mumbled, preoccupied with making sure of the machine. She opened the book on her lap to the first page and set her elbow down to hold the place.

"I said, will you please turn...."

"It's on, it's on," Rosie dismissed her without making a move toward the lamp. "Should I start now?" She cleared her throat theatrically.

"Please do," Yolanda Silverman-Silbermann replied thinly, and then watched with astonishment as the girl reached over and carefully pressed the play button on the cassette player.

"Chapter One. It was the first day of...." The bright, familiar voice of an actress Yolanda couldn't immediately place filled the room. The volume had been set just noticeably beyond the level of normal speech and Yolanda could foresee that this slight elevation would quickly prove irritating. She would have liked to watch the girl, but reminded herself that she had a particular literary purpose in mind. She closed her eyes tightly to listen, "to help me get some insight into the view of the visually impaired," as she had told her agent.

Yolanda was a hands-on writer. The over-arching themes of her own personal history, the minutia of her daily life, the evolution of her every thought and emotion—what were imagination and abstraction to these, indeed what was the wide, wide world itself? In this connection, Yolanda had for some time been seeking a new and more expansive, more direct avenue for her talents; a stint writing the

"Me, Myself, and I" column for Chicago's largest circula-
tion daily would be just the thing, she felt. And this very
morning Mike Katzman had telephoned to announce that
he was exploring the possibility, as he put it, of adding that
feather to Yolanda's cap.

So, in spite of her assumed affliction, in spite of her
avowed literary purpose, Yolanda was feeling upbeat and
unserious. Eyes shut tightly, she was focusing on the identity of the full-voiced actress, and not on "the view of the
visually impaired." She smiled involuntarily at the very
idea that such tones would be thought to issue from that
pipsqueak of a girl. And the whirring of the tape player
— what did they take her for? Her eyes popped open; she
would not have thought it would be so hard to keep them
shut. She gave up and began to watch the girl from behind
her dark glasses.

Rosie was sitting cross-legged now, staring at the book
in the dim light, pointing with her finger at each word as it
was spoken, forming each word with her lips barely a beat
behind the voice of her mentor. Every page or so she would
stop, uncross her legs and lean toward the tape player, looking hard through the little plastic window, and then leafing
ahead in the book soundlessly to make sure she would be
ready. Tom had put a red marking in the margin of one
page as a warning to her that the actress was near to completing Side A of the tape. She must stay alert. At the same
time, Tom had admonished her, she must concentrate on
each word as it was spoken. It was his idea that she might
thus improve her reading, which was strongly marked by
an unbecoming lack of ease. How am I supposed to do

both things at once, Rosie had whined her way through the rehearsal, insisting, though they both knew better, that she could read well enough as it was. Now she forced herself back to the book. Do it for the money then, had been Tom's parting advice.

But her mind was not on the reading. Rosie wondered how her mother was getting along without her. They had rarely spent more than a day apart. Rosie had been her mother's boon companion from the years when Lois had felt it would not yet be prudent to see old friends or make new ones. Indeed, Rosie's erratic schooling had been due more to Lois's desire to keep her with her, than to any contempt for bourgeois education, or their moving about so much. Nonetheless, of course, Lois had been altogether certain that she knew what there was to know about educating her own daughter; she emphasized high ideals, political purity, and natural development. In practice this had meant mainly that she had not allowed her own family access to Rosie, threatening them that she would again drop out of sight altogether if they attempted to contact, corrupt, contaminate, or sully her daughter in any way whatsoever with their money, their religion, or their love.

"Think how much she's learning just from listening to us talk," Lois used to marvel in the early years when her daughter had finally fallen asleep on a corner of bare mattress, exhausted from hours of crawling about among the legs and ashtrays and the wine jugs. And it is true that Rosie was, in her own way, a precocious child; by an early age she had heard just about all she could take of imperialism, racism, fascism, and monogamy. Indeed, she eventually developed her own form of protest, squatting in a corner whenever there were visitors and screaming snatches of garbled rhetoric. Often in the heat of debate, someone or other would retrieve her from the corner and put her on his lap and say to his opponent, "See, Rosie thinks you're full of shit too"; and then Rosie would smile, stick out her tongue, and raise her small fist in salute. Lois, when she gave it any thought at all, was terribly pleased at how well the little girl fit in.

Rosie's mind had drifted by now so far that even this talented reader was powerless to call her back. Her eyes were closed. An image of Willis Washington occupied her. She saw him stretched out on the sofa in the living room, his street hat tipped down over his eyes, his mouth open on a very pink tongue, a small gun nearly invisible, resting in the slight hollow of his belly on one of the heavy dark sweaters he liked to wear. The thought that had occurred to her at once was that perhaps she would approach him quietly, lift the gun away with the practiced hand of a small-time shoplifter, and shoot him to death while he slept. But, of course, Willis had not been sleeping.

Rosie, having spent her formative years around a more middle-class, more loquacious, more self-conscious brand of revolutionary, sensed at once that her mother's present comrades Simon and Willis Washington were different. Perhaps because her own childhood had been quite similarly deprived, haunted, and fatherless, Rosie thought she saw the two men more clearly than did her mother. She kept them at arm's length, spoke to them curtly, if she didn't ignore them altogether, disparaged them on account of their race, and tried out on them with manifest disdain whatever little she knew of flirtation. It had galled her from the start that these black men were frequent visitors to her home, that in a town without black residents, indeed had she but known it—in a state with just a few thousand black citizens in all—two black men were her mother's frequent callers. And she often reproached her mother for it. She accused her of being a freak and a bitch, of being unkind and uncaring, of being without money and without lifestyle—in short, of being un-American.

"I think that will be all for today," Yolanda broke in on Rosie's thoughts, languidly, maliciously.

The girl's head snapped back as if she had been slapped. She scratched at her scalp with both hands. She listened petrified as the voice of the actress flowed on, unconcerned and mellifluous. Her face burned. She reached toward the tape player and then drew back her hand. Perhaps just this once Fate would play a part. Furious, she turned one page and then another trying in vain to find the place.

"You can stop reading now," Yolanda raised her voice purposefully.

"Chapter Two," the actress announced calmly, and took a pause.

Rosie's arm was a flash of lightening. The faint whirring of the tape ceased. "O.K., O.K.," she said with marked irritation, "I heard you. I was just trying to get to a place to stop. You didn't want me to just stop, did you?" She reached for the shopping bag without further ado and dropped in the book and the cassette recorder. It was then that she noticed for the first time a cluster of small painted figurines which decorated the end of one of the book shelves. Those are cute, she thought, and as they were well within her reach, she took one and put it in her bag as well.

Yolanda jumped to her feet, but the girl did not even stop to look up at her, and this returned Yolanda for the moment to her game. After all, they were only cheap little plaster figures, she reminded herself; but the one the girl had taken—that was the cute one, she thought. It did not occur to her to wonder that on a matter of taste she should find common ground with a largely illiterate teenager whose eye had been tutored, and whose taste educated, by daily trips to the shopping mall. When it came to kitsch, there wasn't a snobbish bone in Yolanda's body.

Now there emerged a real, albeit short-lived, conflict within her breast—the writer in her rejoiced at what she had witnessed, while the haus-proud frau demanded revenge. In the event, the latter would not be denied. Yolanda reached for a cane which she had put in the room earlier to lend some simple verisimilitude, and moved toward Rosie, swinging the cane energetically from side to side to clear her way.

Rosie, who was twisting to get into her out-size over-coat, paid no attention to Yolanda's approach. Then, with surprising purpose, Yolanda swung the cane hard against the paper bag, and then once again the cane came down on the bag, this time from the top. Rosie turned in fright, but Yolanda brushed by her without a word.

Rosie picked up the bag and looked inside. Her employer's cane had taken the head off the little plaster figurine, so Rosie lifted the two pieces out and set them on the coffee table. She was sorry that had happened; she had intended to bring the little statue to Frieda Zale as a gift, but now there was no point to that. Disgusted, she flicked at the painted head with her index finger and sent it rolling ear over ear across the table. She reached in and turned on the cassette player to make sure it had not been damaged in the assault as well. "It was just...." She did not permit the actress to hit her stride.

"Zenia!" She jumped as Yolanda's voice came booming through the intercom. "Oh Zinnia," Yolanda's voice fairly fluted now, and there was something so false in that tone, a timbre so theatrical, that Rosie actually felt her skin crawl.

Yolanda awaited her in the hallway at the front door. She tapped one long purple-red petal of a fingernail against the black lens of her glasses as Rosie walked toward her. It was an odd, provocative gesture, and Yolanda wondered at once whether it might not prove useful; after all, a touch of the surreal never hurt anyone, she mused. She wanted to check the girl's face for a sign that might authenticate the move, but Rosie had lowered her head, raised her shoulders, and seemed bent on withholding any more of herself.

"Do you want me to come again?" she asked without a trace of irony. "When should I come again?" she demanded, reaching for the doorknob and twisting and pulling at it impatiently. "How do you get outta here?"

"I don't think that will be necessary," Yolanda answered serenely and as if from a great height. Apparently so into her role was she by now, that she was unaware of how she took the edge off the gentility of that reply when she sought to move Rosie away from the door by the mere interposition of her own body. It was not a graceful move.

"Ooww, get away from me," Rosie snarled, "and give me my money." She had almost forgotten. She snatched at some bills she suddenly saw laying on the antique wooden washstand by the door.

"That's not for...," Yolanda began, but Rosie had already ducked under her arm, squeezed through the partially opened door and found the stairway.

Yolanda was ebullient. "It was marvelous," she reported to Ian and Letty that evening. "It made me terribly vulnerable to myself. Yet at the same time I felt absolutely on top of things. I had that cozy, curled up feeling; the velvety darkness, that burrowed-in, rainy-day feeling, the wilted lettuce quality of feeling in touch. It was a wonderfully useful exercise."

"Mmmmmm," her husband affirmed. "Carla McIntyre's coming in to tape this week. Really knows how to use the medium—all that yelping and hissing—powerful stuff."

Yolanda smiled encouragingly, but preferred to keep the conversational focus on her own professional life. "You know what came out of it, the gift of memory—do you remember that fur stole?! It came from Grandma? Do you remember what it smelled of? Do you remember the bald spots? I can still feel it on the back of my neck." Here was the stuff of Yolanda's fiction. Even her earliest work had shown this pronounced weakness for material detail.

"That was before my time, Sweet." Ian was shuffling through the day's mail.

Yolanda half-closed her eyes. "I remember just the way mother's hand looked when she smoothed the fur back and forth," she went on, her voice thrilling with professional purpose. Though she knew Proust only by reputation, she did wonder just for an instant whether she was not here coming very close to him. "Do you remember mother's hand, the way it was then? I can still see the wrinkle of flesh between her thumb and forefinger; I can feel...." Yolanda shivered girlishly.

Though Ian's thoughts were far away, he had not taken his eyes from her face, and he could not help but feel that girlishness did not suit her. "Sad to say, Sweet, I remember neither the woman's hand nor the stole."

Absentmindedly, Yolanda drew her daughter to her and lifted the child onto her lap. Immediately Letitia was on her guard. "No bed," she said. At her mother's pleasant reply, which incorporated a promise for the morrow to balance a strong suggestion bearing on the lateness of the hour, the Young-young Person climbed down and crawled under the dining room table.

"Let me tell you the best part," Yolanda addressed herself to Ian who had bent double in his chair to poke his head under the table, showing himself ready to pursue negotiations at whatever cost to his digestion. "The absolutely funniest part was she ran off with the singles I had left out as a test...you know...for....the..." She stopped with a glance at Letty who was just emerging onto her father's lap, wishing to spare her daughter the knowledge that they employed a domestic worker, before continuing "The...ah...la femme... uh...la senora...ah...the uh new girl."

"New girl? No baby here!" Letitia waved her arms in all directions at once to protect her singularity. "No baby! No, no, no new girl!" she wailed.

CHAPTER TEN

Courting

Paul Silverman stopped at the newsstand and bought a paper. Several days had gone by, but that fatefully choreographed square dance of a shoot-out was still big news. There was something about it that made him sure he could discern Lois's hand therein, something about shared responsibility, about full participation, about equitable distribution—that was Lois all over, he thought; and talk about grass roots! So that's where Lois had been headed. From the first, the newspaper accounts had mentioned a get-away car parked about half a mile from the house. It stood to reason, Paul felt, that Lois was the driver of that car; his sister Lois, the most abiding revolutionary of them all.

Hold a good thought, he said under his breath with something of his old sharp-tongued conviviality. Why, he had often wondered, had his stock-in-trade badinage deserted him all this while. Certainly his attempts to find new employment had been severely hampered as much by this sudden lack of fluency as by his predilection for African place names. Of late, he thought he had noticed that the admonishments he addressed to himself were gaining something in pungency. He took some heart in that.

The digital display at the corner of the bank building showed not quite noon. It was remarkable to him that his way with time—or was it really time's way with him—had altered so radically. In the old days he had never been on time, never even attempted it. It had been his conviction that accommodation was his due. He had been clear in his own mind that he always gave more than he got. And in so far as it was true that, as he had believed, he was smarter and more energetic and more socially imposing than those who waited for him, he might be forgiven for imagining it to be a fair trade. In the old days everyone wanted "a piece of him," in the old days he was always "running late."

Now, more often than not, he was early. Even Paul himself, who saw no especial profit in the examined life, understood this to be a fundamental shift. Time was money, of course, but there had been more to it; he had taken a more sophisticated approach. He had been a master of the illusion of omnipresence, of the forced expansion of time through over-commitment and over-scheduling. Clearly, too, space was money, and he had been into real estate as well. But the breakthrough, the realization that had brought him up to the majors, was simply this: Everything is, was, will be, or can be, money. That was the fundamental truth.

Yes, thought Paul, that lesson had surely been brought home to him during a weekend trip to Paris with the mentor of those palmier days. Upon catching sight of the Louvre Museum, that individual had cried out enthusiastically, "That's where the money is, Paul, that's where the money is." What a trip that had been: the best of everything—the Concorde, the Ritz, Taillevent—life had been sweet.

"Zo vat happened?" Paul asked himself, continuing down the street toward Nini's Pizzeria. The burlesque did little to take the urgency out of the question. He checked his watch. Well, for one thing, he had played his game very close to the edge, without perhaps knowing himself just how close, protected by his own conviction that he was more far-seeing, more far-ranging, and more charming than anyone else. There did finally come a moment, however, just when the very intricate strategies he had pioneered and developed were in full bloom, that he beheld the abyss—no place to stand, neither for rest nor vantage, and the constant sound of a rushing wind where there was no air to breathe at all.

Even later, months after his own departure from the firm, his colleagues, baffled and cowed, were still so in awe of his profits and of the unmistakable legality of his maneuvering, that they were as far from seeing what he had seen as ever. It was a bit of unacknowledged grace, then, that Paul's soul should have seen fit to recognize and shrink from an extremity of refinement so absolute as to simulate nothingness.

Paul checked his watch once more and felt he might now at last fairly turn to that centerpiece of his daily life which was his lunch hour. He crossed the street only to find the restaurant entrance suddenly blocked by a large red chow attended by a slender well-dressed man, the leash taut between them.

"Sorry, no dogs," Nini had rushed to the door.

"Jupiter, did you hear the man?" The dog pulled on the leash, growling, and Nini took a step back. "All over

Europe," the man turned, complaining, to Paul, "people are allowed to eat with their dogs. That's what I call civilization," he reached down to give his fierce companion a reassuring pat, "don't we Jupiter."

"Try the Chinese down the street," Paul suggested with unwitting cruelty as he hurried through the open door. Behind him the man blanched and bent to his pet, speaking honeyed words of comfort to this descendant of an ancient Chinese delicacy.

When Frieda emerged to set down Paul's water glass, she found the Formica tabletop partially covered by his open newspaper. In the early days of their courtship, she had brought him the menu and the breadbasket along with the water glass. But it soon occurred to her that she could make the most of their time together if she performed each task separately with all the leisure he would tolerate. She saw with regret that a menu was already on the table.

If Paul was on to her, he had said nothing, nor had he given any indication that he was not perfectly pleased with the service he was getting. And in fact he was never in a hurry, for there was never any place he had to be. Actually, though he had yet to face the fact, there was currently no place he would rather be than here at Nini's Pizzeria with a newspaper for company and Frieda occasionally by his side.

"Clipping," Paul said, lifting a delicate, mother-of-pearl handled pen knife. Then he greeted her more formally, more warmly, aware that such abruptness seemed to suit her rather more than it did himself. He smiled at her. He noted and not without pleasure the way she hesitated, even blushed just slightly, before smiling back.

"That's a nice knife." Frieda put the glass down on an empty table and held out her hand for the knife. "Don't worry," she said, although he displayed no hesitation to part with it, "I'm a waitress."

He had from the very first been taken with this penchant of hers for the deadpan. It made for a great change from the more animated and sprightly sort of woman, the more socially literate sort of woman, the more successful sort of woman he had been used to know.

"Why?" he asked her then, having not dared before to probe the matter of her career choice.

Frieda rubbed her thumb back and forth along the handle of the little knife. "I deal in cutlery; I'm a waitress," she answered him simply. She had conceived an intense, inexplicable, child-like craving for the knife. To what could she liken this desire? Years ago, a neighborhood boy had flattened a penny on the railroad tracks.

Paul studied Frieda's thumb. It had the look of the never-manicured, but he was pleased to see, it also had the look of the never-bitten. "No, I meant why are you...."

She held the knife to her cheek for a moment before returning to him the first true artifact of their relationship. "Is that called mother-of-pearl?"

"It is; but the question is, what exactly is mother-of-pearl? He gave her a vaguely conspiratorial look. "It's like the veal," he reminded her, smiling, I don't have any idea what mother of pearl is either."

"I'll get your bread," she told him, turning away, stunned, thrilled as always at the proof that they did indeed share a past.

He watched her return with the breadbasket, walking through the increasingly crowded restaurant with an odd stiffness he had noticed before. The moment he caught her eye, she hesitated for just an instant in her progress, she moved the basket from her right hand to her left, she put her hand to the back of her neck, she shook her head almost imperceptibly as if he were a catcher and she were shaking off his sign.

"Look at this," he pointed the pen knife at the open paper. "I should clip this article for my sister."

Frieda, an only child, listened closely. His sister—was it she for whom he had declined her invitation that fateful first evening.

He pointed at the paper again, very nearly stabbing at the news photo with the little knife. "This guy used to be in the so-called Movement with her." He looked up as if to gauge the effect of his announcement.

But Frieda had spent the early seventies in a prolonged spasm of ill-timed adolescent preoccupation, nor had she given much thought to things political since. Now for the first time did she regret this lack immensely. She was stymied. She stared unseeing at the article. "Anyway," Paul half-got-up to reach for the water glass, where Frieda had left it, "now this guy is going to sponsor a celebrity golf tournament out at Lakewood Country Club. Listen to this, he's naming it for his father, in memory of his father, quote inventor, entrepreneur, philanthropist, unquote. This is a guy, according to Lois, who used to brag about how he stole money from his father and used his credit cards; besides, of course, signing the money that came from his trust fund directly over to the Panthers on a monthly basis."

He stopped talking suddenly, unused of late to this feeling of fluency. He took a sip of water.

Frieda bent to look at the newspaper photo, so close to him she thought she could feel herself breaking the electric field that seemed to define the space between them. "Blood is thicker than water?" she suggested, straightening quickly, too aware, at the moment, of her own blood to provide a more thoughtful analysis.

"Well," he sighed, barely remembering that he had dealt with like sums on a daily basis, "or maybe it's just millions and millions of dollars, your basic estate on the North Shore, an apartment at the Ritz Carlton, a place in Charlevoix...."

"Who's Lois?" It so pained Frieda to think she knew so little about him, that in the moment she forgot what little she might have reason to know.

"'La Silverman,' I think it was *Time* magazine called her; my sister Lois." He continued along his own line of thought, "I think it meant something to her to be on an equal footing—revolutionary, of course—with this upper-class Wasp type. You'd never see Lois as Jewish as when she was talking about this guy."

Frieda thrilled to these musings. It was, she was certain, the first time they were having a conversation of this kind. Responses tore through her mind eagerly, accelerating, whirling, finally useless in the event. Her heart was full too."Mogadishu," Paul said. "What's for lunch?"

Frieda stared at him. Mogadishu. It sounded in her ears like some quaint endearment. It couldn't be, of course, but.... "You know the other night," she began as he studied the menu, "what I wanted to ask you was if that was why you left—because Lois Silverman was related...." Frieda felt oddly emotional about it. "And now she's your sister."

"Any specials?" Paul asked, innocently, if rather bluntly.

Frieda felt herself blushing. "Oh, any specials. I see." Clearly she had overstepped, she had misgauged, she had misunderstood. "O.K." she said grimly, hurt in her voice, "The Special today is the Osso Bucco."

Paul looked up from the menu oblivious. "Next time I'll ask you in and we can look at pictures of Lois in the old family album." He surprised himself with this spontaneous invitation which he knew at once, despite its tone, to be absolutely genuine.

"Can I take your order now?" Frieda asked dully, vowing never to be taken in by him again. How mismatched they were! How out of tune!

Suddenly Paul knew that everything had changed. It was as drastic and as chilling as the sun's retreat from an Autumn sky. "What happened?" he asked, helplessly, "What's wrong?"

"I want to take your order now," Frieda continued to insist, finding some small pleasure in her intransigence.

"Oh for Christ sake! Give me the Osso Bucco."

Halfway to the kitchen Frieda was already filled with a deep sense of regret, and a feeling of futility as well. After all, she was a waitress; why shouldn't he ask her about the Specials. So it suited her purpose well when Nini informed her that they had just run out of Osso Bucco.

"I'm sorry to say that there's no more Osso Bucco," she began formally, sorry for much else beside.

"No problem," Paul answered casually. "I'll try the manicotti."

If Frieda had been hoping for a substantially different reaction, which she had been, she managed not to let on. And this made fer feel a bit better about herself as she turned away toward the kitchen.

A second waitress was at work refilling the cheese shakers, checking on the hot pepper flakes and the oil and vinegar cruets, bending a step here and stretching a step there, exercising as she worked her way around the room.

She was a small-boned blonde from Idaho working to put her husband through graduate school, a tight-lipped, all-business creature, in training for the Chicago Marathon. Frieda habitually referred to her as 'The Biathlete,' although as far as Paul knew the woman pursued only the one sport. Coming to an abrupt stop directly in front of Paul, she stretched her left leg, heel to the floor, and bent over it.

Paul gave her a casual, vaguely appreciative glance and she moved on.

Meanwhile, Frieda was bursting with an awareness of this attention to her colleague. Had he not, only days earlier, assured her that she was not alone! Her heart had leapt at that possibility. Perhaps she had read too much into it.

She thought suddenly, and with unusual charity, of her Francophile suitor. From him she had learned about the French idea of hell, and now she was able finally to make full sense of the concept: A waitress, her lover, and a Biathlete locked in a pizza parlor forever.

CHAPTER ELEVEN

And Then There Was One

Following the plan in every detail, Lois, after much touristic feinting and tacking, finally reached home. And not a moment too soon, for she was aware that though she had managed to keep her wits about her, they were by no means as sharp as they might have been. On the bus coming out of Portland, a large, florid outlet-shopper had struck up a conversation, and Lois had answered her friendly queries unthinkingly, truthfully, for the first time in years. Still, she had dealt with the unexpected as well as she could, leaving the car (which Simon was to have switched) parked on a South Bend street, and throwing the tiny turd of a gun into a dumpster near the airport. I am every woman, she thought; I move through your streets unseen. Walking through the security scan she had nearly started to cry. Simon's gun.

The second leg of her trip home had been delayed by snow in Philadelphia. Why am I going through Philly? she had whined at Willis, knowing that Willis was often devious beyond all purpose. City of Brotherly Love, he had snarled, launching into a familiar lecture on the revolution's symbolic agenda. Of the three, Willis had the finest mind. They had made him minister of travel. In the departure lounge her fellow travelers read USA Today. "Michigan Shooting Linked to Obscure Group." There had been a time, Lois remembered, when the ultimate high had been to watch the commuters open their papers the morning after an action, or to tune in the evening news with acquaintances who didn't know who she was.

Though a pervasive feeling of fear rarely left her during that period, it had bit by bit and imperceptibly become so much a part of her as to be a given of her daily life. Indeed, though sharing something with paranoia, it was a fear on the whole more positive in effect. Requiring the utmost of awareness and alertness, more sustaining ritual than dread discipline, it had lent the world around her a heightened, nearly surreal, quality which did much to affirm the consequence of her actions.

Sitting in her cold, shabby living room the night she got home, Lois was no doubt grateful that, along with some of the energy and generosity of her youth, the years had taken the edge off some of that intensity as well. And yet she felt quite keenly enough that she was bereft, betrayed by fate, that she had come very possibly to the end of this particular road. There wasn't a time Lois could recall when things had been so bad. She was alone. It was untenable. It was politically incorrect. What of the People? What of a better world?

And she mourned alone, which was, if anything, even more painful. To whom could she turn. They were men, she sobbed over and over, they were men. But the phrase eventually lost its power to comfort. Of Simon's family she knew nothing, but Willis, she thought she knew, had a mother, a school teacher in Washington D.C. The telephone operator for District of Columbia information laughed at her request. There were, she happened to know, "584 names of the surname name of Washington" in Washington D.C. Fuckin' slave names, Lois sobbed, setting the receiver down hard.

She pulled her coat tightly around her and sat in a corner of the sofa under a portrait of the great Indian Chief Crazy Horse. A red plastic cassette player was at her feet and she stirred through a pile of tapes with the toe of her boot. Let me hear Otis Redding, she prayed, putting her cheek against the sofa's worn fabric. "Let me hear 'Dock of the Bay,'" she said aloud because it was past time for magical thinking. She leaned down and put a tape into the player. But it wasn't Otis Redding and she stopped it with her foot. Oh c'mon, c'mon, c'mon, what am I gonna do now, Lois aimed her anguished whisper up toward Crazy Horse; but the Chief only stared off at an angle toward Malcolm on the far wall. What confidences those two must exchange when she was away, Lois had often fantasied. And you too, Fidel, she hastened to add, feeling his piercing gaze on her now.

She went into the kitchen. She wanted to drink something warm. She thought she should drink something warm. Harry Silverman would have urged her to drink something warm. A cup of tea with milk and honey, or a mug of coffee on which she could warm her hands, or hot spiced apple cider, or cocoa with whipped cream. The kitchen was dark and dreary. The cabinets were brown, the appliances green, and three of the four bulbs in the ceiling fixture were burned out. The refrigerator was virtually empty, but most especially it did not contain any whipping cream or apple cider. She put the kettle on.

All at once an enormous weariness overcame her as she faced the consequences for Third World peoples of her appetite for coffee beans or tea leaves or cacao or Indian spices. In fact, the more she had come to understand of exploitation, degradation, expropriation, and depredation, the more trouble she had pleasing her finicky little rich girl's palate. There was, however, a certain satisfaction in that, in taming degenerate white-skin desire, in keeping her figure trim without diet.

She poured some hot water into a tea cup and added a slice of lemon. She studied the lemon. Picked by migrant workers, she had no doubt, but decided, not without some difficulty, to draw the line there. She carried her cup into the living room. The scene inside that house by the St. Joe River presented itself to her mind's eye. Willis, too cool and confident, would have insisted on reading the two men "the charges" they had drawn up, before he called on Simon to pull the trigger. She saw the elegant mask that his face would have become at that moment, noble, contemptuous, taut beyond bearing. Willis, she nearly cried aloud, for it was a face she loved.

It had been, of course, this nicety on Willis's part, this devotion to rhetoric, this righteous arrogance, this assertion of emotional disciple and dignity, that allowed the third man, approaching, surprising them all, to finally set the tableau in motion. So lost were the antagonists in terror and the high drama of the moment, that his mere footfall triggered the action. Driven outside by cabin fever, or perhaps returning from a lovers' tryst or from some official government business, he alone of all of them was aware, on the one hand, that there were fewer than one thousand right-wing-whackos currently being monitored by the FBI, and, on the other, that race war was not the imminent threat.

Nor was Lois herself more realistically informed than any one of the four martyrs, as disinclined to believe the reporting in the Fascist Press, as the Last White Men in America were distrustful of the Zionist Media. Yet she knew what she needed to know. She knew there was a way a man ought not have to live; and she knew, too, there was a way a man ought not choose to live. She herself had chosen, had rejected her destiny as Capitalism's darling, had denied Babylon its death grip. Choice had opened the door to revolution, choice had come before the facts.

She took a sip of the hot water and lay down on the sofa, pulling her knees up and tucking the coat around her. There was no longer any way she could avoid the thought. It was nearly beyond believing, but she was convinced that the third man, the newspapers' unidentified witness, the gunman who had ordered her out of her car, was none other than Randall ("Rip") Parks, infiltrator, instigator, impregnator, G-man extraordinaire. Yes. She knew his aftershave. It was Harry Silverman's aftershave. Had he recognized her too, had he sensed her nearness, had he picked up her trail, had he truly loved her after all?

She thought of the time they had all done LSD, all of them together; it was a way, they thought, of getting an informer in the house to expose himself. Rip had been there—he had passed the test, no questions asked—instead, one of the others, Lois tried to remember who, had drawn suspicion to himself. Rip had spoken eloquently, beautifully in his defense; Lois thought it likely that she had actually fallen in love with him that evening. He was brave and pure and full of goodness, and if only he hadn't been an agent for the FBI, they would have lived happily ever, she was sure. In fact, he had wanted to marry her anyway, to rescue her from herself, to redeem her for America, to marry her anyway, to marry her anyway....

Lois sat up with a start. The telephone was ringing. Then it stopped ringing. Had she fallen asleep? In any event, though her body was tense and weary, she felt more settled in her mind. She went to the bedroom, changed her clothes, and took the last five hundred dollars from the cache. She emptied her shoulder bag on to the bed and repacked it with more of a view to sentiment, jamming an envelope of snapshots, a tiny Cuban folk doll, a letter her father had written her the day President Nixon resigned, and several cassettes in among the necessaries. She entered Rosie's room for a last poignant moment. The room was just as the girl had left it. Lois got down on her hands and knees and looked under the bed, but found only several enormous dust balls. On closer inspection, however, she saw that one of these balls had formed itself around a tiny gold earring. She pulled the heart-shaped bit of gold free and put it in her left earlobe. She felt better for that.

Turning off all the lights, she started out the front door to the car parked by the side of the house before remembering that she would not be driving her car. Willis had long ago provided a car for a contingency such as the one she now faced. They kept it in a dilapidated, long-unused shed on the vacant property behind the house and very late at night Willis and Simon would drive it along the back roads to make sure it was always ready for action. Lois walked back through the house and out across the yard to the shed.

"I'm outta here," she echoed Rosie, starting the car. Her daughter had been strangely absent from her thoughts over the last several days. Nor was she at all anxious now to consider the possibility that they might never see each other again. After all, Lois had no idea where Rosie was, and now Rosie would have no idea where Lois was. She tried to push these thoughts from her mind. She put a tape in the car's tape player. "Dock of the Bay." "I'm fuckin' history," Lois said aloud, heading for the Interstate. Her heart was beating hard with a mixture of excitement and dread at the very thought.

• • •

Meanwhile, Special Agent Randall Parks had spent the last several days catching up on the Radical Left since his own unexpected and wrenching departure from its ranks. Over the years and as his assignments permitted, he had been gathering material. In this effort he did not hesitate to make use of the Bureau files and its copying machines until he had a couple of scrapbooks full of clippings, random pages of intel, and his own notes on several popular histories of the period. Now in a small room on the second floor of his rented house he studied each page closely, certain he would find what he was looking for without quite knowing what he was looking for—bombings in eastern cities in the mid-seventies—the activities of the so-called October Coalition—a bloody escape from a police paddy wagon—the destruction by fire of the Calvin Coolidge homestead in Plymouth, New Hampshire.

He had known of course that the so-called Movement had changed, would have had to have changed, and yet his study left him even more dispirited than he expected. Randall Parks was a man of feeling. Even as he had burrowed away from within, he had been aware in those days that there was between him and them large areas of agreement. He had chosen his path as they had theirs, full of purity, intensity, and the highest ideals. Indeed, his own quest was nothing but to build a better America. Winning the appointment as a Special Agent of the FBI was for him only to secure backup for that mission. He loved his work.

That morning he had found in a rubber banded packet of old snapshots one photo in particular he had known must be among them. It was a picture of himself—on the back someone had written "I sing of Olaf glad and big." He had been a kind of a shining young man inside and out in those days. Big and very blond with a prominent jaw and a prominent smile. It had been an easy job really for him to burrow into the very heart of the group. They needed him. Sometimes he was the only one in the house with money for groceries. More important, of course, action was the cry, and they were at the time he arrived very far from action. As far as practical affairs in general were concerned, mechanical things and electrical things especially, the group was, he saw at once, totally inept. There was a lot he had had to teach them, or even do for them, in that line.

He knew too well who had taken that snapshot, who had written those words on the reverse. It had been her in the car, he was certain of it, felt it in his bones. He took a deep breath now—half satisfaction and half alarm—when he thought of what he should have done and had not done. He had not mentioned the white woman in the car, had reported simply a car driving away as he approached, reported its make and a partial plate number. When they found the car in South Bend, they called him down. They had connected Simon Washington to the October Coalition, that network of black ex-cons and white left-wing women which had been considered largely decimated. Could it not have been a white woman driving the car? they pressed him a bit. And what about the broken window? Could have been, Special Agent Parks assented, could have been.

While he was there, he looked the car over. Nothing definitively useable, he had been told, but on the other hand, there was something—something that told him everything he needed to know. Tracings on the windshield which could speak to him alone. Drawn in condensation, turned invisible by evaporation, he was able to make the letters out quite clearly in the bright morning sun. Over all the long years the ideograph came back to him—the double lines, "B" for the black cashier, "W" for the white cashier, the checkout dilemma. How often she had worried him with that puzzle, but he had always come down for the black cashier. It seemed safest in the long run.

After the fiasco of his exposure, after detailed accounts appeared in the alternative media around the country, he had been useless to them for the political end of things altogether. He was assigned elsewhere. He wanted her to go with him, to marry him, to wait for him in a clean white house with clean white sheets; they would be Americans together. Instead she had quoted at him, screamed in his face, beat at his chest, "'I will not kiss your f-ing flag,' I will not kiss your f-ing flag," as if suddenly she and not he were big, glad Olaf. She had been off her head that day, and for many days after, unable to deal with the shock of it, unable to come back from the betrayal.

"You're making a mistake about me," Special Agent Parks had protested. Somewhere in the house that sad day there had been music—James Taylor singing "Fire and Rain." When it came down to it, all he could tell her, comfort her with, was this—"At least I'm not a fascist pig," he said plaintively the day he left town, "You know I'm not a fascist pig."

"Oh, don't worry," she had responded bitterly, "I understand your pigdom totally, I understand it completely, a pig is a pig and you are a pig." Actually, she did not understand it totally. She did not, for example, know that the radio in his van had been installed by the Bureau with a view toward broadcasting whatever took place whenever the van's ignition was on. And the van's ignition had been on. Fittingly, perhaps, there was also one thing he did not know about her. She was pregnant with his child.

Eventually, of course, he had married someone else, and now he was a bachelor once more. Not that he had thought of Lois very often over the years because he hadn't; but now that their paths had crossed again, it seemed to him that maybe he had thought of her more often than that after all.

Then, when he had spent some years doing white-collar investigations and RICO, performing well, finishing each assignment off with meticulous care, but not quite loving his job, in a surprise move the office decided to return him to his first love. He was put in touch with someone who put him in touch with someone who put him in touch with the LWMA, right-wing whackos trying to organize themselves in several mid-western states. More gray then blond now, but big still and still an easy smiler, he proceeded with great skill and prudent dispatch to worm his way into the confidence of The Last White Men in America.

He had helled around with them for the past three years now, and they like him; but the job is not over yet. He is some lucky SOB he was able to tell them with total honesty, to have the john back-up before supper, so he could be out taking a leak instead of getting his fuckin' head blown off by a couple of Niggers. They all agree that "the Ripper" is some lucky SOB; and sit down to watch the Saturday Night Movie. I'm burning out, Special Agent Parks thinks, eyes shut, I really am. He holds the cold beer can against his forehead. Again, he has said nothing about the white woman in the car.

CHAPTER TWELVE

Frieda Entertains

Frieda had not seen Paul since the day she had taken refuge in the pizzeria kitchen in the face of his imagined attention to her co-worker. Presumably he was lunching elsewhere. Nor apparently had he seen fit to come to the Castle on recent evenings. That did seem to Frieda a bit extreme. He could at least, she thought, have shown her his confusion, or maybe his concern, or she might even have settled for his curiosity. As it was, Frieda had passed through disappointment and was growing despondent. Finally, she had turned to Julius for advice. Julius, who had wooed in conditions of scarcity and lost his bride to malnutrition and disease, suggested she invite Paul to dinner.

It was not the first time she had confided in Julius. At twice her age he was nonetheless her peer in his capacity for analysis and romantic intrigue. He came by it naturally and honestly, the years of silent graveyard-listening had brought him more than his share of intimate revelations, nasty speculation, trivial anecdotes, rumor, distortion, and fantasy. There were the melancholics and the suicides, the bachelors who did or did not love men, the converts, and the Viennese Jewess who married a Maharajah and rode an elephant across the

Indian subcontinent. Indeed, Frieda's confidences paled in comparison with what Spitzer had once been used to hearing. Still, there was quite enough to hook him, to quicken his taste for machination and satisfy his need to give advice.

Much discussion preceded the issuing of this invitation, for although Julius had conveyed his a priori regrets, he was not averse to debating the guest list with her until the appropriate mix was achieved. Rosie and the B.T. received verbal invitations within the day and accepted unconditionally. But Paul, whose invitation had been hand-delivered to his mailbox, was not heard from, and Frieda began to fear for the future of their relationship. Against her better judgment, she left a message on his answering machine, she slipped a note under his door, she stood watch for his car, all to no avail.

The day arrived and she moved ahead with her preparations. She went to the supermarket. She went to the supermarket again. She dusted the television and scoured the bathroom sink. Fighting despair, she worked at these household chores with a kind of perfect faith—and she was rewarded. Leaving the apartment for yet a third trip to the supermarket, she met Paul in front of his apartment door.

Immediately he pulled from the pocket of his overcoat the piece of notepaper on which she had written his invitation. "I can come." He smiled at her. "It's tonight, you know," Frieda replied with a vestige of irritation.

"I'm going to take a nap." He touched her on the arm.

"Were you away?" Frieda asked, finally seeing the suitcase at his feet.

"Couldn't you tell?" He pushed the door open and bent

to pick up the piece of paper she had slipped in the day before. "I'll come, I'll come." He backed across the threshold thrusting his arms out toward her as if to ward off her further entreaties.

"There's a message on your machine too," Frieda said dully.

"Will you be cooking kidneys," he asked casually but knowingly, reaching for his suitcase.

Frieda understood in a moment. She felt herself blushing. He remembered. She had made an impression on him then. Perhaps he even cared. She thrilled at the thought. Nevertheless, she looked at him blankly, as if without comprehension. "Actually, it's going to be chicken," she said feebly, regretting at once her meaningless subterfuge.

"Well, I'm going to take a nap," Paul reiterated; and so, in spite of her intense curiosity about where he'd been, and his silent wish that they might lie down together, they took leave of each other without further ado. Now that Frieda's prayers had been answered in so timely and material a manner, no less urgency attended her preparations than had been the case when she was simply going on faith. She could see, for example, that she had been mistaken in concluding that the apartment did not require vacuuming. Deciding on the spur of the moment to do without the parsley, she climbed the stairs again, hoping that Rosie would choose to absent herself in the face of a growing list of housewifely chores.

Rosie, however, remained where she was at the dining table, her headphone firmly in place, staring at a half-eaten toaster waffle. The vacuum cleaner was wedged behind a screen of outer garments in the hall closet. Frieda dragged it out, bringing a small suitcase and a plastic bag filled with rubber bands out with it. These she kicked back into the closet without so much as a glance. Sighing, she bent and jerked the electric cord from its housing, pulling the machine toward an outlet. Rosie looked up as the vacuum bumped the leg of the dining table. Her waffle remained half-eaten. Frieda would have liked to have taken a bite, but forbore on account of the illusion of intimacy it might create. Instead, she stepped on the pedal and the vacuum sprang to life. It began well enough, the little machine gliding smoothly behind her, as she worked the bedroom, the short hallway, and the kitchen floor; but all too soon she was forced to move in among the closely constellated furniture of the living-dining room. Now the machine started to buck and stall, and she, without even turning, to yank brutally at the hose pulling the canister over, around or through each obstacle. Finally, it struck her in the ankle without warning. Frieda kicked the vacuum hard, the plug popped from its outlet and the machine faded from existence.

"What you need is one of those Dust Busters," Rosie said blandly. "Or you could have less furniture. One or the other." She got up, stretched, and shoved the remaining piece of cold waffle into her mouth.

Frieda opened the door to the balcony and leaned outside to cool her face. She felt that these episodes with the vacuum did not bode well. She closed the door again and lit a cigarette. "How does it look," she asked Rosie reluctantly.

Much of the furniture had been selected, with more imagination than good sense, from the houseful which had been left at the untimely death of her parents. The statement it had made in their home, dust-free and color-coordinated, had been parsed here into unintelligibility. There was the multi-color leather ottoman, for example. She had chosen it for its name; had they called it a hassock, she would certainly never have taken it. Ottoman. It was clearly the less Protestant, the more allusive word; and while Frieda was not the least bit well-informed in any general way, she had managed to develop an entirely idiosyncratic body of allusions. So, though she had not seen fit to take along its matching easy chair, the ottoman had come home with her. The Turk stands alone, the Turk stands alone, she had sung at the time, and this moment of dry mirth had given an edge to her mourning.

"When are you gonna start cooking?" was Rosie's response. Had she calculated that she could thus throw into sharpest relief the far-reaching inadequacy of her hostess, she could not have done better. She moved to the sofa and sat down next to Frieda's cat.

Frieda went to lie down on her bed for a few minutes, to conjure up, as her cookbook advised, a plan of attack. When she awoke, however, the apartment was dark; it was winter after all, she sought to calm herself; still, high-time to start cooking. Rosie, who had threatened to help, had apparently gone out. Nevertheless, with a can of beer on the counter beside her, Frieda was able to manage quite well on her own, and soon the One-Dish Dinner was in the oven. There remained, however, one problem which Julius Spitzer had not been able to solve. She went to the bedroom and opened the closet. No gesture ever made her feel more hopeless. The outfit she finally chose to wear differed from the one she was wearing only in so far as she had yet to put it on.

The B.T. was the first to arrive. He brought two white candles, a loaf of challah and a bottle of wine. "It's Shabbos," he noted, putting the bag down and taking off his heavy coat. He wore a jacket and tie.

Frieda, looking at his fresh face above the nearly mature beard, feeling the cold air rise from his coat, smelling the bread, was tempted to kiss the B.T. on the cheek. But instead she said, "I don't have any candle sticks."

The B.T. busied himself with the challah and the wine, hiding his disappointment that Rosie did not appear to be at home. "We've missed the candle-lighting time anyway," he told Frieda.

"Who told you to say 'Shabbos'?" she responded, suspicion, perhaps even accusation, in her voice. "You've never said 'Shabbos' before."

"It's the real way. You know," he admonished her casually, without even turning to look, "a rabbi said that a man should have one suit of clothes for the workdays and one suit of clothes for the Sabbath."

"Well, fancy that," Frieda replied, stung for no reason she could name. She began to set the table.

"Am I early?" The B.T. opened the balcony door and stepped out. He looked across the yard toward 54th Place thinking he might catch sight of Rosie. He was doubly anxious to see her just now; he had news for her. "Where did Rosie go?" he asked, stepping back into the room.

Frieda stared at him through the open archway between kitchen and living-dining room. "Shabbos! Don't you feel things might be getting out of hand? If you're going to go whole hog—not hog, of course—your whole life is going to change. Don't think you're going to solve your problems that way."

"All I said was 'where did Rosie go'," the B.T. complained with just a trace of belligerence.

"I'm not talking about Rosie." She gestured irritably toward the Challah on the table. "I'm talking about Shabbos, etc. I can't believe this is happening. I'm sorry"

"I'm sorry too," the B.T. told her mildly, but she could see the hurt look in his eyes. "Anyway, you have to start somewhere, and separation is very crucial. Separation. The weekdays and the Sabess...." He blushed at the stumble.

"Oh, I see, separation. Just what we need. It's not enough to have the White Sox and the Cubs, poisonous mushrooms, South Africa, Parochial schools, non-smokers...." She tried to hold him off with a gimlet eye while she lit a cigarette, but as the B.T. had in any case been unimpressed by her line of thought, he had no qualms about interrupting it.

"I don't think you should be so quick about it," was his almost gentle reproof. "This may be something you don't understand."

"And you do," Frieda challenged with a bitterness that surprised them both. She walked to the window, pulled the drape aside, stepped behind it, and held her forehead against the cold glass. I'll stay in here behind the drapes for the rest of the evening; she toyed with the thought. But then the doorbell rang and she swept out, her heart in her throat, to open the door.

Paul held out a bouquet of flowers. "T.G.I.F.," he said, jovially, but hypocritically, too.

Frieda had to suppress an involuntary shudder at this false note; hardly much of an effort, however, in light of how truly handsome he appeared to her at that moment. "Not only do I have no candle sticks, but I also have no vase," she said, covering conversational ground, re-introducing the two men.

"Call me Issachar," instructed the younger.

"O.K., Ken, whatever you say." Paul was feeling good. For one thing, he had grown tired of eating out. "But do you mind my asking why?"

Not only did the B.T. not mind, he had actually been quite put out that no one had been moved to ask the question before.

"'Issachar is a large-boned ass.' That's in Genesis."

Frieda carried the flowers into the kitchen. "Well they got it half-right anyway," she called out.

The B.T. blushed, but he pressed on. "Sturdy to bear the yoke of the Torah. That's the comment on that verse."

"And presumably that's where you come in," Paul said pleasantly, urbanely, sitting down on the sofa.

From the archway Frieda tried to make amends. "Aren't you sturdy to bear a joke, too? Come on!"

The B.T. continued to ignore her. "Do you have a Hebrew name?" he asked Paul, who answered rather gracelessly that Pinchas might have been chosen but he could not say for sure. "Pinchas was zealous on behalf of his God," the B.T. annotated.

"That's good to know," Paul replied more seriously than he had intended. There was about the B.T., mild-mannered and affable as he was, something which discouraged levity.

As another man might glide with conversational ease from his golf score to the price of a new SUV, so the B.T. went on. "God created the world by the Torah. It was His blueprint." The B.T. checked his watch. "Everything is in it." Except, he thought fretfully, the whereabouts of Rosie. "It distinguishes us from the goyim...."

"Who told you to say 'goyim'?" Frieda burst out again, angrily. She turned to Paul. "He's been going up to Rogers Park. They're in their own little ghetto up there. A certain Shlomo has taken him over. 'Shabbos.' 'Goyim.' What world are we in?"

It was not until sometime later, indeed not until they had tired of waiting for Rosie and sat down to begin dinner without her, that an answer to Frieda's question began to suggest itself. First of all, it turned out, as the B.T. explained, that in addition to 'this world,' there was also another world, 'the world-to-come.' And then, as if this revelation were not enough to sustain ten such dinner table conversations, Paul rode his African hobby horse into the fray with particular attention to wage and price structures in the sub-Saharan portion of the continent. How do you measure the worth of a man, he asked them.

Gradually Frieda was able to understand that her own lack of appetite and impaired conviviality were not the common condition; she began to relax and enjoy herself, pleased with how, after a rocky start, a dinner party had indeed come into being. And this in spite of the fact that the B.T., while only picking at the food she had prepared, ate countless slices of Challah. Frieda wondered briefly at this, but the religious explanation did not suggest itself; thus, perhaps fortunately, the possibility that the B.T. was now eating in the kosher way remained unexplored, and the general good feeling unimpaired.

Her satisfaction was short-lived, however, for she had not thought to provide dessert, and now found she had nothing in either refrigerator or cupboard to make up the deficiency. Her spirits plummeted; she took herself to task. Her guests, seeing her thus embarrassed, protested that they did not mind in the least. Paul proclaimed his satiety. The B.T. was emboldened to reveal Rosie's absence as his only lack. This went a bit too far for Frieda's taste, but she was in no position to complain. In any case it was at this moment that the door opened and Rosie entered.

"It's cold out," she said, looking nowhere in particular. "I woulda helped, you know...." She shrugged her shoulders in the direction of the bedroom as if to suggest that Frieda had let her down. She approached the B.T. with a half-smile. "Don't you look nice; gotta date?" She pulled a piece of Challah from the loaf and studied it briefly before putting it in her mouth.

"I thought we...," the B.T. tried to pull himself together. A vein was throbbing at the edge of his pale forehead. "What did you do instead? Where did you go?"

"You have a different idea of a date than I do," Rosie lied. "Besides I started talking to this guy and he was telling me all this stuff about the sixties. For all you know this guy could've been my father," she punched the word up, "and all you care about is this dinner. Look at Frieda; she doesn't care."

"You ask Frieda. I was worried about you. You were supposed to be here."

Frieda had begun to carry the plates into the kitchen. Ordinarily she would have availed herself of their invitation and thrown herself into their quarrel with great vigor; but tonight her heart was not in it, her mind was not on it. For here was Paul rising from the table, here was Paul bringing the One-Dish Dinner dish into the kitchen, lowering it carefully into the sink, smiling, complimenting her on her cooking. Why, who was to say that this could not be the very pattern for every night of the rest of her life. Not only could, Frieda thought, smiling back at Paul, but would, would!

"Where did you go, by the way, where were you?" Frieda hated to ask, but she could put it off no longer, hoping only that the high spirit of the moment would cushion her against whatever might lurk in his response.

But Paul demurred. He had something to ask her about the girl first, about Xenia. No, she insisted, you tell me first. Then Paul turned deadly serious in the blinking of an eye. "I was married once," he began without preamble.

"You were not."

"Well, I was. It was a short marriage." He smiled self-consciously. With Frieda standing there before him, he was himself having a difficult time just then lending credence to that union.

"Are you serious?" She wasn't breathing right. "I don't believe you."

"It's true. Why don't you believe me?"

"Because I would have known that already. You would

have already told me that." At once the recognition built quickly and powerfully within Frieda that Castle's University Tavern was the only place she wanted to be at the moment. She made known to her guests her intention to depart. Indeed, she had her coat on and was out the door, before any of them rightly understood what was happening.

CHAPTER THIRTEEN

Without Brandy,
Without Cigars

After Frieda left, Paul rolled his sleeves back and began to wash the dinner dishes. Intuition led him to it. He was filled with a kind of anxious wonder at her storming out like that. What was she trying to prove? It did not seem very likely to him that anyone still found a previous marriage worthy of such histrionics. How better to counter her theatrics, to undercut the drama of the moment, than with this homey task, this honest, responsible pose. He washed quickly and got the dishes clean enough, but not nearly as clean as Frieda, who was a stickler for the clear final rinse, would want them. No doubt it would have made some difference to Paul to know this, for he found himself, even elbow deep in greasy water, wanting very much to mollify her, to please her. A rack full of boiled-clean dishes might have helped.

Unready to return to the dining table, he sat down for a moment on a painted wooden stool so low to the ground that it served no discernible purpose except to be in one's way wherever one stood in the small kitchen. It's useless, Frieda had admitted to him, but on the other hand it's not likely to tip over. That's clear enough, Paul thought, resting his chin on his knees and looking out the full-length window into the reflected kitchen. The sky appeared profoundly dark. But not dark enough. In Sirakoro Meguetana, Paul thought, how much blacker must the night be; Sirakoro Maguetana, the African village where cooking fires had lately been replaced with wood-burning mud stoves—how did they measure the wealth of a man?

The flowers he had brought Frieda lay on the counter still wrapped in their green paper. Perhaps Frieda's own lack of a previous marriage accounted for her not owning a vase. This, he thought, seemed a plausible explanation for he himself had at least two to show for his marriage; he would go down to his apartment now and get a vase; he would show her by example the benefits of maturity and rationality. That was the right way to finish off the evening.

Suddenly he thought of other evenings he had finished off—his wife on his arm, a limo at the curb, the world at his feet. That would be the First World, of course, he reminded himself. His wife on his arm—he might as well have said his sleeve on his arm, so weightless was she, so perfect a fit, so suitable as to seem nearly a creature of his imagination. What a shock, then, it had been when she dumped him, when he came to understand of a sudden that far from her being a character in his play, he had in fact been a character in hers. A beautiful young woman of pretension and ambition, she had lost what little patience she had when the curtain did not go up on his second act.

She was not without her sensitivities, however. And as she could conceive of no greater shame than that attaching to such a fall as his, she had offered Paul as a consolation, as a part of the settlement, a place to hide, a small dilapidated farmhouse that had long been in her family. At the time too far from the city to be considered susceptible of reha-bilitation, time had revealed the place to be suddenly just far enough away to be truly fashionable. Now she wanted it back. Paul's trip had been in connection with this business. He was ready to let her have the house, he told her; the only thing he asked was that she keep away until he gave her the go-ahead. What he did not say was that he had once had a copy of the keys made and given them to Lois.

"Did you know that Jewish mourners sit on low stools?" the B.T. asked, poking his head into the kitchen. "Is there any food left? Xenia's hungry."

"That's the problem with one-dish dinners." Paul twisted to look up at him. "In Nigeria they eat a pot of yams, for example. When it's gone, it's gone"

The B.T. grinned mysteriously. "Did you ever eat cholent?"

Paul heard them making plans to leave. Struggling to rise quickly from the low stool, he knocked askew a framed magazine photo on the wall behind him—Anna Freud, her chow, her garden. About this picture Frieda had told him simply, "That dog is still alive!" He was strangely moved by her appreciation.

"Wait," he called out to the others; he wanted to bring the vase up from his apartment. But what he saw when he entered the other room stopped him in his tracks. The din-ing table was covered with papers. The girl, Xenia, seemed to be stirring these about in an aimless manner, her eyes half closed, as if she were in a trance.

"Is that her? Is that her?" the B.T. chanted compulsively, showing her a succession of photo copies.

Paul picked up a sheet of paper which had fallen to the floor. It was a part of the *Time* magazine article which quoted Lois Silverman on the subject of the Tupamaros, the Uruguayan urban guerillas. Perhaps it was this Latin American connection which had inspired the reporter to dub her "La Silverman." The name did not catch on, how-ever, and Lois had continued to live in the media shadow of those radicals who were—as *Time* described them—"sexy, rhetorically accomplished street-fighters."

"What's all this?" Paul asked as casually as he could, and here his years on Wall Street stood him in good stead. And yet his mind had jumped at once to Lois eating a hot turkey sandwich at the Interstate Rest Stop.

"Xenia has come to Chicago to look for her father," the B.T. answered happily.

Paul took a breath. "Her father?" he repeated with heavy surprise. "What do you mean 'look for her father'?" But he thought he knew only too well what the B.T. meant; in fact, he had a better idea of what he meant than either the B.T. or Rosie had themselves. "Her father the pig," Lois's words were on the tip of his tongue, or as close to the tip as the exigencies of investment banking would allow them.

The B.T. was proud. "I got all this research material for her. We think he was someone from The Sixties."

"I've seen some of these before," Rosie mumbled, wip-ing several sheets of paper aside with a languid gesture. "I'm hungry."

"How could you have seen them?" The B.T. picked up

a photo of a crowd of protesters shouting at a line of police-men. "Is that her?" He pointed at a tiny female head at the center of the group.

"What do you mean 'her'? I thought she was looking for her father." Paul continued the charade unthinkingly. He stared at the girl. Clearly Lois's daughter; no question now.

Rosie ignored him, addressing the B.T. "Mom has a scrapbook. She used to look at it with me. We had clippings. There were some Polaroids, you know, no developing. She gave him a practiced wink. Sometimes something would happen, maybe on the news or on the phone or something, and she'd go screaming around the house, cursing like crazy, and she'd find the scrapbook and rip out stuff. She'd get real depressed, you know, about Babylon excetera."

"Babylon?" The other two said in unison.

"It's a political thing," the girl assured them politely.

Paul felt just vaguely weak in the knees. He pulled a chair from the table and sat down. "Is your father in politics?"

Rosie gave him a strange look, perhaps truly taking in his presence for the first time that evening. "I have no idea. He could be a Capitalist, that's all I can think of because...."

"A capitalist?" the two interrupted again.

"You know, Imperialism, Capitalism, Racism, excetera. I'm hungry," she complained again to the B.T.

"What's your father's name?" Paul asked her, almost embarrassed now to hear it for the first time knowing what he knew. Lois had never called him anything but The Pig.

Rosie rolled her eyes at the ceiling in irritation. "Well, it says Randall Parks, but I'm pretty sure that isn't his real name. Now can I eat?"

"And what's your real name?" Paul asked her, going for the jugular. This was as close as he cared to come just now to addressing the fact that this girl was unlikely to be someone other than his niece, Rosie.

"Xenia Sills," she said, and proceeded to stare him down.

Paul needed time to think. He felt anxious suddenly, as if a sixth sense were predicting the souring of a deal. It occurred to him that he might go over to the Castle to gather his thoughts. He decided to take the flowers with him.

"I was thinking about something," Rosie said as soon as the door had closed behind him, "do you know how the other day you said something about how 'they didn't change their names,'?"

The B.T. looked at her mystified. Here she was turning to him for the very first time, and he sat helpless. Help, he prayed silently, nearly reaching out to stroke her hair.

"You said something about their fathers. I was just wondering what did you mean about their fathers, you know."

The B.T. pinched the bottom of his beard. "Maybe I didn't mean their actual fathers; maybe I meant their fathers meaning Abraham, Isaac and Jacob," he ventured.

"Don't you mean Abraham, Martin and John?" Rosie looked puzzled, thinking of the song, the golden oldie which memorialized those three victims of political assassination. Before the B.T. could fully appreciate the chasm which separated them, a more philosophical line of inquiry had suggested itself to Rosie. "What about 'the good they die young...,'" she sang the phrase from the song. "Do you think that's true?"

"Well!" He put his chin to his chest and his thumb to the bridge of his glasses. He closed his eyes and blew tiny puffs of air out the side of his mouth.

"What is your problem!" Rosie said under her breath, scorning this burst of theatrics. But still, while she had the chance, she took a close look at him. The beard was reddish-blond; it had turned out even better than she had expected. But the best thing about him, she thought, were his eyes. "O.K. time's up," she mocked.

The B.T. raised his head and blinked at her. "Just preliminarily, I think one could say that 'the good they die young' is true in a way that '_only_ the good die young' is not true. However," and here he actually pointed a warning finger in the air, "if 'the good they die young' actually means to imply a causal connection between their being good and their dying young, then, uh...," he stopped suddenly. "What were you thinking?"

Rosie stared at him.

"I might have more to say at another time," the B.T. speculated.

She rolled her eyes and walked over to the sofa dropping onto the soft pillows. "So anyway, what were the names of their actual fathers?"

He sifted through the possibilities. "For instance," he tried to be casual about it, "names like...Gershon, Kehath, and Merari."

"And probably Randall, he fits right in," she said, reaching into her knapsack for the envelope containing the birth certificate. "Let me show you this." She held up the piece of paper, but the B.T. remained where he was at the dining table with a faraway look in his eyes. Rosie half got up, but only to rearrange herself, sitting again with one leg tucked under her. "Here. Look!"

The B.T. found her particularly appealing when she sat like that, but still he did not move. In his mind's eye he saw the Children of Israel encamped in the desert, the families of Gershon, Kehath, and Merari, situated by God's command around the tabernacle. He saw the twelve tribes beyond, with their division banners and their flags. He saw the flag of Issachar planted on the east side of the encampment, a sun and moon on a black field. So unaware for an instant was the B.T. of his actual surroundings that it was almost as if the Lord Himself were holding an old View-master up to his eyes.

CHAPTER FOURTEEN

Soused

At the Castle, a drink before her and Julius Spitzer squinting judiciously at her side, it did not take Frieda long to see that storming out of her own apartment without explanation ("antics," Dr. O.H. called that) was unlikely to produce the result she desired.

"What did you think, he would come running here after you right away? No. A man does not do that." Spitzer took another cigarette from the package that lay on the bar between them. "What, a crazy woman is so fascinating, so irresistible?"

Frieda's face went stony. She lit his cigarette and then her own. She drained her glass and pushed it forward for a refill. As befit her earlier rashness—whether as reward or punishment she could not tell—she was drinking tonight with cinematic abandon. "I was hurt."

"You were hurt. That is established." He sighed, for she had communicated hardly anything other than this fact. "Now if I may inquire, why should you already know that he was married once. Does he already know, how shall I put it, that you were not married more than once? What's the big rush!"

"It's not a rush." Frieda mustered her dignity. "But just for instance, he's told me more about certain things than I want to know, about a river for example or an anthill—he just didn't happen to tell me about being married."

"Zalechen, Zalechen," Spitzer's voice was filled with mock solicitude, "I am sure you will have many other rooms to rush out of and doors to slam. Believe me."

"Oh, fuck off," Frieda said angrily, grabbing her cigarettes and her pocketbook and departing the bar blindly for any table of familiar faces. She noted without alarm that she did not feel altogether steady on her feet.

Left to his own devices, Spitzer undertook a leisurely review of his troops. He liked nothing better than to pluck one or another from the graveyard ranks and inspect him for signs of fiction. Still unsung, for instance, was the young genius who had left Brno to study at the University of Vienna, and died early of tuberculosis. Many years later he had become a favorite of Spitzer's. Sometimes, when Spitzer had in mind a little piano melody the boy might have composed, he could not lose it even if he wanted to.

Then in quick order stepped forth an innkeeper from the village of Nennowitz, a young doctor travelling the Pusta, a provincial actor, a touchy anarchist, and a world traveler stranded by war. Geography, history, politics—these were inciting Spitzer to attempt ever larger canvases. He had already recreated a ski holiday in the Tatras, refurbished a hunting lodge at Nova Paka, rescued a Romanian textile factory from oblivion, returned a grand spa to its former glory, and reestablished the Austro-Hungarian navy at anchor in the harbor at Pola. Spitzer viewed his creations with considerable pride.

"I'm buying," Frieda announced to the table at

large—the Finnerans, Kevin-for-crying-out-loud, Wesley Abbas, attorney-at-law, and Tommy Tee, part barfly, part gadfly, part Native American.

"There's the fucker," the latter said morosely, nodding up in the direction of the television screen where the President of the United States was beginning an address to the nation. "Oh Christ – 'his fellow Americans'—what a piece of crap. 'I come to you this evening'; Where the fuck from? Answer me, you creep." But the president preferred to address the nation as a whole. Tommy Tee caught Finneran's eye. "He don't know shit, Man."

"The guy's a mole, Tom, face it, he's a sleeper," Finneran said dismissively.

"The mole is my brother," the other replied simply.

Frieda brought the drinks back from the bar one at a time, carrying each one with a self-conscious care which was, however, no match for sobriety. Finally she sat down at the table to join them.

"We are a people like any other," Wesley Abbas was saying. Abbas appeared at the Castle from time to time to argue the Palestinian case. "The Irish have Ireland."

Frieda focused her eyes, unseeing, on the sleek, attractive lawyer across the table. "Oh Ireland," she sang in an undertone, with an uneven ersatz brogue, "saaad is thy lonely soulllll hmmmmmmm."

"There's your problem right there then," Finneran told Abbas with just a hint of condescension, "because in fact the English have Ireland."

"So you say, so you say," Abbas murmured. "There is, however, the matter of the land. No small matter." He smiled at Frieda whose eyes appeared to him fixed with rapt attention. He saw her lips move but could hear nothing amid the general racket.

Mrs. Finneran turned to engage Frieda. "Sometimes I just wish Finn was, like..." pensive, she paused, searching for a proper antidote to the Irish condition, "like...from Finland. He would be so much happier if he weren't in an ethnic group, you know what I mean?"

"Hmmmmmmmmm," sang Frieda without acknowledging this apercu, "'came Scofield's mennnnn, and his body tennnnn,'" she took a long draw on her cigarette, "'wearin' jackets greeeennnnn....'"

"Everybody's gotta be somewhere," Tommy Tee attempted with drunken precision to define the issue; and a careful listener would therein have understood an allusion to certain lawsuits demanding the return of Native American land. "And *somebody*'s gotta be everywhere."

"I didn't say that," Abbas put in quickly, his nose twitching as if at a sudden odor. "Remember, we are Semites, too. I'm saying simply that we are a people like any other."

"Sometimes I wish you would talk about Polish people. What about Polish people?" Ignored by Frieda, Mrs. Finneran addressed this complaint to Wesley Abbas.

"Quit while you're ahead, honey," Finneran suggested to his wife, not unkindly.

"Well, some Semites are and some Semites aren't," Tommy Tee maintained perversely. "I mean that in the best way."

"What way is that?" Frieda said sourly, eyes on the table.

Abbas turned his urbane attentions to Mrs. Finneran.

"The governments of Eastern Europe are very important to us in our struggle," he told her. "Tom may mean what he likes. The fact remains they have driven us from our homeland and we must have it back."

"What he likes," Frieda echoed; she felt she was on to something. "What kind of a world would it be if we all meaned what we liked?"

"It works for the A-rabs," Finn answered jovially, giving Abbas a good-natured clap on the back.

Frieda leaned forward, planting one unwitting elbow in a green metal ashtray. "What if we liked what we meaned for a change," she speculated.

Wesley Abbas shrugged his shoulders and averted his eyes from her. "We are a people. We must have our rights. We must have a flag and postage stamps and our own currency."

"Zlotys," murmured Mrs. Finneran sympathetically.

"Hey, what about if we even knew what we meaned," Frieda maundered on. "On our stamps it would say, 'We Know What We Mean.'"

"Philately." Kevin-For-Crying-Out-Loud spoke for the first time.

Finneran turned and told him sternly, "We'll have none of that talk here, boy-o."

"No, this is amazing, Finn." Kevin's voice started to crack with emotion. "My mom sold the whole stamp collection." It was a betrayal the pain of which he re-lived on a daily basis as a substitute teacher in the city's public schools.

Ashes drifted from Frieda's sleeve as she took a sip. All at once she was no longer having quite as good a time. "I thought Muslims don't drink alcohol," she challenged Wesley Abbas with a sneer.

"We are a people like any other," he answered smoothly. "Some of us do, and some of us don't."

"Well there's your problem right there," Finneran said again. "Slainte!" He raised his beer and turned to his wife with a wink. "Don't tell me the worst part."

"You know what the worst part was, Frieda?" Kevin-For-Crying-Out-Loud forged ahead.

"The worst part was she didn't give you any of the money," Frieda said unfeelingly.

"Yeah, right, the worst part was she didn't give me any of the money." His voice was filled with the awful wonder of it.

"Don't give me that crap," Tommy Tee was saying as the president wound up his speech, "You're a goddam fuckin' mole."

"This discussion is going nowhere. I leave you, people." Abbas stood up, his eyes accusing Frieda.

"Abbul," Mrs. Finneran said quickly, "don't be discouraged. I think we were all really listening."

"Wesley," Abbas corrected her, ice in his voice. Then he leaned toward Frieda in what she at first took to be a little foreign bow, and brought his face close to hers. "It's purdah for you," he told her with silky assurance before walking away.

Frieda, with no idea of what purdah might or might not be, nonetheless took satisfaction in his departure. She leaned back in her chair and stretched her legs. She blew smoke at the pressed tin ceiling. Prince Wesley, she said more or less to herself, he reminds me of that asshole Prince Wesley.

But who the hell is Prince Wesley, she was trying to remember when a bouquet of flowers landed in her lap. Her heart was racing, but she looked up at Paul Silverman with apparent calm. "Who's Prince Wesley?" she asked gaily.

He watched her put her nose into the bouquet of flowers and breathe deeply. The futility of the gesture appealed to him. But he took in at once how it was with her and urged, "Let me drive you home; maybe 'It Happened One Night' is on TV."

Nevertheless, Frieda and Paul were instead among the last to leave the Castle that evening. In the meantime, their conversation had gone far afield, and, while avoiding the subjects of his previous marriage and her abrupt departure, it had seemed to both of them, none the less intimate and important for that. Whether by way of apology or not, Paul was more forthcoming than ever before, and it was soon apparent that they shared a desire for a sympathetic brand of human companionship. There was satisfaction in this discovery, and, too, an increase of tension, temperature, and sexual terpsichore.

Frieda left her car keys behind in the charge of Frank Castle himself, and entered Paul's car for the first time. The bouquet of flowers in hand, she sat close to him and put her head against his shoulder as he drove. For several moments together Frieda now approached a benign thoughtlessness which, though it verged on the unconscious, she took to be a variety of happiness.

She followed him silently up the stairs, but when they

reached the second-floor landing, she stopped there in front of the door to his apartment. "I thought we were going to watch 'It Happened One Night,'" she said with just a touch of belligerence. Paul unlocked the door to the apartment and ushered her in.

The living room was still crowded with moving cartons, on one of which sat a color television set. A sofa stood opposite and a large canvas by an up-and-coming Ghanaian artist leaned against the wall of the dining alcove. Paul's cat lay in one corner of the sofa. Frieda did not enter this room but turned without comment to a door on her right and, opening it, walked into a closet containing a pair of skis and a camel hair coat. Her host, equally wordless, took her by the hand and led her to the bathroom door at the end of the short hall.

Inside, she picked up a section of newspaper from the pile on the clothes hamper; focusing her eyes with the greatest difficulty, she read a squib about Queen Victoria's dogs, how many of them she had, and of what breeds. She washed her hands and face and rinsed her mouth. She looked in the mirror and, although her face appeared an odd shade of yellow-green, she was less displeased than she should have been with what she saw.

She had turned on the television and was lighting a cigarette when Paul came in carrying a glass vase into which he had stuffed the bouquet of flowers. He studied her as she stood absorbed in front of the soundless TV set, wreathed in smoke, her hair disheveled, her turtleneck drooping. His ex-wife, he recalled, had been the most social of social drinkers. The downside, of course, was that she had been as well the most social of social scientists, dismissing Africa to his face as a fad whose time had passed. He followed Frieda's gaze to the screen. What he saw there alarmed him.

"'It Happened One Night,'" he exclaimed, putting the vase down on a carton marked "miscellaneous."

"I know," Frieda answered placidly, backing away toward the sofa. "I knew I could trust you," she settled herself on the sofa pulling up her legs. All was right with the world. The future seemed secure.

Paul found a glass ashtray in yet another carton marked "miscellaneous." He held the ashtray toward her.

Frieda smiled what she took to be an intimate smile, and toppled slowly sideways until her cheek touched the rough fabric of the sofa. Paul's cat leapt to the floor. "But I want to know what I mean...." Her voice was muffled, directed down into the front of her coat, and she slept where she lay.

Paul took the still-burning cigarette from her fingers and put it out. He found a blanket in a carton marked "miscellaneous" and spread it over her.

Earlier in the evening, before leaving for the Castle, Paul had, for the first time ignoring Lois's instructions, tried to telephone her. Now, late as it was, he tried again. Still no answer. Though he was convinced of her involvement in the Michigan shootout, this alone would not be grounds for attempting to contact her. But now he thought he had found Rosie. Actually, he knew it was Rosie.

It was not quite 5:00 a.m. when Frieda woke with a start, her turtleneck damp with sweat. One might imagine that she came-to disoriented, with no sense of where she was or why, but in fact, quite the opposite was the case. She was aware, it seemed, even before waking, of something profoundly unpleasant in her circumstance, and this caused her head to pound, her limbs to be suffused with fear, her mind awhirl with dread possibilities. She threw the blanket from her and was up and moving in a single frantic motion.

Revulsion, disgrace, embarrassment, mortification, humiliation, remorse, hopelessness and panic accompanied her upstairs, where, because life itself now lacked any attraction except a bed of one's own, it was only fitting that she should find the feckless Rosie, not on the living room sofa where she belonged, but sprawled on Frieda's own bed, mouth open, snoring lightly.

CHAPTER FIFTEEN

At the Mall

Lois did not like to face the fact that she was all alone. How desperate and corrupting that was. How pathetic ideologically. But it was difficult to keep up the appearance of visiting old friends when old friends made themselves, for any number of reasons, impossible to visit. Many had simply disappeared; but others, settled folk, sure of themselves, made excuses, or put her off with talk of the environment, or even pretended they were not home at all. In any event, no one had been truly happy to hear from her.

No one, that is, except Fizz Hoban, at the start of her wanderings, and now—was this the end?—Ernie Blyda here in Pittsfield. She had been able to locate Fizz without any trouble. He was a New Yorker born and bred, still at the same address. He had welcomed her warmly, insisted that she share what little he had, offered to show her the sights. This had raised her hopes cruelly at the start. What's more, which had put him at the top of her list to begin with, Fizz read no newspaper, was without radio or television, without friends, without curiosity, and, as it turned out best of all, without any clear idea of just who she was. Of course, it was not as though they had ever been good friends, but they had shared more than a few joints, and it was even likely, Lois realized with growing disbelief, that they had slept together once.

"My brains are rot, man, but I like a lot of what I see," Fizz told her straight off. All to the good, Lois thought grimly, as she watched the rapid practiced motion of his hands as he readied a fix. Over the next several days, whenever he was aware of her presence, Fizz discoursed on the subject of fire and ice and their work in the world. "That's nice," Lois murmured at regular intervals, staring down five stories at the East Village street where the lives of The People dribbled and coursed. It soon became evident that his interest extended only to the Four Elements—he had come to lack the human touch—and any phrase which struck Lois's ear the least bit comfortably—his offer to show her the sights, for example—was only a scrap of dialogue left over, along with a psychedelic wall-hanging and an empty window box, from another time.

She might have stayed longer—it had been very cold that week, and the fact that she and her host were themselves unable to construct a common past seemed to insure a double measure of security—had it not been for how terribly thin he was. It was that which forced Lois's early departure; she found she was unable to eat in his presence. Nor did he ever eat in hers. This tended to strain the bonds of sociability, and made Lois think sadly of the old days when great groups of them had gotten together and eaten stew and drunk red wine and fallen in love with themselves and each other. In those days, of course, she had been worried about her own weight, in thrall, as she soon understood, to a decadent vision of the female form, foisted on her by The System and the men who gloried in it and later gave their names to hospitals. Harry Silverman himself had built a synagogue.

Lois did not worry that this urgent need to leave might put into question her theoretical underpinnings, not to mention the political imperatives of her very existence; but she was perfectly capable of feeling badly about it nonetheless. "I'm a shit," she told Fizz Hoban, thinking specifically of her lack of compassion, humanity, commitment and guts. Here was suffering, here was drug addiction, here was poverty, here was illness, here was no hope and no power. What more could she want? She thought about that. Did Emma Goldman want to dance? The question presented itself. Did a Nazi Commandant play Beethoven? Did Mother Theresa visit her parents? She struggled to find some reflection, some illumination, in that piquant modern triptych.

"I gotta go meet a dude," Fizz had drawled, interrupting her reverie.

But wait—Lois could not let go yet, selfishly, pettishly, aggressively, seeking her own comfort—I'm no social worker. She sneered at the thought. How could she have forgotten how much she despised their bureaucratic, stopgap, finger-in-the-dike, confrontations with a sick society. No, it was The System; The System had to go. It was the only way. Put all the social workers out of work. Now. She thanked Fizz for his hospitality, and forced herself to put her arms around his body for a brief moment, to feel that collection of bones shift at her touch in their loose sack of skin. Yes, there was much work to be done.

Lois spent that night on the streets, among the homeless, as she counted it. She had the car, of course, and actually spent a good part of the night, after the movie let out, driving the well-lit streets of mid-town, deciding what to do and where to go next, nourishing her resolve on the burnished brownstones of East 63rd Street, on the limos at the Regency Hotel, even on the broad, imperial steps in front of the Metropolitan Museum. Before daybreak she was driving north out of the city, tired, but confident that in her pursuit of a worthy goal she would find succor whichever way she turned.

Now, however, on the outskirts of Pittsfield, with her cash reserve dwindling, Lois found herself truly weary and discouraged. She dried her eyes on the sleeve of her parka. The week before, the car had had a flat tire as she drove the length of Cape Cod on a tip from a friend. She had changed the tire, and now her sleeve was stiff with grime.

Little Ernie Blyda lived in Pittsfield. She had hoped that she would not have to resort to Ernie Blyda. Their paths had crossed once too often, she felt. True, at the beginning, he had merely been a friend of a friend; but now it was more than that. It was his van and his wheelchair and his apple butter—and, of course, there was no one but Ernie to thank for the recent illfated action. Nevertheless, Lois's hunger for comradeship had begun to disorient her, and she had telephoned Ernie from a phone booth early that morning. He apologized profusely, he conveyed his condolences, he spoke of the future. But best of all, Ernie was happy to hear from her.

Around her the parking lot was beginning to fill as the end of the day brought people from every direction to The Mega-Mecca Mall. They did not dawdle, but emerged from their cars smartly, walking purposefully toward the entrance of their choice; and before Lois knew it, she was inside too, staring into a display case filled with sunglasses.

This is America, Lois thought wandering along the Mall's upper level, and these are the American people. She was momentarily heartened by the thought—how poorly they looked, how authentic, how ripe—smoking their cigarettes, dragging their pale children, downing their Cokes; and yet, she noted cynically, with it all, buying, buying, buying. She unzipped her parka. Climate control, she thought.

But it was not all climate control. She felt suddenly ill at ease, overwhelmed, even light-headed. She rode the escalator down into The Food Court and bought a donut. Perhaps she was only hungry. Sitting on a slatted wooden bench, watching the capitalist commotion as people milled among a multitude of fast-food outlets, she thought suddenly: all Americans must have equal access to the world of the Mall. She conjured up those citizens who still had to shop in narrow dingy storefronts, pawing ill-assorted merchandise, paying cash. No waterfall for them, no see-through elevator, no hope for the future. For The Mall seemed suddenly to be, and the very thought confused her, a kind of hopeful place, indeed, a place of peace and plenty.

She studied the people who clustered at the hotdog cart, who ate their tacos outside the Cactus Cantina, who purchased pizza slices or swallowed down fish and chips. Dignity, the thought struck her; if, as she knew, the availability of material goods was crucial to a life of dignity, this could well be dignity. For her own part, personally, she had always considered dignity to be something quite different, had, as she groped her ideological way, thought it probably a cross between the Native American's nobility and the gaunt-faced miner's pride; but perhaps it really was here, here amid this abundance of material things, that man could truly move in dignity.

Her mind was in a muddle. The theory presented itself that the air of the Mall had been infused with a mind-clouding chemical agent which did not agree with her. It was likely intended, she thought, to intensify the consumerist urge, part of the government's effort to shore up the economy. She sniffed but smelled nothing other than a stomach-wrenching mélange of the food of many nations. A perfect camouflage.

Suddenly there was shouting from above. Lois looked up to see a white banner being lowered over the railings of the mezzanine level. "Not In My Backyard," it read. Perhaps a dozen women leaned over the rail chanting, "Not in my backyard, not in my backyard." Lois stood transfixed. A group of diners began to coalesce around her. "Shut up and shop!" they shouted, "shut up and shop!" The issue was joined. Here was Main Street, Town Square, Village Green, here at The Mall, here where every man, woman and child in America could take his rightful place in the economy of the nation, could exercise those personal freedoms which are most profoundly realized in the realm of the shopper— choice and expression—could walk with his neighbor in the fellowship of plenty. No way, no way, Lois muttered, getting up distractedly, brushing the powdered sugar from her slacks, and, along with it, this disturbing vision of The System at work.

Suddenly, with a start, it came to her as if conjured up by that miasmic American Dream just whose friend Ernie

Blyda had been; he had been a friend of a friend, true, but that friend, she recalled now, had been Rip Parks. Betrayal. In her world that word was like no other; it took in the whole conceptual universe, and attached itself with equal ease to an idolized father, a G-man's All-American smile, and the promise of democracy. Spooked, she began a circuit of the Mall's lower level, browsing through one store and then another, her mind on a future which seemed suddenly open to interpretation. Then at the end of a long aisle, in an establishment which had more the aspect of a cornucopia than a pharmacopeia, while calling itself a drug store, she saw a small bottle of spot remover. This would be useful for cleaning the sleeve of my parka, she thought. With a casual motion she picked the bottle up and put it into the pocket of her jacket. She made her way slowly back to the store's open, door-less, anti-exit, and was just about to break into the stream of passing shoppers when a corpulent dark-skinned woman stepped in front of her. A small badge identifying her as Mall personnel was nearly invisible on the vast plain of her bosom.

"Please remove the bottle of spot remover from your pocket and step this way," the woman said in a deep hushed voice.

"I was just about to pay for it," Lois protested.

"Come with me, please." She held Lois firmly at the elbow and walked her through half the Mall matching her stride to a tune Lois strove without success to recognize. Behind a standard, hinged door, possibly the only such one in the Mall, was a small beige room with several folding chairs, a TV set, and a video tape player, as close as Lois was likely to come to the Star Chamber. The woman opened a gray binder and checked the name Lois gave her against a multi-page list of names, only to learn that Sarah Loomis had never been caught shop-lifting in this or any other mall belonging to Mega-Mecca Management Group. As Sarah Loomis had died in infancy a dozen years before, this was in no way surprising.

There was a knock at the door and the woman moved to admit a uniformed policeman. "Got anyone for me, Sister Deb? Or is she going to the show?"

"I got no record up here," she tapped the binder, "but you don't never know when a fingerprint will tell a different story." The woman named Deb sounded simultaneously hopeful and ominous.

"Look," said Lois, mustering all her calm and conviction, "I swear to you I've never done this before. I don't know what happened; I wasn't feeling well." She did not sound calm.

"The only problem is," Deb paused for effect, "this." She put the small bottle of spot remover on one meaty palm and stretched her arm toward the policeman who examined the bottle closely.

"Non-prescription," he joked, looking Lois over. "Next time try taking your garment to the cleaner. There's one right here in the Mall."

"But what if I can't afford a cleaner?" Lois whined, unable to resist the opening.

"I was joking, ma'am," the policeman replied pleasantly.

Pigs are always joking, Lois thought, except when they shoot you down in cold blood. She considered for the briefest moment bringing that into the conversation, but satisfied herself by saying haughtily, reproachfully, "Not being able to afford something is no joke."

The officer did not like her tone. "Look," he gestured toward the woman, "Sister Deb has you down for the show, but if you got something on your mind, something you want to discuss," he hissed his contempt for the very idea, "you can go in with me for the prints."

"But why can't we discuss it here?" Lois was whining again.

The woman sighed and inserted a video cassette into the VCR. "You just sit and enjoy this," she ordered as the title "Malls Are For Shoppers" appeared on the screen, "and I'll be back for you." She popped a mint into her mouth and held the door open for the policeman. For just an instant Lois had a glimpse of the outside world, and it looked to her, shut away, facing re-education, suddenly, poignantly, like Christmas.

The woman named Deb was true to her word. In this as in other, lesser, matters she reminded Lois of the woman of color who had worked for her parents during her growing up. Less than half an hour later she returned holding two skinny white girls by the hand, and Lois was released to do her worst in the world. "Next time—when you gonna come up in here," Deb warned her warmly in parting, "remember, it's your little red wagon."

This colorful threat was denied much of its power, for Lois had grown preoccupied with an awful thought that had come to her in the middle of "Malls Are For Shoppers." She had been set up. She was walking into a trap. Indeed, who but Ernie Blyda did she have to thank for the recent, ill-fated action, she thought again. It would be a mistake, she was certain now, to follow-up on her telephone call to him. She needed another plan. Yet there was, oddly, a feeling of regret mingled with her relief at the discovery.

Over the several weeks, the desire to remain at large, which had heretofore been the be-all of her daily life, had slowly, subtly been co-opted by the desire to see Rip Parks once more. The odor of his after-shave, the proximity of his gun on that bitter, starry night, had done their work. Rip Parks had come into kinder focus during her lonely hours on the road, as fragments of fantasy and of her former good opinion of him began to reassert themselves. Now, sitting in her car in the dark, the Mall parking lot crowded but silent, she imagined him waiting for her at Ernie Blyda's faded cottage, standing in the shadows, standing absolutely still and strong, waiting for her.

CHAPTER SIXTEEN

Grilling Rosie

"She's my niece," Paul told Frieda.

Frieda, half-way through the open door, stopped short with surprise, less at his announcement than at his presence in her apartment.

"She's his niece," the B.T. echoed excitedly, entering from the kitchen waving a sheaf of news clippings.

"You." Frieda recoiled, blindsided. "Why are you here?" She stepped into the room and closed the door carefully behind her, an oddly willful gesture in view of her turmoil; and she did not let go of the doorknob as she glanced around in search of other surprises. "Who let you in?"

"His niece." The B.T. grinned, so caught up in his own enthusiasm as to be completely unaware that Frieda would find his grin a provocation. "Rosie Silverman." He said her name as if he had just been initiated into a secret society and were now giving the password for the first time.

"Rosie?!" Frieda looked toward Paul who looked toward her. Had she been able to take it in, she would have seen on his face an aspect which spoke of his pleasure in seeing her. "Don't look at me that way!" she was caused to say instead. Only then, turning, did she see Rosie outside on the balcony, looking off into the dusky distance, thinking who knew what dark, familial thoughts. "Why aren't you saying anything?" Frieda pressed him.

"I am saying something. I'm saying she's my niece." Paul folded his arms across his chest. At this moment, in his pressed khaki trousers, crisp collar and Italian sweater, a satisfied smile on his lips, he seemed very nearly a picture of his former self. If he needed any reassurance that this was a superficial judgment at best, Frieda Zale was close at hand, shrugging her shoulders comically, energetically, as if escaping a carapace far more confining than a navy-blue wool coat.

In spite of the B.T.'s straight-forward presentation, Frieda was having trouble taking in her houseguest's true identity. "When you say 'she,' do you mean...," she stretched her neck toward the window.

Paul nodded. "Remember my sister Lois? Her mother."

"I was instrumental," the B.T. asserted, picking up a thick book from a stack of books on the table. Its title was *The New Left: How It Was.* "We'd been discussing names. She would have confided in me in a day or two, I'm certain of it. But Paul confronted her with it now; she just got up and went outside."

"Confided?" Frieda lit a cigarette. She tried to get her attitude in order, but, being unaware that her attitude did not in fact address their discovery of consanguinity at all, she was at a disadvantage here. "I'll have a beer," she temporized, moving around the table toward the kitchen.

"Look at the index," the B.T. commanded, misunderstanding, thrusting the book at her as she passed. "Lois Silverman. Look at all this...," he pointed, "*passim.*"

Paul joined her in the kitchen. "After you fell asleep the other night, I tried to call Lois...."

"What was I like?" Frieda asked dully, and this question should have given her some indication as to the real source of her distress. She rubbed her cheek quickly as if it were yet marked by the pattern of ridges the rough fabric of his couch had left behind. Frieda's stomach turned queasy at the memory; she felt herself blushing

Paul put his hands on her shoulders; Frieda allowed the upper half of her body to lean stiffly toward him until her head rested against his chest. She held onto the book tightly, awkwardly. Paul spoke into her ear. "I haven't been able to talk to Lois.... She's probably all alone and has no idea where Rosie is."

Frieda stood limply, head bowed, a penitent. "What was I like?" she asked again.

"You were asleep," Paul tried to pull her to him, but Frieda did not know in which hand she should hold *The New Left: How It Was* in order to make their embrace possible. He stepped back, frowning, and took the book from her. "Can we try and focus on Rosie now?" Paul was showing impatience for the first time, anxious perhaps for some reassurance of his own.

Frieda reformed herself at once. "At this point if her mother isn't at home, Rosie obviously wouldn't know where her mother is, right?" Frieda felt a flare of sympathy for a girl thus suddenly bereft of her parents.

"But maybe she does know. I hadn't thought of that. I just assumed, as you did, that she wouldn't." He patted Frieda on the head. "Smart girl."

"That sounds very convincing." She reached up to touch her hair where he had touched it.

"Soft and silky," Paul assured her. "I'm right; you were thinking about it, your hair, right?"

Frieda did not know what to say. Was he really coming to know her? "Fortunately, I'm not trying to make a first impression."

"I like your hair. I liked your hat, too. You made a good first impression; it was the second impression...." He smiled.

"And I like your hair." Frieda was back on her own turf again. "What about her father though. I mean, she wasn't looking for an uncle!" Paul reached out to tease her with another pat on the head, but she backed away nimbly, boosting herself up onto the counter out of his range—only to land half in and half out of the half-full sink. They were both laughing now. She took the hand he offered. "You're driving me to sink," she said, feeling suddenly very good about how things were between them.

"Our graduate student is going to do some further research and see what we come up with. I've told him what little I know about her father. Which, however, I don't want Rosie to know right now. The main thing first is finding Lois."

The researcher in question had meanwhile set aside his books and papers and stepped out to join Rosie on the balcony. Scooping snow from the railing, he let a rough ball drop through three stories of darkness into the blue-shadowed yard. "Uuuuuhhhh," he said to her back, imagining for just an instant that she would turn and fling herself into his arms, "do you feel O.K.?"

Rosie did not turn around. "The thing is," she answered

plaintively, hewing to what was apparently the distaff party line, "I wasn't looking for an uncle. He seems like he would be all right, you know, but it's not the same thing."

Puzzled, the B.T. stood at the railing next to her. "It's just a bonus, that's all. We're still going to find your father." He felt compelled to have her share his excitement, almost as if it were he who had discovered a long-lost relation instead. "And now he can help us too. He might have some information," he added disingenuously.

"No," Rosie said with heavy finality, "he said he didn't. He said he never even heard his name or anything. Let's start the hibachi," she moved away quickly, kicking at the little barbeque in the corner of the balcony.

"Wait, wait, but we already know his name, so...."

"If that's his name. If. Frieda, I need matches," Rosie ordered through the open door.

As the B.T. studied her motionless silhouette, a vestal virgin awaiting only a flame to tend, he put the two bits of biographical information together one way and then another and always came up with one indisputable fact— Randall Parks, Rosie's father or not, had been an informant for the FBI, maybe even an agent—they had read it in one of the old news reports. The B.T. actually stroked his beard at this point. Moses, it occurred to him out of the blue, had married a Midianite woman. From the corner of his eye, he received the impression that a figure was standing in the doorway at the far end of the courtyard, looking up toward the very balcony on which he stood. He focused just in time to disbelieve the sight, or else imagine some such shadow slipping away around the corner of the building.

"If that's his name," Rosie repeated with emphasis, as if she were following his thoughts.

"Were you given a Jewish name when you were born?" the B.T. asked, recalling suddenly that if you live with a gentile woman you were liable to be slain by zealots.

"Who said I was Jewish?" Rosie tilted the bag of charcoal into the hibachi." I'm not even Jewish, so why would I have a Jewish name?"

"Your mother's Jewish," The B.T. pointed out smugly, squatting by the grill, making a neat little pyramid of the briquettes.

"Who said she was Jewish? She's nothing, no religion, that's what she told me. I'm gonna make barbeque chicken wings," she said to Paul who had come out with a box of matches." I know a great way someone showed us." It was the first time since she had heard about the Michigan shoot-out on television that she had had a kind thought to spare for either Simon or Willis Washington. Or indeed a thought at all, as she pushed the event further and further from her with each day that passed without getting Lois on the telephone. She had been on the phone at all hours of the day and night; the moment Frieda closed the door Rosie had the receiver in hand dialing the number at home. But there was never any answer. Whenever she thought of that, Rosie felt nervous about the future.

"Who?" Paul asked bluntly.

"Some guys my Mom knew...I mean, you know, knows. They showed us. I have to go to the store now and get some barbeque stuff." She started for the door but Paul seemed to be blocking her way.

"Where is your mother now?"

"Home, I guess." She squeezed past Paul. "Probably barbequing."

On the verge of a retort, Paul suddenly saw this for the bit of bravado it was and let it pass. "I don't think so," he said mildly and followed her inside. "I've been trying to get her on the phone for days and I haven't been able to."

"I don't believe you."

"Why not?"

"Because no one has our telephone number. You don't even have our telephone number."

Paul recited the number then. "I've dialed it so often lately I know it by heart."

"Who gave you that number?"

"Your mother did. For an emergency."

"O.K., so you're her brother." Rosie feigned resignation. "Can I go now? I'm getting hungry."

Paul suggested that Frieda go to the supermarket instead, and Frieda went without a remonstrance, that dreary task suddenly burnished by intimacy, shining even with the promise of future domesticity. Rosie lit a cigarette and sat down on the sofa with the current issue of *People* magazine. The B.T. cleared a place for himself at the table. He readied a pen and a yellow legal pad. It seemed however that the page was destined to remain blank, for Rosie claimed to be totally without knowledge regardless of the matter Paul chose to pursue.

She had not heard, seen or read anything about any shootout in Michigan, she told him. What's more, she was by no means certain of the existence of such a state, let alone of its geographical location, or any predisposition it might have to hosting cells of right-wing extremists. No, again, she did not know of two black men who might be friends or confederates of her mother's, knew indeed only of white friends and of women friends at that. As a sign of good faith, she then told them about how their neighbor, a white woman she emphasized, had driven with Lois to a nearby college and how after that the two women had started collecting hip hop tapes.

Paul groaned. "That's Lois. Hip hop."

"So, what's your problem?" Rosie demanded hotly. "She likes all kinds of music."

The B.T. drew three columns on his legal pad. In the first he wrote "neighbor," in the second, "local college," and in the third, "hip hop tapes."

"What about around the time you left, can you think of anything, any phone calls, people, anything she talked about?"

Again, no. Things were just as they had always been, she assured him. Everything was just the same. She went on to detail the physical reality of her home, moving slowly through time and space, catching herself up in the rhythm of her effort, in the sarcastic monotony of her refrain. "Missing thumb tack...Indian guy...TV...sofa...Cuban guy... ashtray....Ernie's apple butter...pile of socks...."

"Who?" The B.T. wrote "Ernie" on his pad in column one.

"What?" Paul and Rosie asked in unison for neither had been listening to her monologue, Paul because he was irritated by her sullen rhetorical excess, Rosie herself because she was pretending to have an out-of-body experience. Paul bent over the B.T.'s shoulder. "Who's Ernie?" he asked now. "Ernie who?"

But the girl denied knowing anyone by that name, nor would she admit to so much as having spoken the name aloud, or even, she added for good measure, having it in her thoughts. "Why should I even believe you just because you say something," she started again.

Once again Paul, feeling like a spymaster, recited the telephone number, and Rosie who was about to give full vent to her injured feelings, abruptly chose silence instead. She might have wished that cunning had been hers as well, for the B.T. had at once taken up one of the volumes on the table and begun to read avidly through the lists of footnotes at the back.

"Wait," he muttered, "there may be something. Here. No. One of these guys did a lot of interviews. Hold on." For the first time in nearly a year—ever since he gave up pork in fact—he understood that he was not a graduate student for nothing. He picked up another book.

"I don't think you know what you're doing," Rosie accused, but this time more in sorrow than in anger. "If she wanted you to know where she was, she would call you. She knows what she's doing, so just...."

There was no response. Rosie threw the magazine across the room toward Paul's head; the clippings on the table floated and scattered in its draft. Paul turned and gave her a close look. Suddenly he felt very much in charge; after all, he had done his share of negotiating in his day.

"You're right," he said to her surprise. "If you don't mind

not knowing, then I don't mind either. There's more than one flight to Gaborone." This expression had yet to become proverbial. But it was not so easy to fob off the B.T. who in this respect perhaps proved himself to be more a scholar than a gentleman. "I mind," he broke into their colloquy, "I'm going to keep looking."

"Oh great," said Rosie, having turned on the television in response to the apparent finality of Paul's response. "What's your problem!"

"This could help us," he said, changing ground, giving up on knowledge for its own sake." I mean maybe this Ernie knew your father too. Anything's possible. You never know."

"My father would not know Ernie," she said placidly, mind elsewhere, eyes on the television screen. "If I think you're a nerd," she mused unthinkingly to the B.T., "well you should see Ernie."

Paul walked over to turn down the television sound. "Who's Ernie? Ernie who?" he asked in passing, innocently, as if the question had never been raised.

"Do you have a hearing problem?" Rosie inquired with studied impertinence. She slithered the length of the sofa in the direction of the TV set, her sweater riding up over her bare midriff. "I said Bee-Tee not Er-Neee, B.T. is a total nerd." She could not suppress a laugh. "Right B.T.?"

Her laughter, and it was rare enough, became her, Paul thought, made her look a lot more like his niece. What a life she must have led. Was it not likely that the FBI knew all about Lois's daughter? Were they on her trail even now? Clearly this had been in Yolanda's mind when he had called to tell her about her niece. "What a life she must have led," Yolanda had said excitedly, "come to dinner with her. Come to dinner soon. I must meet her, I must meet my niece," she had finished off soap-operatically. He had yet to extend the invitation to Rosie.

As the B.T. had not responded to her provocation, Rosie got up from the sofa and swung past his chair into the kitchen. She did not bother to adjust her sweater back down over the top of her low-slung jeans, indeed while out of sight in the kitchen she may very well have hiked it up just a bit all around to create a more complete impression. She returned with a handful of pretzels, half of which she deposited on the table next to the B.T. When he still did not look up, she took one of the pretzel sticks and poked at his bearded cheek with it. "It's really growing now."

The B.T. raised his eyes from the page and twisted his body to the right until he was looking straight at her smooth, naked belly. He tilted his head back a bit, took off his glasses and looked up at her, naked in his own right. "We sat by the flesh pots," he quoted, "we, of course, being the nerds." He wriggled his shoulders and stretched, the fingertips of his right hand just grazing Rosie's bare skin as she skipped back out of reach. "I'm not getting anywhere."

"Give up," the girl encouraged him. Just outside the door Frieda could be heard shuffling about. "You can help me do the barbeque. I hope Frieda got a lot of chicken wings." But Frieda hadn't gotten any chicken wings at all. The supermarket was out of chicken wings. As it turned out, however, this never became an issue. Two men had entered the apartment with her.

"They're FBI agents," Frieda told the others.

"Paul Silverman?" Someone had to have been driving that car, the FBI had reasoned when Special Agent Parks had confirmed the presence of a get-away car. Lois Silverman was one possibility. Hers had been one of the names on the October Manifesto, yet The Bureau had all but forgotten her, had been unable to tie her to any criminal activity before or since, had for some time no idea whatsoever of where she was. But now, of the five signatories of that seminal document, three women and two men, one was dead and the other three had been arrested in connection with an armored truck robbery. So, Lois Silverman, they decided, was one possibility.

Paul determined instantly that he would not give his niece away unless the men already knew that Lois had a daughter, and he were asked a direct question about her. Then it would be better to tell the truth, for it was no good being caught in a lie by the FBI. He had lied inadvertently—too smooth for his own good—when agents had been around to see him in the early 'seventies, and it had caused him no end of trouble. Paul felt now that this time Lois had reached the end of the line. He didn't know what would happen, or how it would happen, he only hoped it would happen in the best possible way.

Rosie identified herself at once and the agents took down the name Xenia Zale without any apparent interest. But Rosie's interest in them was intense; she studied them closely. Might one of these men know her father, be her father? Never had her material been so ripe for speculation. Though the B.T. stood to block their view, the men were equally uninterested in the books and papers on the dining table. Finally, Frieda, feeling painfully outside things, felt compelled to help by supplying the men with Tom Waggoner's name; for the sake of completeness, she said. Tom, whom it had taken some time on the road to fully break the spell of his erstwhile travelling companion, would shortly find himself caught in a more unpleasant sort of snare. The agents then, with all due courtesy, requested Paul to join them in his own apartment.

CHAPTER SEVENTEEN

Cousins

If the truth were known, and Rosie did everything in her power not to let on, she was in fact anxious to accept Yolanda's invitation to dinner. One summer day—home early from her job at Saco River Canoe Rental—she had walked in on her mother unannounced, and discomfited Lois badly. Lois had only been reading a book, but Rosie, seeing at once that she had embarrassed her, was determined to press her advantage. Lois shut the book quickly, pressed it cover-side to her breast, and stumbled up from the sofa all in one motion. But Rosie stopped her before she was able to get out of the living room and took the book from her.

It was a novel entitled *Her Crowning Glory* by one Yolanda Silverman, her aunt, as she had badgered Lois into revealing at the end of a long evening filled with unrelated arguments and tearless recrimination. That summer, Rosie had actually tried to read *Her Crowning Glory*, did read much of it; that is, she got the jist of the novel, although she did not come away with any insight into what had gone wrong with Yolanda's first marriage, or—a higher level of criticism yet—what Yolanda's desire for a child had had to do with it.

I know this building, Rosie thought vaguely as she and

Paul entered the vestibule. "What are you doing?" she asked as he pressed the bell marked "Silverman-Silbermann."

Letitia's precise little voice came through the speaker. "Are you my cousin?" she asked with controlled excitement. A dog barked in the background.

"It's Paul. Can we come in, please, Letty."

"Are you my cousin or not?" the child persisted, and Paul felt his body tense for another rejection.

"Does a blind lady live there?" Rosie asked Paul in an undertone. "Does she live there too?"

"I'm waiting," came the little girl's voice, managing to catch in her own register all her mother's ominous forbearance. The dog continued to bark.

"Let...!" came Yolanda's voice. The speaker cut off then, the door buzzer sounded, and they went in to ride the preternaturally slow elevator in silence, Rosie fearful now, without a clue to what lay ahead.

Paul could offer her no comfort for his thoughts were elsewhere. Frieda had not been herself when he came to the apartment this evening. Or perhaps she had been herself. With Frieda, he acknowledged, it was difficult for him to be sure. Actually, he might not even have noticed—he did no more than stand in the doorway for a moment or two while Rosie dawdled—had Frieda not brought it to his attention by mentioning casually, too casually he saw now, that he should not expect to find her at the Castle later in the evening. O.K., was all he had said, but had he not known at once that something was wrong!

The elevator door opened to reveal little Letitia Silverman-Silbermann. "Ta da," this young-young person said by way of embellishing the moment of their arrival. She wore a floor-length flowered skirt over what appeared to be a bathing suit. A large scarf decorated with a horse-head motif provided an elegant cape-like wrap for her narrow shoulders and back. As Paul and Rosie stepped from the elevator, she took the latter's hand and led her into the apartment. "Look," she said triumphantly to her mother, "she's a girl. I wanted her to be a girl." Behind one of the doors a dog barked frantically.

"I told you she was a girl," said Yolanda dully, looking with a wild stare from Rosie to Paul and back again at Rosie. "You mean this is Rosie," she asked him, "Lois's daughter?" She closed her eyes briefly, massaging her right eyelid.

"I got a new bed," Letty looked up at her cousin, "do you want to see it?"

Rosie turned to Paul. "It's her but she's not blind." It was a minor point of information, but enough, she must have felt, to put herself in the best possible light. "Is she my aunt?"

"Do you want to see it?" Letty asked again. The dog, who had apparently stopped to catch his breath, began to bark all over again.

Yolanda smoothed her hair and smiled a gracious, mature, take-charge smile. "Let's start again, shall we. Hello, Rosie. Yes, I'm Yolanda. Your aunt." She stepped forward, put her arm through the girl's arm and pulled her to her side.

Rosie, who had feared being kissed by this once-blind stranger, was pleasantly surprised by the controlled intimacy of her aunt's gesture. *"Her Crowning Glory?"* Rosie looked Yolanda right in the eye, daring her, "I read that book."

"Oh, I'm so glad," Yolanda virtually gushed as she stared back at her niece. In a pig's eye, she thought. "How did you like it? Letty, go tell Daddy they're here."

Yolanda drew Rosie down the hall at her side. The dog's barking increased in ferocity, and he scratched at his door with great vigor as they passed. "Stop that," Yolanda ordered in a tone of great sweetness, "now you stop that. Ian, Ian-love," she bent to the intercom, "they're here. Paul," she kissed him on the cheek, "let's all sit down."

She felt very relieved. The girl seemed willing, and for good reason too, Yolanda thought, to buy into a conspiracy of silence. The experiment in blindness, that of course Ian knew something about, but she had not come completely clean about the fate of the little painted figurine. Ian had loved that kitschy set, and she had encouraged him to think that the tiny statue had been dropped by the new cleaning woman. Her fabrication was lent unlooked for credence when this same woman broke a second figurine a week later. "Letty, honey, go tell Daddy your cousin's here."

"I'm waiting for her. Do you want to come with me?" the little girl asked Rosie.

"O.K." Her cousin spoke to her for the first time.

The girls out of ear shot, the brother and sister immediately took up the subject uppermost in both their minds. The FBI, Paul had learned on the telephone, had been to visit Yolanda as well. Having had no contact with Lois at all for many years, Yolanda was genuinely happy to cooperate with the FBI. Indeed, had cooperated fully during a visit years before when a local bombing had been under investigation. She made this clear by asking the men a great many more questions than they asked her. Their responses were, however, perfunctory, and no appeal to their vanity did Yolanda any good. They had interviewed writers before; what's more, they told her stoically, had been interviewed by them; indeed, had been quoted extensively in a recent book as "agents in a Midwestern field office."

Close-mouthed, unwilling to share, the men from the FBI left Paul and Yolanda none the wiser as to why they were looking for Lois, what progress they had made in finding her, or what steps a brother or sister might or might not take to frustrate a nationwide man-hunt. The discovery of Rosie's identity, Paul told Yolanda now, had left the agents virtually licking their chops. They could hardly believe their luck; they had simply assumed that the daughter was on the lam with her mother. When they had returned to question her, Rosie had been as determinedly uninformative as ever she was earlier in the evening. Yet she told the truth.

The dog took up his warning bark once more. "Does the damn dog bark all the time or is this a special treat?" Paul asked, hunching his shoulders against the noise.

Yolanda picked up a book from the little table to her right and showed him the spine. "*Mrs. Dalloway*," she said, opening the volume where a slip of paper marked the page. "Listen to this. 'Admirable butlers, tawny chow dogs, halls laid in black and white lozenges with white blinds blowing, Peter saw through the opened door and approved of.'" Yolanda's face was aglow. "We're calling him 'Dolly.' It's not his official name, of course, but we wanted something suitable and female for Letty. He's got a pedigree a mile long."

"How does Letty like him?" Paul did not think that this change of name and gender boded at all well for the dog's adjustment to his new environment.

"Her, Paul," Yolanda reminded, "she hasn't seen her yet. We're giving them a chance to, hmmmm, smell each other out shall we say?" She raised an eyebrow and smiled at her brother. Her look of self-satisfaction was so intense that Paul literally braced himself against its impact. There was, however, no follow-up as she rose and excused herself to see what was keeping Ian. As she started down the hall, the dog resumed his barking. Yolanda turned back. "She's a watch dog, Paul. They're famous as watchdogs."

Yolanda was out of the room no more than a moment— the dog had barely ceased before duty called him once again—when Ian Silbermann entered carrying a plate with a circular white cheese on it. The two girls trailed him, Letty with a 19th century straw basket full of potato chips in her arms and Rosie with a platter of assorted crackers.

"My handmaidens," Ian said. "Caviar spread. Delicious." He tilted the plate in Paul's direction so that the latter could appreciate the pinwheel design the black caviar made in the white cheese. "Over here, Rosalee," he ordered casually, indicating where he wanted her to set down the crackers.

The girl smiled at him. "Sure," she said.

Paul's heart sank. There was more of ease and intimacy in this brief exchange than in anything he and his niece had been able to manage over all the past days. Was it true,

Paul had wondered of late, that stripped as he was of power and position, he had lost as well his much vaunted "way with people?" Not now, he complained, just when he really needed it, just when he was beginning to want to make himself known anew. He thought of Frieda, for it was after all to her specifically that he was increasingly desirous of making himself known. Perhaps it was his good fortune that this odd woman seemed so resistant to whatever fragments of his old charm he had been able from time to time to muster. Yet she would, it appeared to him from all indications, be amenable to a prolonged, multi-country African honeymoon. He was glad he had met her.

"So, what do you think of the new addition to the family," Ian began with his usual bonhomie.

"Well," Paul lowered his voice. He had not yet formulated his real feelings. "She reminds me a lot of Lois, her hair." Ian was laughing. "I doubt that very much." A book was open in his hands. "'So she intimated,'" he read in his radio voice, "'standing at her doorway; handsome; very erect; while her chow stretched behind her....' etc., etc."

"Oh," Paul said, unembarrassed, "him. How can you take the barking?"

"Her." Ian handed Paul the book and stooped to spread some of the caviar and cheese on a cracker. "She's a watch dog. That's the point. You'll see him later." He put a finger to his lips and swiveled his large head to indicate the current policy position on this question. Behind him Letty and her cousin sat on the piano bench with the potato chips between them. "I got my hands on a case of great new beer." Perhaps it was Ian's enthusiasm that led him to suppress the fact that this had been by no means difficult. "Never tasted anything like it." He left the room and the barking began again. A man like Silbermann did not seriously entertain the possibility that his guest would choose to drink anything else; after all, when a man is known for his fierce pursuit of the best, who would not wish to share his taste, even when, as happened so frequently, Ian himself had already come to reconsider his early enthusiasm.

Paul leaned forward for a cracker. Letty played a scale on the piano. Yolanda came back into the room with a wet paper towel in her hand. "I never have time for this," she said without a glance at her brother. Approaching the large Dracaena plant, she knelt and began to wipe its leaves with the paper towel.

Paul sniffed the air and checked his wrist watch. "Need any help in the kitchen?" The odor of cooking food was noticeably absent. He walked over to the piano bench and took a handful of potato chips from the already half-empty basket.

"Don't eat too many chips, Letty," her mother called over her shoulder. "No thanks, Ian's getting things set up. He's cooking tonight." She crossed the room to an immense jade plant in a hand-thrown ceramic pot. "Have we told you about our friend who does these marvelous pots?" she asked, squatting in front of the jade. But she got up suddenly and faced him, her hands on her hips, the wet paper towel, dangling from one finger like a flamenco scarf. "Now that I come to think of it, she would be perfect for you, Paul. Of course, she's married; but if I have any insight into these things, and I think I do, that won't last."

"What won't last, Mommy, what won't last?" Letitia, nostrils flaring, ran to her mother's side.

But while Yolanda paused to take thought as to just how best to characterize the condition of modern marriage for a young-young person, Ian entered the room with a tray of drinks.

"Coke, Daddy, Coke." Letty was in a state of high excitement as she danced impatient attendance on her slow-moving father.

"Have we told you about our good friend who throws these marvelous ceramic pieces?" Ian asked, setting the tray on a fine little mahogany table and pouring the beer. Paul turned for confirmation to Yolanda, but she had left the room.

"Ever taste anything like it?" It was second nature to Ian to heighten the particularity, that is the desirability, of all that came, in whatever way, into his possession. He sat down heavily in the center of the sofa.

Paul shook his head, eyes glued to his beer stein. His brother-in-law, he worried, seemed to have forgotten completely about dinner. Nevertheless, shortly after 8:30 p.m. and many exits and entrances later, they were all seated in the dining room and the meal was on the table. Paul ate his rabbit ragout hungrily; Letty and her cousin, on the other hand, having done their share of eating before dinner, begged to be excused from the table after only a bite of couscous and an obligatory taste of the unnamed other. Their hostess requested that they return in time for dessert, and this they agreed to do.

"Who is this Frieda?" Yolanda asked at once. "Is she suitable?"

Paul looked at her strangely. "For what? She doesn't make ceramic pots, if that's what you mean." He could not help feeling defensive.

"Oh Paul, please! Is she a suitable guardian for a teenage girl? We have to think of the future. I don't mean to be pessimistic...."

"What about her father," Ian broke in, "if we were able to locate him?" Clearly Ian had had a word with the girl. "From what I could tell, she hasn't brought any real resources to bear. She hasn't gone to the media." The word hung above the table for an instant and then shattered into a million fragments of light, of grace, of power.

"What are you thinking of, your show?" Yolanda, a hearty eater, helped herself to a bit more of the ragout. She pushed the serving dish toward Paul. "Mmmmm, I'm glad the girls weren't hungry. Help yourself. Well," she said addressing her husband once more, "the radio is a possibility, but I was thinking of," and here she paused to ensure the attention of both men, "I was thinking of my column." She looked expectantly at Paul, who smiled back weakly, compliantly. Yolanda sharpened her gaze; such an attitude of anxious accommodation had characterized their childhood relations. As far as Yolanda was concerned, it behooved her now to take advantage of it in any way she could. She raised both eyebrows and tilted her face up slightly to signal that she required a further response.

"Career move?" Paul inquired then just negligently enough to rein Yolanda in.

"You bet your ass!" Ian put in proudly.

"The 'Me, Myself and I' column. Do you remember

that night you were mugged? It's a wonderful piece; I'm thinking of using it as my debut. Ian-love, what do you think? I could do Rosie."

"You know what might be interesting," the professor-cum-communicator mused, "why don't we both try it, that might make a useful little study, print versus broadcast, it could prove valuable. How does that sound?"

"It might be fun to work together," Yolanda assented, amending in the process. "Under the circumstances," she drummed her fingers on the table, musing, "perhaps she should move in with us for a while. Letty would love having a big sister...."

"And we'd love having a babysitter.... It's a great idea. I'm for it." Ian rose and began clearing the dishes from the table.

Clearly, Paul saw, Yolanda and Ian were under the impression that the world remained under their control. He needed time to think. Why should he take it so much to heart that Rosie might move in with them? Bobo-Dioulasso, he thought, as if to give substance to his opposition in the face of their certitude.

"It is perfect for me," Yolanda agreed with a forgiving smile.

Paul wondered what exactly, if anything at all, he had just said. It was not that silence was unusual with him these days. But the company of Ian and Yolanda often filled his mind with rude observations and unpleasant feelings, and it was difficult for him to believe that the greater portion of these remained unexpressed.

"Just for instance," Yolanda continued vibrantly, "I'm

thinking of examining my habits as a writer in some detail. There's some fascinating material there, including a wonderful opportunity to highlight Letty as an inspiration as well as an object of my creativity and nurturing instincts." She gazed off into the middle distance, composing like crazy.

There was the note she had made just that morning which might be brought to bear. It recorded the reddish-brown peanut-casings which often festooned her daughter's tutu. 'Festooned,' how apt the word was in Yolanda's motherly ear, how she admired its connotation of festival and airy grace. How well it reflected on herself and on what was hers. She was much-praised for her endearing ability to elevate the homely image, to make a literary language safe for the forces of delayed motherhood.

The expensive, hand-tooled-leather-bound journal into which Yolanda had entered the above observation was a gift from Ian; she had often complained about snagging her baggy woolen sweater-dresses on the spiral notebooks she liked to jot in. But Ian had not remembered that. Nor was she the only writer then selling between twelve and fifteen thousand copies to wear a baggy woolen sweater-dress. Ian returned from duties elsewhere with a pot of coffee. "You'll talk to Frieda Whoever about Rosie's coming here, and I'll talk to Rosie," Yolanda told Paul, pulling herself back to the present. "By the way, any idea at all where Lois is? We should try to get this done," she added more to herself than the others, "before they pick her up. It'll be easier all around."

Paul got up and stretched. "And if they don't pick her up, what then? Did you say anything to the FBI about my driving out to see her?" Paul took a turn around the table before sitting down again. Were things moving too quickly or was it just his imagination?

"Do you know that I forgot about that completely," Yolanda said, expressing neither chagrin nor surprise. "What did she say about the picture of Letty and me?"

"What picture, Mommy, which one?" The cousins joined them at the table then, and ate the pear tarte a la crème fraiche with great gusto.

"This food is real different," Rosie said, baffled, wondering, "but it's pretty good."

Yolanda had her opening.

CHAPTER EIGHTEEN

A Blow Is Struck

The Castle, heedless of Frieda's intention to deny it her patronage that evening, was unstinting in its welcome—the place was open and there was room at the bar. Her confreres were in position and her drink was poured without delay. She was already glad she had come.

"If you don't mind." Julius Spitzer broke into her thoughts, pulling a cigarette from the pack that lay on the bar between them. "The mistake your friend makes, if I may say so," he began without further preamble.

"You may," Frieda invited, simply happy that Paul should have been brought into their conversation thus easily and early.

Spitzer took three short puffs on the cigarette to get his thoughts in order. "He does not understand with historical knowledge. This comes from his days of..."

"...of Wine and Roses," Frieda mumbled automatically.

"...of high finance. There he had to be always up-to-the-minute. Now he is with this Africa business. In Africa I can see only chaos and disease and dancing. I must know him better." Spitzer, Eurocentric to the bone, might have done as well to know Africa better, but that was not to be.

"So must I," Frieda replied soberly. And being younger and more open and undoubtedly in love she added, "I should learn something about Africa too." She tapped a finger to her temple several times to indicate that she was willing to work with her head as well as her heart. "He has ideas, you know...."

On Frieda's left, the B.T. stirred at these last words. "Oh, sure," he grumbled, mocking. A certain feeling of superiority where these earthbound secularists were concerned had begun to trouble the B.T. of late. He turned away suddenly. Moses was the most humble of men, he reprimanded himself. Surely a Ba'al T'shuvah has enough to do just to focus his mind on a minute examination of his own thoughts and behavior.

For what seemed to Frieda like the thousandth time that hour the B.T. reached up to finger the little circle of crocheted wool that sat on top of his head.

"It's still there," she said bitterly, although she had promised herself she wouldn't give him the satisfaction of commenting at all. "Are you going to be fiddling like that for the rest of your life?"

"I'll get used to it," the B.T. said with great determination.

"Why should you?" Frieda parried. Often, as was the case here, someone who wants something is resentful of someone who has found something, no matter if what he has found is something completely different from what she wants.

Again the B.T.'s hand went to his head. "'A male person must not walk even as much as four cubits while being bareheaded,'" he recited, "that's the Law." How the B.T. loved the dignity of that reply. And yet he saw that this was only a partial answer. The yoke of the kingdom of heaven, he thought. Accept it.

"Can I expect to see you in a black hat and coat any time soon?"

A year ago this English graduate student would certainly have quoted carelessly in response, 'You call me misbeliever, cut-throat dog, And spit upon my Jewish gaberdine." But in the event the B.T., even thus challenged, said in a tone of pleasant moderation, "First things first. First, I have to stop coming here. I'm sorry, but I just can't be here anymore." He did not meet her eyes.

"Woe is you." Frieda held her elbows, rocking herself back and forth on the bar stool to convey timeless public grief. "Woe unto you. Is that sufficiently biblical? Finneran," she grabbed his arm as he passed, "say a prayer for the B.T. He's leaving us."

"O Saint Wilma," Finneran turned to face a cartoon portrait of Wilma Castle inked by some long-gone patron, "pray for this sinner," he raised his beer to his chest, "and also for Finneran. Kenneth, lad," he looked him over, "what's with the coaster top?"

The B.T. flushed. Never having heard the nomenclature before, he nonetheless understood instantly what it referred to. This is crunch time, he thought, He has separated us from the peoples. "Yarmulke," he said loudly, "Jews wear them."

"Hey, hey, hey," Finneran cautioned in honeyed tones, "I'm not gonna let you leave the Holy Father out of this one. When you're talkin' Holy Father, you are talking regulation beanie, you are talking Holy Roman Apostolic Beanie, you are talking," he eyed his wife, "little-Polish-lady-on-a-pig-farm-with-a-beanie-wearing-son beanie."

"Let's get a table, Finn, honey," Mrs. Finneran, blowing smoke through her nose, did not rise to the bait.

The B.T. held his peace. Pig farm, he echoed silently, how the words leapt out at him. He was feeling a bit strange tonight, overheated, vaguely exalted, suddenly an outsider. Was it this eventuality, he wondered, that had drawn many Jews into the hospitality professions.

"Julius," he called out, "who owned the restaurant, the one Himmelfarb stopped at...on his way to...."

Spitzer leaned forward across Frieda. "On his way to Koniggratz. Yes." The B.T. was one of his most devoted listeners, perhaps even, eventually, Spitzer had fantasized, a professorial repository for these stories he had rescued from the grave. "Himmelfarb's father," he explained to Finneran, "was a wealthy man and a religious one. He arranged to buy his son out of the army; but young Himmelfarb preferred to fight for his Kaiser. Fortunately or unfortunately," and here Spitzer smiled at the simple-minded ambiguity of fate, "he had run up a very large bill with his tailor."

"His tailor," Finneran mouthed the words at Frieda in mincing disbelief.

"Himmelfarb's father, instead of advancing Himmelfarb the money, paid the tailor a premium to have his son jailed as a debtor. In later life Himmelfarb always made a point of owing his tailor money," Spitzer paused dramatically, "but of his father he seldom spoke."

Finneran, released, fled without a word to the table his

wife had claimed for them. When it came to money, he told her, when it came to fathers, he told her, this Himmelfarb was no patch on Beak Finneran. As the younger Mrs. Finneran knew only too well, this proud assertion was merely prologue to a long, boozy, evening of Beak-bashing.

"Was it a kosher restaurant, do you happen to know?" the B.T. asked, at least in part to cover Finneran's ill-mannered retreat.

"Under no circumstances," Spitzer assured him with a degree of spite. "No. The owner took great pride in that." Spitzer had once had high hopes for this young man. Now, he saw, he would have to look elsewhere for an archivist; he needed another kind of Jew. Himmelfarb, Feuerbaum, Siggy Steiner, Kurt Glaser, these men did not know from kosher.

"Who told you that you can't come here anymore," Frieda wanted to know from the B.T. "Have you been brain washed? I warned you those people have certain ways. Who told you not to come?"

Now the B.T. felt just the least bit uncomfortable. "I'll tell you later," he muttered, anxious to keep the others from hearing. He was barely used to the idea himself.

"You can tell me, I'm Jewish," Frieda joked. "Or would you say I'm a Jewess?" She ordered another drink. "Why can't you come anymore?" she demanded again, turning to face him squarely. "Oh-oh," she mocked, "I just had an awful thought; what if I can't come here anymore either." She readjusted her hat, giving it what she took to be a Holmesian set. "Tell me," she ordered, tugging at his sleeve.

"He separated us from the peoples," the B.T. said softly, leaning toward her, "that's why."

"He separated us from the peoples," Frieda echoed. "That doesn't sound very American. Look around," she did not take her eyes from his face, "in America we're against that."

"'You shall be holy,' it says. Which do you think He cares more about, being American or being holy? I'm serious."

Frieda was beginning to lose interest. "Finneran," she nudged him as he squeezed up to the bar, "you can quit praying now. We've lost the patient."

"Ah ha. Mr. Leopold Bloom. Oh yeah, Mr. Leopold Bloom," the Irishman quite unexpectedly clapped the B.T. on the back, "'he ate with relish the inner organs of beasts and fowls.'"

The yarmulke flew from the B.T.'s head at this friendly blow, but he palmed it quickly, damp now from the bar, and pressed it again to his curls. "Well," he said, looking meaningfully at Frieda, as if to say, you see, can you really expect me to live among them!

"Relish. 'Hold the pickles, hold the relish,' Kevin-for-crying-out-loud, interpolating the hamburger jingle, unwittingly gave Joyce a new twist, "'special orders don't upset us....'"

"It's 'hold the pickles, hold the lettuce,'" little Mrs. Finneran corrected at once. She had come up to the bar to see what was keeping her husband, but it was Kevin-for-crying-out-loud who returned to the table with her.

"Listen," Frieda was unaccountably enthusiastic, "I once made kidneys." What was it Paul had said in connection with those kidneys? Every word which had ever passed between them was retrievable, and, she believed, capable of sustaining complete and repeated analysis.

"Sweetbreads," Spitzer joined in then, "you know who liked them? Moritz Sternberg. A boiled potato with it. His mouth was watering."

"Who cares?" Finneran asked irritably. "Who the hell are these people Julius is always talking about?"

"The dead," Spitzer said. "If you don't mind." He held Frieda's empty cigarette package up to draw the bartender's attention.

"'Lily, the caretaker's daughter, was literally run off her feet,'" Finneran quoted casually, aptly, as the bartender approached.

"'The Dead,'" the bartender said in response, bringing Frieda her cigarettes.

Meanwhile Spitzer had become quite agitated. "What craziness. Thank God I had no daughter. If so, I would not have stayed. With a daughter I would have left straight-away. But I had my responsibility. A caretaker, do you think that was something for me. Living in a graveyard. But alright. I did it. And for what?! For this Ihrlender to say 'who cares.'" He fumbled with the cellophane wrap on the new package of cigarettes.

Finneran was listening closely. "I care about mine; you care about yours."

"When the stones spoke," Julius continued heatedly, "it was of life and not of death. My old uncle often said it—we are a peculiar People; but I can tell you one thing, that our life did not begin with the...Holocaust." He spoke the word as if it had been foisted on him by an unsavory Berlitz instructor. "There were boiled potatoes before, generations and generations eating boiled potatoes. Let the others talk about horrors and make docu-dramatics. What I am telling about comes from before. Before."

Finneran put a warning hand on his shoulder. "Don't tell me about boiled potatoes, pal. We had our share of potatoes, boiled and every other which way. You ought to hear Beak Finneran on that subject. Besides, there was also a time when we did not have our share of potatoes--and then we starved. I mean famine, pal." Finneran winked at him as if to say, I got you coming and going, pal; and departed directly for the table where it appeared, even from the distance of the bar, that Kevin-for-crying-out-loud and Mrs. Finneran were enjoying each other's company.

"So why don't you leave already?!" Frieda said to the B.T., exhaling a great cloud of smoke. Apparently there was truculence in the air.

The B.T., with no sense that he was a blind man approaching a cliff, leaned behind her to tap Spitzer on the shoulder. "The Lord warned them, he began information-ally, "He warned them, He would turn his face away. It was a punishment according to Shlomo." So innocent was he, so ripe for the picking, so bereft of any sense of what he was talking about was he, that he did not even pause to take breath. "Frieda," he tapped her in turn, "I wish you would come with me sometime for Shabbos at Shlomo's."

Julius Spitzer meanwhile had gotten down from his bar stool. With one hand on the back wall to push off, he low-ered his head and ran full-tilt at the B.T. who was just shift-ing his body to settle in for a chat with Frieda. With a burst of energy born of who knows what bit of history, Spitzer thrust his bullet of a head forward into the B.T.'s chest, butting him right off his bar stool into the press of bodies surging along the bar. "Punishment?" Spitzer choked on the word. Then, with a kind of wail, he turned and walked back past the kitchen and out the backdoor.

Whether it was, as Shlomo later suggested, simple anti-Semitism or not, the fact remained that as the B.T. toppled backward, the crowd instinctively stepped back as well, and he fell unhindered to the floor. The B.T. did not know what hit him. He got to his feet slowly; Frieda slid down from her stool to rescue his yarmulke from the floor as the customers began to press in again around them.

"I don't understand," the B.T. said forthrightly. "I better catch up with Julius. Ahavas Yisroel. It's very important to love your fellow Jew." In spite of this proclamation of urgency, the B.T. walked out slowly, alternately rubbing his left elbow and his left buttock, though more in puzzled meditation than in pain.

Frieda was equally baffled. However, as this feeling was to her as the breath of life itself, she merely carried her drink and her cigarettes to the table where Finneran held sway, and determined to get on with the evening. The incident at the bar, she knew, would go unmentioned, if it had indeed been noticed at all amid the general melee; this was the code of the place.

"Where's Peter?" Finneran asked as she sat down.

"Who?" was Frieda's disingenuous reply, for she knew at once about whom he was inquiring. How thrilling to be asked that question, to be thought of thus, to be expected to know.

"Your friend in the downtown coat."

This was not quite the description Frieda had been angling for. "You mean Paul?"

"You rob one, you pay the other. Better for him to be Paul, then."

"Why do you ask?" Frieda inquired formally, hoping against hope to get him back to the point.

"Ah, who cares!" Finneran did not appreciate the interruption. Had Frieda been just slightly less relentless in pursuit of her own amatory agenda, she might have noticed that little Mrs. Finneran, nursing a diet coke, was deep in conversation with Kevin-for-crying-out-loud. Could this account for her husband's lack of good humor?

"Not me certainly," Frieda answered, her heart aching. "He's having dinner at his sister's," she could not resist adding as a simple sop to her vanity.

"Yeah, I wanted to ask him about that Ian Silbermann. I've got a couple of ideas for his show." Finneran drained his glass.

Ordinarily Frieda would have shown considerable and genuine interest in these ideas of Finneran's, and this in spite of having heard them more than once before. It was one of the delights of the place that such a conversation should not only be possible but should be positively pleasureful. Not tonight, however; for Frieda had earlier in the evening seen fit to set an arbitrary standard of proof for the unwitting Silverman, and now she was increasingly anxious as the hour grew late, that he would not meet it. It was, she thought, a simple enough test—he must show he cared by arriving at the Castle sometime before the hour of closing. Nothing else would do. She took money from her pocket and gave it to Finneran who was headed for the bar.

Alone with her thoughts, she counted up the ways in which Paul Silverman might have been seen as displaying some degree of caring—his daily lunches at Nini's, for example, or his frequent appearances at the Castle, the flowers he had brought her, the dishes he had washed, what he had hinted about her not being alone. She picked them over one by one. Alas, she noted sadly, they did not amount to much. No, he simply must show up at the Castle before closing, otherwise she would understand that he was as indifferent to her as she had all along believed him to be.

Kevin-For-Crying-Out-Loud, Frieda was suddenly aware, had begun to speak in a significantly raised voice. It was a sign she had learned to recognize. "Philately," he proclaimed for Mrs. Finneran's edification, "philately is a very sexy word."

"As I suspected," Finneran muttered, returning from the bar with the drinks.

Frieda and Finneran drank on then in a silence each fashioned from his own well-tailored thoughts of betrayal. But suddenly, mercifully, Frieda remembered that she had herself told Paul Silverman that he should not expect to find her at the Castle that evening. Her brow furrowed. How differently did her condition at once appear. Her heart grew light. Now his not arriving could be seen in a wholly positive light, as a confirmation in itself. Why should he come, believing as he did that she would not be there?! That was it, surely that was it; there could be no other explanation.

From the depths to the heights, she thought smugly, weren't these very gyrations and mood swings just what one read about when people talked of being in love.

Meanwhile, little Mrs. Finneran was gaining in vigor. She had in her possession, as it turned out, a stamp collection. Well, not precisely a stamp collection, but rather a shoebox full of miscellaneous stamps her grandfather had collected for her. "A lot of them are Polish stamps," she murmured delicately.

"You ought to have someone go through the box and have a look," Kevin-For-Crying-Out-Loud said with an authority his students rarely saw him display. "You don't know what you might have."

"I know what she might have," Finneran broke in heavily. "She might have a lot of damn Polish stamps, that's what she might have. Who the hell cares."

"Look, her grandfather saved those stamps for her," Kevin rebuffed him sternly. Mrs. Finneran blushed at these words. How long it had been since someone had stepped up on her account. The stakes, she felt, had just been raised.

"'It's with O'Leary in the grave,'" Finneran muttered, studying the palms of his hands.

And thus did the time pass more pleasantly for some patrons than for others, until suddenly, silently, Paul Silverman stood at Frieda's elbow. She sensed him there, but so comfortable had she become with the construction she had put on his absence, that the mere sight of him now cast her instantly into the depths of despair. So, he had come after all; so, his presence could henceforth not be linked in any positive way to her own; so, just as she had feared, all was lost.

CHAPTER NINETEEN

A Mother's Letter

Ernie Blyda lit a joint. He had known what was coming from the first. True, Rip Parks had been in touch once or twice over the years—the theory being that the Bureau could locate a private citizen if it had a mind to—but they were hardly on visiting terms. Now Rip Parks was visiting.

"Long time no," Ernie remarked, rolling in from the kitchen. A large square opening cut into the wall between the two rooms had been left unfinished. It was unclear whether this outsize doorway was a matter of handicap-access or simply a naive stroke of interior decoration aimed at bringing some light into the low-ceilinged, dark-paneled living room. In the bright kitchen, Ernie's wife was weighing and wrapping fudge by the piece. Several people sat at a round table on which three large I Ching coins had been cast.

Ernie handed his guest a can of beer. He thought it likely that he was the only one who bore the G-man no ill will. Ernie's loyalty had been to the music after all. As far as he was concerned, politics was a by-product.

"You once mentioned you saw Lois around," Special Agent Parks said matter-of-factly, popping open the beer.

"Well, not around." Ernie, prepared, was all innocence. He wheeled himself to the stereo. The cheap brown carpeting appeared pressed nearly napless by Ernie's active chair. Along three walls raw wood cases held his enormous collection of records. "Maybe I saw her once. I've been travelling a lot and all." He set a record on the turntable.

"This isn't official," Parks anticipated him with considerable brusqueness.

Ernie craned his neck. His music-born appreciation for the nuances led him to wonder whether Parks was telling the truth. He relit the joint and closed his eyes to get a better fix on where their conversation was headed. Much would depend on that. The music began.

Parks held out his hand for the joint. "I must be having one of those middle-aged crazy things," he said. "I have this idea I want to see her again. It's really been bugging me. That's all."

Ernie opened his eyes. "I can dig it, man," he said softly, sleepily, seduced by Park's atavistic cliché. His ear for subtleties of tone and phrasing notwithstanding, he decided to play it cool for the moment; he did not pick up the conversation. The two of them sat, each with his own thoughts, and listened to the sitar music. It was more or less through music that Parks had first approached Ernie, claiming to be from Chicago, claiming to have known Butterfield. Ernie, who was short and doughy and already heavily into weed, had nonetheless had a positive response to such a fresh-faced, friendly Nordic type, and he had quickly bound himself to Parks by all manner of trivial service.

"This is good stuff," Parks said finally, looking for an in, passing the joint.

Ernie pursed his lips and nodded to the music. "No way was I ever caught in the Western web, man. Right now I'm pretty eclectic and all."

Parks, though relieved to have gotten him talking, had no thought to follow this conversational tack. "There's something else too. I want to see Lois's daughter. She's my kid." This fact, which he now dropped so casually, had struck him with the force of a stroke when he had first come across the information that Lois had a daughter of a certain age.

"Yeah," Ernie nodded, jiggling his chair back and forth. "No shit!"

"I've got this daughter out there somewhere and I want to see her. It's like a goddam talk show, for chrissake."

"'Kin-A, Jim." Ernie felt himself weakening. This was elemental stuff, and he had always been partial to the elemental. Instinctively, he tried to buy some time. "You want a snack? Some smoked fish? Apple butter? Goat cheese?"

"No, Man. How's the business going by the way?" I've got time, Rip Parks thought, I'm in no hurry now.

Suddenly, and for no reason he could name, Ernie seemed to capitulate. "Did you read about what happened up in Michigan, LWMA and all?"

"Yeah, I read about it. Why?"

Ernie looked him clear in the eye for several instants before continuing. "Who do you think went in there and all? Do they have any idea who went in?"

Parks swallowed down the last burning fragment of joint with a sip of beer. "I don't know what they think or what they know. But I'll tell you what I think. I think someways Lois was involved. That's the thing. I want to find her, see her first. See my daughter. Before they do. That's all."

"Hey Man," Ernie rolled his chair to the window and back, "I'm down with that." The Blues had long ago taught him to respect the proudly primal, the not always sanctified nature of such a connection. "Lois called a couple of days ago. She said she was around. She said she would call back."

• • •

Not too many miles away, across the New York state line in a county so rural as to have been only recently certified by the New York Times as suitable for country living, Lois had found final refuge in a dilapidated farmhouse ripe for rehab. She had never been there before, but the directions Paul had drawn were still legible, and the key he had given her still fit. It was a white clapboard house up on a little knoll a quarter mile beyond the school bus turn-around. This much may be said for the state of Lois's mind—or perhaps only for her soldierly stolidity—the obvious symbolism—here was the end of the line—did not oppress her. At the bottom of the ragged meadow behind the house was a rapidly thawing pond.

Lois had arrived and set to work with a housewifely will she half-attributed to her own legendary Latvian grandmother, a woman, according to Harry Silverman, of pronounced managerial skills. Even now, Lois shrank from this convention of her father's. Harry Silverman had but to say the word "managerial," for his daughter to feel instantly deprived of her rightful babushka-crowned, low-to-the-ground, salt-of-the-earth, immigrant grandma. Indeed, as far as Lois was concerned, Harry Silverman had but to speak and the world became a bourgeois hell. She did not like to acknowledge—nor did she often remember—that there had been a time when she had felt herself unthinkingly happy there.

Lois had toured the premises at once, opened the window in the bedroom she chose—who knew with what imperatives—for herself, checked for supplies, and plugged in the refrigerator. That first evening she slept well between musty sheets in the room at the top of the narrow stairs, exhausted by her travels and strangely pleased by her circumstances. She had not known what to expect. The fact that her hideaway was a farm house rather than a cabin, a cottage, or a split-level had raised her spirits considerably. I could have ended up in one of those, she thought, remembering perhaps the fiery end of a certain West Coast liberation army.

She had actually knelt down in the kitchen that first morning to finger the worn linoleum in front of the oven, coming one more time to worship at the shrine of authenticity. What pies and biscuits she imagined had come out of that oven. How apparent had the identity of flag and food been in the America of her childhood—one had only to visualize Mrs. Crocker, Betty herself, beaming, bearing biscuits, to understand fully all that being brave and free implied. Those were the days. Sure, Lois thought bitterly, and just where the hell was Aunt Jemima supposed to be all that time?!

It rained all day and this pleased Lois too. She sat at the kitchen window with a cup of hot tea balanced on the blistered sill and looked at old magazines. It was dark and gloomy outside and the wind blew the rain past the window, but the kitchen was filled with an intense yellow light, the rich, golden light of hearth and home. In the late morning she fell asleep at the window, her head upon her chest, and dreamed a short dream—Simon and Willis, black faces pressed against the glass. Then in the afternoon she drove through the rain back across the state line and bought a ticket for a twi-light show in the six-cinema complex of the Mega-Mecca Mall. After the movie she shopped at the supermarket and drove around a bit before she could find two working payphones. How long had it been since one day had seemed so fine? Nevertheless, she did not sleep at all well that night.

In the morning she walked down through the muddy meadow toward the pond. The sun was out, the air was very fresh and it smacked definitively of Spring. She examined a lingering patch of snow where it lay heaped against the shaded side of a desiccated tree stump. After all that rain, still there; it struck at her heart. I can't remember a day like this, she thought. When had she seen such intensity of sun and sky, felt such a determined yet bracing wind? Someday every man would have such weather, every woman be heartened by such a wind, every child fly his own kite, dream her own dream.

Now she could think of Rosie again, had in fact to think of Rosie. And yet, she did not feel she was ready to sit down and write the letter. I've got time, she thought, I'm in no rush now. Indeed, a kind of calm had descended on her upon arriving at the farmhouse, edged, when she came to consider it, with a hint of anticipation, irrational expectation it was really.

"Dear Rosie, (she began to compose as she wandered) Maybe this is the only letter I've ever written to you because we've always been together...."

Turning back for a view of her solitary homestead, she wished suddenly for a camera. She would have liked to take some photographs for Rosie—that last patch of snow, the white blistered paint, the single high cloud over the pitched roof. This uncharacteristic urge to document was no more than an intense desire to share with her daughter such a rare moment of solid tranquility, for Lois did have an obscure inkling that there had been far too few of those in their life together. But she had no camera with her, and no time anymore to have pictures developed, and, worst of all, no idea where Rosie was.

"Do you remember the picture of me with a blond man standing in front of a van? (she proposed to continue) I want you to know that we loved each other. But in the end a pig is a pig. If the pigs are good for anything, I hope he will find you and bring you this letter."

In spite of the deep-down surge of joy and well-being she had felt in the face of this early Spring day, Lois had never been much of one for the out-of-doors. Wandering hither and thither aimlessly she had nonetheless managed to make her way back to the house without wasting too many steps. So engrossed had she been in her letter that she identified the sound of a car stopping on the gravel drive only as she approached the corner of the house.

Could it be that he was already coming for her? A confusion of possibilities overwhelmed her for she had given scant thought to the moment itself. She stopped in her tracks. She held her breath. A car door opened and was slammed shut, surprising her. He doesn't slam car doors, she thought at once, the years melting at the sound; how struck she had been by his knowledge of and respect for his van—Harry Silverman knew nothing about cars, except, that is, that he had to have a new one every year. Then a second door was opened and shut. Tears sprang to Lois's eyes, for although she had not thought a great deal about their meeting, she had thought enough about it to know that he should be alone when he came for her.

She forced herself to take a quick look around the corner of the house. What she saw relieved her, disappointed her, frightened her. A woman, tall and willowy, dressed fashionably for the city, posed as if for an advertisement next to an expensive car. She wore large-lensed tinted glasses against the bright Spring sunshine, and these were focused on her companion, a short, muscular man dressed in perfectly draped black slacks and a short black leather jacket who had taken up a position at her side. He had a camera with him.

"It has the charm of the absolutely ordinary, my chick," said the man, squinting in the sun. He raised his hand to his brow to shade his eyes. "Ordinary is back. I've said it before and I'll say it again. I see wicker and wonderful picnics. Check out the weeping willow. You could have warned me!" He directed her attention to a spot directly behind Lois who flattened herself against the side of the house.

"I'm so glad you like it, Raymond," the woman answered frankly, perhaps even leaning on her relief a little. "I think it has real potential. Needless to say, my ex-husband has no sense at all for this kind of thing, so I imagine we'll find things rather distressed."

"Lucky Chickee," said the man shaking his head sympathetically. "Let's take a look." He started for the house.

"Hi," Lois called, stepping forward.

"Heh-lo," the woman answered, stopping where she was to glance first over one shoulder and then the other. "May I help you?"

"A friend of mine is letting me stay here. It's his house."

The man who had continued to walk toward the house, paused at these words and looked back, surprised. "There must be some mistake," he said.

"And your name is?" The woman approached Lois.

"Sarah Loomis."

"And your friend's name is Paul Silverman?" At Lois's nod she waved the man named Raymond on about his business. "Actually the house is mine, Paul's my ex-husband; I was letting him use it as long as he needed it, and I've decided he doesn't need it anymore." She chuckled appreciatively at this charming admission of her absolute power.

"Well, I won't be here much longer," Lois said stonily, eyeing her erstwhile sister-in-law with interest. Reasons of state, as it were, had prevented Lois from attending the wedding. She had no intention of kowtowing to this rich bitch, that much was clear. After all, what did she have to lose? And then she remembered what she had to lose. "Would you mind if I stayed another couple of days?" she asked in an altered tone. "I'm almost finished."

She was a photographer Lois explained, with an interest in rural life. It had never ceased to amaze her how easily even her most spur-of-the-moment, off-the-rack fabrications were swallowed. Why, she wondered, did not the sophisticated ex-Mrs. Silverman ask to see her work, or at least inquire after the kind of camera she used. Self-involved, bourgeois bitch was an explanation with which Lois found herself comfortable. They walked companionably together into the house. The woman complimented Lois on a fascinating career choice, and agreed to allow her to remain until the following week. Then she would be returning with her builder and her architect and her interior decorator, who even now stood at the foot of the stairs fondling a sturdy newel post. "I see blues in the bathroom," Raymond Della Casa told his employer.

Long after they had gone Lois could not get this sentence out of her mind. "I see blues in the bathroom, I see blues in the bathroom," the words were mimicked over and over inside her head. Suddenly the calm she had been feeling all day evaporated and was replaced by a more familiar state of mind. Not since the day she had sprayed her outrage across the entrance to the Chicago Board of Trade had she again been seized by this specific desire. But now, this house, her house, so organically authentic, so plainly American in its simplicity and guileless serviceability, was under attack by the forces of white-skinned consumerism and bourgeois adventurism.

She knew what had to be done, and, though it was late in the afternoon, she got into the car and drove into Pittsfield. "'The words of the prophets are written on the subways walls, tenement halls,'" she sang as she drove. Once in the hardware store, however, she had a change of heart. Why bother with the paint at all, she asked herself, why not just burn the place down. That was the stronger statement. But in the end she went back to the paint. You want blue, she railed silently at that effete minion of the ruling classes, you see blue, you got blue. After leaving the store with her purchase, she went to one of the telephone booths she had located and called Ernie Blyda. From him she learned to her intense satisfaction that Special Agent Randall "Rip" Parks had already been around to visit and would return. "Tell him I'll call," she said quietly. "I'll call when I'm ready." This is perfect, Lois thought. Indeed, to simply contemplate that eventuality was nearly enough to make her forget her package on the floor of the telephone booth, thereby raising at least the possibility that the sanctity of private property might yet be upheld.

CHAPTER TWENTY

Footnote to History

A few cartons still remained on Paul Silverman's living room floor, and these he was unpacking slowing, reluctantly, as if he were unwilling to give up such a palpable reminder--not of his old life--but of his commitment to the new. For, oddly, the cartons themselves and not—as one might expect—the emptying of them had come to stand for the great change he had experienced. There would have been a time when, with the strength of ten men and the will of twenty, he would have unpacked them during one feverish twenty-four-hour day right after the move. And not just unpack them either, but put things where they belonged, and understand why they belonged there and nowhere else, and explain why at some length to colleagues who in all likelihood would never be invited to see them in place. He bent to a carton now and pulled out a great ball of packing paper and threw it past a visitor in the direction of his cat.

The B.T. flinched. He needed rest sorely. His lids were heavy and his shoulders ached. How he wondered did the men of an earlier era stay up through the night to study. Shlomo had told him of the sure-fire, low-tech solution of one saintly rabbi. While he learned, he kept a finger extended toward his candle so that should he happen to nod off, the dripping wax would quickly burn him awake again. The B.T. sighed. He put one foot up on a carton marked 'miscellaneous,' and opened the distinctly secular volume he had brought with him, balancing it across his thigh. He had come to report the results of his research into the identity of a certain "Ernie," although, sad to say, his enthusiasm for the project had undergone a substantial diminution.

"Here it is," he said, "In a footnote. 'Conversation with Ernie Blyda.' This author interviewed an Ernie Blyda on September 10, 1980. Judging from the context, he must have known your sister in the 'Sixties."

Paul looked up from the polished copper bowl he was unpacking to praise the B.T. for his scholarship. "It could be him," he allowed. Had he asked for the copper bowl or had it been his wife's idea that he take it? And to what end? Egg whites, he remembered; a bowl specifically for the whipping of egg whites—indispensable, terribly expensive, never used, a symbol in other words, of her working kitchen. He drummed on the shiny bowl with his fingernails to encourage his companion's attention. "Did you ask Rosie? She might at least corroborate his name for us."

It was a step the B.T. did not want to take. A long conversation with Shlomo the evening before had planted a seed of doubt in his mind. Perhaps Rosie was not after all the right wife for him; because it was in this light, he had been amazed to learn from Shlomo, that he must now begin to look at a woman. Indeed, had not Shlomo hinted that he had just the woman in mind. From *The Sayings of the Fathers*, Shlomo had instructed him that "At five years old one is ready for the scripture, at ten years for the Mishnah, at thirteen for the commandments, at fifteen for Talmud, at eighteen for marriage...." The B.T. had been plunged at once into the abyss. Marriage was one thing, but apparently it was only one of many areas in which he lagged, in which he had quite desperately to make up for lost time. There's no hope for me, the B.T. thought, I'll never make it. But Shlomo had been anything but discouraged, indeed took the opportunity to explain to him that the more lacking a man found himself, the greater the potential for the heights to which he might rise. So, the B.T. sat down to his studies immediately upon hanging up the phone, and did not leave them until the early hours of the morning.

Paul was put off by the B.T.'s lack of animation, by his apparent distraction. With scant ceremony he took the book from him. "Let me see it," he demanded. "Is there something else?"

There was something else, the B.T. had to admit. Marriage—Rosie had already laughed the very idea out of mind, and, under the circumstances, there was no way he could afford to wait for her. He was already five years behind schedule. Clearly, then, it was not meant to be. He hadn't even mentioned to Shlomo how she had danced before him with her midriff bare, poking pretzels into his beard. The modest Rebecca, he recalled, covered herself with a veil before meeting her husband Isaac. Shlomo would have lectured him on modesty in women, any deviation from which he took to be nothing less than the overturning of God's order. "I wouldn't go that far," the B.T. muttered aloud with a stiff smile, and at that he was only telling half the truth.

Paul did not hear him. He had found something in that brief footnote of which his companion could not possibly have known the significance. "Conversation with Ernie Blyda, September 10, 1980, Pittsfield, Massachusetts." Pittsfield was a town he had come to know well. Of a sudden he knew that Pittsfield was a town that Lois, too, either already knew well or would come to know well in the near future. No doubt about it, it was his sudden intuition, Lois had made her way to the farmhouse, was laying low there, or at any rate soon would be. Hard upon that certain realization the plan came to him all at once—he would drive to see her, he and Frieda, they would take Rosie to her mother. The idea made such a powerful impression on him, buoyed him up so, that he barely stopped to remark on how surely Frieda was part of his planning, how easily he had linked their names. "I think I know where Lois is," he said. "I'm going upstairs."

The B.T. did not respond, nor did he follow at once. He was in a quandary. Shlomo had advised him to simply withdraw from what Shlomo referred to, quaintly, contemptuously, as "your scene." It's very lack of substance, of reality, was apparently manifest in the theatrical borrowing. It could hold nothing for the B.T. now that he knew that he was to pursue the things of this world only with a higher goal in mind. When you eat, you eat, Shlomo told him, but when you eat in order to get strength to study Torah, then you eat for the sake of heaven. It was an exciting prospect. The B.T. trailed up the stairs behind Paul, his heart, for one reason or another, beating rather faster than normal.

Paul, meanwhile, had lost all interest in the B.T.'s state of mind. What, he wondered, did he hope to accomplish by driving all that way to the farmhouse to see Lois? He would reunite mother and daughter, he would attempt to convince Lois to give herself up, he would see if he could be of some comfort to her; but there was something else too. What about the lure of the open road, the culture of a motel, the healing power of a rural scene? What about Frieda? She was an integral part of the plan, he saw; of course he could make the trip without her, but it was in no way what he had in mind.

"How do you know where she is?" the B.T. asked finally, catching up just as Frieda opened the door.

She was wearing a large white apron and her face was flushed, whether from the exertions of her cookery or the identity of her caller one did not know. She would have preferred on the whole never to answer her door, but recently anticipation had begun to supersede dread. In fact, she was in excellent spirits, for though she had been given the apron (gift of the Francophile suitor) several years ago, she had thought to put it on today for the very first time. As the crisp white cotton had become increasingly spotted, so had her spirits risen.

"I have a proposal," Paul said to her with measured intensity.

"I'll probably just say yes," she answered truthfully, but shaded to imply as well, more the fool I; the blood seemed to have drained from her head all at once. "Now what happens?" She mocked her own urgency.

"We get in the car and drive to a farmhouse in upstate New York."

"I love a farmhouse. Is it a white farmhouse?" She followed him into the room already in a high state of excitement. The proposed trip came very near, she had to admit, to her idea of life. If she had not often specifically imagined men and women getting into cars together and taking long drives to white farmhouses, she had dreamed things that came awfully close in spirit.

"Hey," said Rosie, coming out of the kitchen with a can of soda to her lips. "Hey," this to the B.T., "how's it going?" She scooped Frieda's cat up with her free hand.

"Fine," he told her, jerking hard at his beard to give him the courage to acknowledge publicly for the first time the One who was responsible for how things were going, "baruch haShem."

Rosie rolled her eyes. "Ohhhhh-kay!" she said sardonically, "have you died and gone to heaven yet?"

The B.T. maintained a dignified silence. How juvenile she is, he thought, how uninformed, how vulgar.

"I think I know where Lois is," Paul said.

"My mom?" Rosie let the cat go, turning first to the right and then to the left as if she wished to go to her mother's side at once. "Where is she?"

"I'll take you there. Frieda's coming too."

Frieda had not bargained for that "too," but even it could not succeed in bringing her down. There was only one thing more she wanted to know. As if their minds were one, she noted joyously, Paul turned to her now to discuss an hour for their departure.

"I'm ready," Frieda answered him.

"Wanna come, B.T.?" Rosie asked. "We could have fun."

"Shabbos," the B.T. reminded her abruptly, backing toward the door. "Anyway...." his voice trailed off, leaving unspoken the decision of a lifetime.

"Oh come on, you're not doing anything anyway."

Here she touched the B.T. nearly. In his naiveté and ignorance, he had taken Issachar as his model. "Rejoice Zebulun in your going out and Issachar in your tents." This meant, he had read, that Issachar sat in his tent and studied, while his brother Zebulun went out to do business. Now it turned out, however, as Shlomo had read to him straight from The Rebbe himself, that there was a way in which Zebulun's service was actually superior to Issachar's; for it is the profit from his business that makes possible Issachar's study. Clearly, the B.T. had some rethinking to do. Besides, he reminded himself, soon he would have a wife and family to support.

"I'm going up to Shlomo's for Shabbos."

"Shlomo's for Shabbos," Rosie mocked, "O.K. don't come." Had it been her way, Rosie might have been bewildered by her erstwhile suitor's sudden cooling, and she was, she had to admit, just the least bit disappointed that the B.T. wouldn't be coming along. She found his seriousness comforting—after all she had grown up among serious people—appreciated his empathy and persistence; but, still, most of all she enjoyed the knowledge that she was only toying with him until something better came along.

"I'd still like you to come there with me some time," the B.T. offered feebly, a sop, he thought, so unaware was he of the current balance of power.

Rosie did not deign to reply. She went to the closet and took out her knapsack. "I probably won't be coming back," she said to herself as much as to the others.

"I don't know," Paul replied quickly with a sharp glance at Frieda, who, though thrilled by the look had no idea at all of its import, "after all, now you have your family here...."

"I think I'll stay with my mom for a while," Rosie said with a frown, as if she dismissed out of hand the idea that she had any family outside her mother.

"But what about your father?" The B.T. stood at the door now. If he were going to arrive at Shlomo's before the start of the Sabbath at sunset, he would have to leave soon.

"Maybe he's dead. Did you ever think of that? Lately I've had the feeling maybe he's dead." Rosie spoke harshly because contrary to what she had said, the thought had in fact struck her only the moment before and she was devastated. The one assumption she had always made was that he was alive.

"Maybe the time has come for Lois to tell you about him," Paul suggested with his well-honed talent for negotiation, integration and compromise. If, as he hoped, Lois would be willing to give herself up, this would indeed be the time for her to tell Rosie all. "Give herself up"; the words startled him. Would he be asking her to give herself up? That, he was quite sure, she would not do. Nevertheless, his flattering conjecture notwithstanding, it might be thought that the very essence of Lois's self was its compulsion to give itself up.

Rosie turned fearful eyes on him at the words "the time has come." Plainly, while she had said nothing, the idea had crossed her own mind as well. "Maybe," was all she would allow now, and begrudged even that, although knowledge of him had been all her life her dearest wish.

The B.T. glanced at his watch and cleared his throat. He took one last deliberate look at Rosie as she ran a hand through her brown curls. Today she wore black calf-length cycling tights and a t-shirt reading "Shop Till You Drop." Her feet were bare. Modesty was the farthest thing from her mind, the B.T. recognized with just a vestige of sorrow. He sighed, wished the three of them a good trip, and departed without further ado. He would have to hurry. He thought of how God had shortened the way for Jacob, so that he arrived in Haran the same day he left Beer Sheva. What sort of miracles did God perform in this day and age, the B.T. wondered, driving north along Lake Michigan, and, strangely, the road to Shlomo's apartment that afternoon did seem a bit shorter than usual.

Rosie wiped at her brow as the door closed behind the B.T., pantomiming her narrow escape. "Gonzo," she said, seeking to describe the departure of her one-time suitor as it related to the mental as well as the physical dimension. Then she took and lit a cigarette from Frieda's packet to seal the rift.

What should I do now, Frieda asked herself somewhat wildly. She had been wandering in a condition of high anticipation from living room to bedroom and back again while the others talked, but had been able to form no clear idea of what she should do for the next several hours. Her closet door was open but she dared not look in. What did people pack for such a trip? Something suitable—the words echoed in her head. Knowing that one took something suitable, without knowing exactly what something suitable might be, produced a refined state of anxiety which reduced and purified itself quickly into immobility.

"Is something baking?" Paul broke into her thoughts. Frieda leapt toward the kitchen. Life often seemed thus to Frieda, one crisis barely recognized and defined before another began to vie for her attention. She reached the brownies with time to spare, however, and upon removing them from the oven her small kitchen immediately took on, she felt, an additional very welcome reality. Paul and Rosie followed and the three of them watched the brownies cool making desultory conversation. This companionable spirit seemed to bode well for the long drive ahead.

CHAPTER TWENTY-ONE

Disappointments

Yolanda had a room of her own. With a simplicity that did her heart good, she called it her writing room. This room looked out on a brick wall, a circumstance of which she had made much in a paragraph on "architectural influences" for the Book Review's "Summer Reading" number. In fact, she harbored a strong desire to share her thoughts on the room itself, its interior decoration; readers of a women's magazine already knew that the coral-color paint generally made her feel as if she were "deep inside a giant shell," where "my people can whisper to me." Moreover, there was not a stick of furniture without its story, and no story which did not, in the end, have a great deal to say about Yolanda Silverman-Silbermann—the human being. Indeed, there, no pencil fell which did not speak her praise.

Yolanda was in her writing room now, but she was not writing. This was unusual and she made a note. Certainly, it would not be long before she would find an occasion to write about not writing. In Yolanda's eyes there was nothing that Yolanda did that was not worth making much of. How her weaknesses especially endeared her to her literary self—how nearly naively they cohered toward the aim of revealing that she was like any other woman, only, finally, better. This home-made cloak of self-regard that named her writer, together with the awe-struck evocation of material life which was her stock in trade, had 'til now worked well for her. Today, however, it appeared that this artful dedication to the self—or, as Yolanda chose to think of it, this selfless dedication to art—had not been quite enough. For early this morning had come the ominous call from Mike Katzman to suggest that perhaps "Me, Myself and I" was not after all the best "venue" for Yolanda "career-wise just now." Yolanda had not liked the sound of that.

"Something smells fishy," she confided to Letty, who, sensing her mother's angst, proceeded to bargain for the day off from the renowned University Pre-School.

With Letty in hand, Yolanda had walked down to the corner and bought the newspaper to see the column for herself. Standing in a doorway out of the sharp Spring wind, Yolanda tore open the paper. The intensity of her disappointment was such that she grabbed Letty in her arms and dashed heedlessly across the street, struggling through the broken door of an ill-smelling telephone booth to vent her spleen.

"Well, as I said," her agent began, but Yolanda had already hung up the phone. So, she was not to be the next "Me, Myself and I" columnist after all; for that job—and here she rattled the newspaper at the heavens—had that very morning changed hands.

How had she gotten through the day, Yolanda now wondered. This was to have been her crowning moment, and to have it snatched away so near realization was too cruel. I deserve better, Yolanda thought. It had taken her several hours of consultation with Letty before she felt able to sit down and actually read the offending column all the way through. And offended she was. "Letty," she said through gritted teeth, "you simply will not believe this."

Letty looked up wearily from the scotch tape collage she was working on, aware that she was now about to listen not simply to the article itself, but once more to her mother's aggrieved lament; for Yolanda's pique was in full flower. Letty knew her numbers and figured creatively that this would take much longer than she wanted; "I have to go to the bathroom," Letty said, running from the room.

Yolanda threw herself down on the daybed. She was mortified. She searched the column in vain for some mention of the writer's childhood fears, of her high school crush, of her husband's hobbies, of her tawny-haired, brown-legged daughter, of her aging parent. But no, nothing of this kind at all. More disturbing still was an odd stylistic tick. The column was noteworthy for its shortage of certain personal pronouns, and this, Yolanda muttered, outraged, in a column called "Me, Myself, and I." Clearly the writer did not understand what Yolanda was born knowing—that to personalize, to colloquialize, to banish the world, this was writing.

The doorbell rang and she heard Letitia running down the hall. What a sturdy sense of self the child was developing, Yolanda thought, judging by the sound and direction of Letty's footsteps that her daughter had only used the bathroom as a ruse to make her escape. She must remember to tell Ian. My God, she thought appreciatively, I don't think I did anything like that at the age of four. She pushed herself to her knees and stared into the pewter-framed mirror that hung over the daybed, pleased to note there few signs of the distress she felt within. Actually, I look quite triumphant, she thought, putting a hand to her flushed cheek. She made a mental note of the dichotomy.

Apparently Paul had not come alone. Only then did Yolanda remember that she had invited the girl to live with them, her niece, Rosie. Now this would no longer be desirable, would in fact constitute an unwelcome intrusion. But what would Letty say? She would have been a lot less willing to face the wrath of her daughter's disappointment had she not had the video store card, unplayed, up her sleeve. Nevertheless, upon catching sight of Letty, she immediately saw that whatever confidence she had been able to muster was likely to have been misplaced. Letty's face was red, her long hair in tangled disarray, as if it had been but recently twined, Ophelia-like, with wild flowers. For a moment Yolanda quaked at the sight. Much, she sighed, would be demanded of her.

"No suitcase, no suitcase," Letty wailed upon seeing her mother.

Yolanda took in the group. What is she doing here, Yolanda wondered of the pale, ill-attired woman Paul introduced as Frieda Zale. Then she turned her attention to her daughter. "What are you talking about, bunny?" she asked Letty so sweetly, so sympathetically, that the little girl really thought she did not know.

"Look, Mommy," she sobbed, the words strangling her, "n-n-not staying." She took Rosie's hand and pulled her arm toward Yolanda. "S-s-su-suitcase...," she moaned.

"Something has turned up," Paul told his sister with a warning look in Letty's direction. "I think I know where she is."

"I want her tooooo." Letty jumped up and down at her mother's side.

Yolanda turned away with a look of indulgent exasperation to usher the others down the hall into the living room, calling casually over her shoulder, "Honey, Mommy was disappointed today, too, remember. Now you know how I feel."

The lives of other women were largely opaque to Frieda. She wondered briefly whether her hostess, seemingly so self-possessed, had suffered a real disappointment earlier or whether this was merely a mother's pedagogy. Frieda's own sense of accelerating anticipation—the simple knowledge that they were going in the morning—meant leaving disappointment behind among the emotions belonging to another life. All was now prelude. She imagined the things other women did to get ready for a trip, and felt a kinship with these travelers despite her own inability to do anything to get herself ready. I'll get up very early, she vowed, trailing Paul and Yolanda closely, torn in her mind between her own thoughts and the vague desire to make some impression on Paul's sister.

"I don't hear anything," Paul said, stopping suddenly in front of a closed door and cupping his ear.

"Please," Yolanda commanded, and stopped too.

But Frieda did not stop—and stepped with distracted force on Yolanda's heel causing the latter to pitch forward out of her scuffed slip-on and come down hard on one knee. Yolanda rose quickly, awkwardly, declining Paul's outstretched hand, and turned on her pursuer. "What do you think you're...." she began heatedly, lifting her head with a sharp intake of breath and looking down her nose to a point where she expected to see a shame-faced Letitia.

"Sorry, I'm sorry," Frieda was saying, "I was thinking," she did not want to say that she had been thinking of herself as Yolanda's sister-in-law, "I was looking at this, this.... I'm sorry."

"Oh, do you like it?" Yolanda asked graciously, stepping to her side. "It's something we brought back from the Emirates. Ian chose it. You'll find he has marvelous taste in these things."

The social strength in Yolanda's voice acted as a balm on Frieda's flushed embarrassment. For a moment she was convinced that her hostess already cared for her, that she had suddenly become all but part of the Silverman-Silbermann's inner circle; best of all, she heard the promise in Yolanda's suggestion that she would be in a position to discover for herself the quality of Ian's taste. There was futurity there.

How rooted in reality Yolanda appeared to her. The effect was paradoxical. There was comfort in it, but discomfort too. In the implied contrast between them, Frieda's psyche felt nearly weightless in Yolanda's presence, while her body, taking up the slack, felt gross and clumsy. This was not a pleasant way to live.

"I don't know anything about art," Frieda parodied in her patented monotone, "but I know what I like." She smiled to underline her mimicry, but Yolanda had already turned back to Paul.

"We had to return the dog. It was a trauma. It really was. He bit Ian."

"She," Paul corrected maliciously.

"Cats are different that way," Frieda said after a moment, trying her best.

Yolanda gave her a cool, uncomprehending look, and Frieda's heart sank. Why could she not curb this desire to make herself known?! It was always a mistake. Yolanda frowned. "Letty, get up from that floor," she called out. "It's cold." Alone at the end of the hall now, Letty had taken up a position lying on her back in the center of the small foyer. "Letty's been very upset about it," Yolanda told Paul with lowered voice. "I think she had already bonded." Frieda might have murmured something appropriate here, but she did not.

"How is Ian?" Paul asked kindly, provoking an admiring glance from Frieda. She looked forward to the day she might ally herself forever with such a socially adept lover.

"He took it very well. But all the same, we've decided no dog. What if it had been Letty?"

"I won't be coming here," Rosie broke in impatiently, speaking for the first time, "we're leaving in the morning."

"You're giving up your search?" Yolanda reproached her on general principles—youth's selfishness and inconstancy. Certainly this girl would be no role model for her Letitia.

"Just temporarily," Frieda, stung on behalf of her young charge, answered in her stead, "it's going into abatement."

Yolanda gave her a brief, startled glance. "So, what happened?" she asked Paul.

It was only now, sitting in the living room listening, toying with the leaves of the nearby Dracaena, that Frieda realized for the first time that radical politics was alive in

America. According to Rosie, Lois Silverman was the object of "a nation-wide manhunt."

"Slash womanhunt," Frieda emended Rosie's cliché, making a stab at sociability.

Yolanda who had been about to roll right over this interruption, turned and put a cool hand on Frieda's arm instead. "Exactly! Womanhunt!" She looked at Frieda with new eyes. "What do you do, Freda?"

"Frieda," Paul corrected. "Frieda is a waitress," Paul said formally, specifically aware for the first time how little justice this job description did her.

"No she isn't," Yolanda said with absolute certainty.

"Yes, she is. She works at Nini's Pizza," Rosie capped it with her usual stolid factuality.

Yolanda got up and looked down the hall to the front door. When she sat down again, it was at the other end of the sofa next to Paul. "Well, for G-d's sake, don't tell Letty. It's taken me months to convince her she doesn't want to be a waitperson when she grows up."

"Waitperson," Frieda echoed. Her mind was awhirl, but the words refused to precipitate as conversational material.

"I've been eating lunch there," Paul came to her rescue with this heartfelt explanation.

Yolanda leaned forward. "As a woman who is a writer and a writer who is a woman and a mother who is a writer and so forth, I find I often don't have the time for lunch. It's a problem."

Frieda might have said, Oh, how interesting; but neither these nor any other words suggested themselves to her by way of reply, and she remained mute.

"And you live in the same building too," Yolanda mused. "Of course, I don't do much with coincidence, but it has its place. I find it breaks a mood, though."

"That's a coincidence," Frieda joked, relieved, "I do too."

As if on cue, Letty entered the room. She had rolled the front page of *The New York Times* into the band of her skirt and carried a paper cup decorated with a Disney motif. "I'm a orphan," she announced to the room at large. "Does anyone have some little moneys for me?"

Frieda reached into the pocket of her blue jeans for a piece of change and held it out for Letty to see. The little girl approached her, unsmiling.

"Letty knows that's called a dime, don't you, Bunny?" Yolanda put in hurriedly, affronted on her daughter's behalf.

"I'm an orphan, too," Frieda said and dropped the coin into the paper cup.

Letty gave her a surprised look. "You keep this little money," she instructed gently. "You need money, too." She took the dime out of the cup.

"No, you keep it. I'm a generous orphan."

"No, you. Me gerrous, me." She held the coin out. "Do you want to see my room?"

"Not now, Letty," her mother ruled, giving up all hope for a brief visit. It would be inhospitable, she saw now, not to offer their guests some refreshment.

It was a moment Frieda had been waiting for. Indeed she had silently rehearsed an appropriate response. And still she was unprepared. She looked to Paul.

"Ian always has good beer," Paul flattered Yolanda by extension, and Frieda took the cue.

Meanwhile, Letty had been tearing the newspaper from her skirt. "I'm a waitress now," she informed Frieda, running out of the room behind her mother.

"I'm a waitress too," Frieda called after her.

Letty stopped in the doorway and looked back uncertainly. Then, suddenly, she began to shriek, "No, no. Orphan, orphan, orphan." Her face contorted with anger and hurt and she started to sob.

Frieda's heart sank once more. Clearly, she lacked the common touch. Then Rosie, with a reputation to maintain where child care was concerned, took her cousin by the hand promising that they would do again all the things they had done together on her former visit. Letty, who even at that tender age was not immune to the allure of an earlier, better day, went with her willingly, but not before throwing a final betrayed look in Frieda's direction.

"Alone at last," Paul said, walking over to put his hand on the nape of her neck.

Frieda jumped at his touch. Did his remark signify pleasure or complaint, she wondered automatically, irrationally, and was relieved to find that a reservoir of confidence in the simple meaning of his words did seem finally to be building. Thus she was able to swallow an uneasy retort, and relax for just a moment against the steady pressure of his hand.

When Yolanda returned with the drinks and a bowl of unsalted nuts, she was surprised to find Paul seated on the broad upholstered arm of Frieda's chair. It occurred to her that perhaps this pale, awkward Frieda would be making the drive out to see Lois with him. How could that be, she wondered, seeing in Frieda no trace of the polish and style to which Paul had formerly aspired. She decided to inquire after his route, hoping thereby to gain a general description of the travel plan.

"We'll drive as far as Ashtabula tomorrow," Paul said.

"Why on earth Ashtabula?

"It's a place to stop, and Frieda...."

"I've always wanted to spend a night in Ashtabula, Ohio," Frieda broke in now that Paul had broached the subject.

"Whatever for," Yolanda asked with ill-disguised disdain, looking full into Frieda's eager face.

Frieda smiled at Paul. "The reason is obscure." She attempted to engage Yolanda. "Have you ever noticed how often that's true?"

"As a writer, of course, I know that obscurity has its uses." Yolanda watched Letty walk across the room toward the piano bench holding a glass of coca cola before her. That girl is a ballet dancer in the making, she thought. She noticed that Paul's eyes were on Letty as well. "Ballet dancer, don't you think," she said to him in an undertone as Letty passed.

Paul's thoughts were far away. "Kigali," he replied.

"Is she the one who just defected?" Yolanda asked, nearly impressed.

Frieda looked her straight in the face. "Your brother can be very obscure," she observed confidentially, happily.

Later that evening Yolanda went back to her writing room. The electric typewriter hummed at the ready, companionable, welcoming. It was law with Yolanda that once the machine was on, a sheet of paper inserted, it stayed on until she went to bed. Though she did not quite attribute a religious significance to this habit of hers, she had seen fit to include it in a short piece she had written on "a writer's rituals." She let the room stay dark now and sat down in front of the typewriter, a world unto herself. She sighed deeply, letting her fingers tap lightly, almost idly, one key and then another. Soon the page was filled with words. And there was not a one of them, from the shortest to the longest, individually or in combination, which did not speak well of her.

CHAPTER TWENTY-TWO

Waiting for the Sunrise

Rosie had decided to remain in her room. She had never stayed the night in a motel before. Though she and Lois had travelled a great deal, motels were anathema to Lois. They might use the bathrooms and the telephones Lois had explained to her; but we use them, they don't use us. Rosie sighed. Lois would stay with friends, or friends of friends, or even enemies of friends, or she wouldn't stay at all. Sometimes this meant driving miles—even states—out of their way, but Lois was adamant. Rosie could remember one hot, hot summer when they passed up countless motel swimming pools and inviting air conditioned rooms to end up in the middle of nowhere in a sweltering attic bedroom where, as Rosie heard it, large bats dove against the flimsy window screen all night long.

Luxuriating now, Rosie tuned the television set and lay back on the bed to watch, and wait for tomorrow. Her skin prickled at the thought. These motel walls are thick she noted, for she could hear nothing of Paul and Frieda next door preparing to go down to the Wagon Wheel lounge. She had been half-surprised at their sharing a room, for study them as she might—and she had damn little else to do all day in the backseat of the car—she had discerned few signs that this man and woman were any more linked to each other than either of them was to her. Nor had she been aware of any particular signs of their intimacy in Chicago, although this perhaps reflected the general state of her consciousness as accurately as the generosity of her imagination. Yeah, but are they making it, Rosie asked herself idly.

What a bore the day had been. She had wanted them to just drive the hell wherever they were going, but, no, Paul was determined, as he told her, to make the trip interesting. "I'm not a nerd," Rosie had remonstrated. Nevertheless, he had insisted on leaving the interstate highway outside of Sandusky, Ohio to visit the birthplace of Thomas Edison near Milan, and again beyond Cleveland to make a stop at President James A. Garfield's home. "What you think is interesting I think is boring," Rosie had told them frankly when they returned full of facts to the car where she was waiting. "A," she said as they resumed their trip, "the only Garfield I ever heard of is a cat."

Now she tried not to think about Lois. When that seemed impossible, she urged herself to think only of Lois as she had been, cursing in the same breath Simon and Willis who were, she was sure, the agents of their own destruction. And responsible for all that—nameless—which would now follow. Soon she began to weep. I told you not to think of that, she admonished herself tearfully, flipping the television channels against the future, seeking comfort and stimulation at once.

I've had a strange life, she thought, as she watched a young boy eat a dish of Jell-O pudding. Who else in the world had a mother who didn't eat lettuce or grapes, who read magazines no one had ever heard of, who made pieces of torn flag into potholders, who threw food at the TV during the nightly news, who hung out with two black guys in the middle of Maine. Freakin' Maine. She cried all the harder with the full force of knowing that this life-style was almost surely at an end. That's the part I told you not to think about, Rosie said aloud, focusing her tear-filled eyes on a Pontiac Firebird.

"Shhhhh!" the voice of an unseen hucksteress advised, "the Barbie Dream Bed comes with its own canopy...." Now suddenly here was Barbie enjoying breakfast on a tray in her Barbie Dream Bed. Rosie pulled her own pillow out and put it behind her head for a better vantage. Image followed image as her mind wandered between past and future. Everything looked so good to her—vital, glittering with potential, the very essentials of the good life. Yes! Things! she confirmed what had previously been but intuition, people want things. And here she echoed unwittingly the general sentiments of her grandfather Harry Silverman, who from modest beginnings had built a name and a fortune around things. Now came his granddaughter Rosie with a vision to do his heart good.

She reached for the brochure on the bedside table and held its pages to her forehead, invoking a touch of the adolescent sorcery Tom Waggoner had found so irresistible. What she was after was room service. A lifetime of television, not to mention the well-documented escapades of rock stars on tour, had left her with a very definite impression of the good life. I wish there was room service, she conjured with the energy of the fantasist. This refinement of her pleasure was to be denied her, however, and she settled for the soft-drink machine located specifically for her convenience just down the hall. As she approached it, a tall man carrying a cardboard ice bucket appeared in the dim corridor. He ran his hand back over his graying buzz-cut and smiled at her. He could be my father, Rosie thought automatically.

Indeed, hadn't she been feeling all day that they were on converging paths, that somehow it had been fated—she must lose a mother to gain a father. Yes, that would be it; after all these years, of course it was bound to be something unspeakably dramatic. Fate was not an everyday thing. Earlier, in the car, Paul had not said much about it; but it did seem that the plan for the morrow might include a glimpse—perhaps just time for a snapshot—of the well-regulated and blissful family unit that she had long projected as her own.

• • •

Lois's admiration for the work of the urban graffiti artists, already substantial, was growing by leaps and bounds. Though she had long since overcome her bourgeois bias against the desecration of private property, this did not, in the event, compensate for her lack of artistry. She sat on the edge of the bathtub, disconsolate, and studied her first attempt at the form. On the floor of the tub in large, shaky letters of cerulean blue she had written "create new institu" and then run out of space. "Righteous Violence" she tried again, this statement consorting poorly with the rubber daisies a former owner had appliquéd along the length of the porcelain. These homely yellow flowers, significantly the worse for wear, moved her inexplicably. "Love," she wrote on the mirror, and stared at herself for a long time.

She thought with amazement, as she had so often, of the time not so very long ago when the collapse of honky-Amerika had seemed imminent, a virtual certainty to her, to them all; no dream, it was going to happen—Power to the People—everybody taking to the streets, no longer afraid, it was definitely happening. She remembered the feeling. It was a high like no other.

And yet it hadn't happened. No matter what they did, it seemed, it was not enough to get the job done. Neither their love nor their hate, not commitment or confrontation or acts of crazed courage, not bombs, not miles of burning slum, no amount of dope or of rock or of fucking would bring it down; Amerika stood, ripe as ever. Lois nodded at herself in the mirror. Deep in her eyes she thought she could still detect a flicker of that innocent hope. She grimaced, reaching out to mark the mirror with her brush, and narrowing her eyes she attempted to sketch two eyes on the silver surface. "Keep the faith," she said aloud. Yes, I'm still out here. But not, she knew, for long.

She shook one of the spray cans and pointed it at the shower curtain, applying the paint with lazy circular motions of her arm, recalling brief moments of righteous ease, aiming at the wholesale recreation of the curtain in blue. It was a pure gesture, calm, controlled, destructive and satisfying. She sprayed and sprayed trying to reach every crevice in the cracked yellow plastic, listening to the sound of the spray, to the venomous hiss of the spray. And what about the toilet bowl, what about all that shit? Lois smiled somberly. Without moving, very relaxed now, just stretching out her arm, she aimed the can past the end of the shower curtain and the blue spray drifted where it would onto the white fixture.

With no place to sit now, she leaned back against the door and took in her handiwork, disappointed to see how little of the small bathroom remained untouched by her art. But, much as their empty walls beckoned, she would not consider moving on to kitchen or bedroom. No, the little man had said very clearly, 'I see blues in the bathroom.' In order to be effective, her protest must be clear and focused, must not be open to interpretation. She thought back to the Convention and the debate that had raged among them— where to plant the little powder charge. The implications of choosing the hotel's Ladies' Room instead of the Men's Room were discussed at length. And what message exactly ought the Ladies Room mirror to bear, that too was debated fruitfully. Her own choice, she could still remember, had been, "Off the Pigs"; in the end they had gone with a quote from Che, and Lois herself had written it on the mirror in a large, lipstick hand.

Her understanding had been imperfect at the time; nevertheless, she still had the distinct impression that Che's sentiment must be as true now as ever. Her own idea of reality, if it came to that, was less a Marxist and more a practical matter. I see what I see, she noted for the millionth time, then dipped a new brush into a can of midnight Blue enamel and printed Che's words on the inside of the bathroom door: "We must work so love of humanity is transformed into deeds."

The letters were smaller, less bold than she intended; and yet for Lois a better world would always be the big idea.

Suddenly, she wondered what time it was. She must work on her letter to Rosie. She tipped the paint can over and around the bowl of the sink. Blue enough for you, you bitch? Her ex-sister-in-law, she had no doubt, had always voted to benefit the rich and disempower the poor. Lois let the can fall to the floor.

She sat down at the kitchen table with a coffee-stained pad she had found in one of the drawers and began to write immediately: "I'm shot Rosie. These days I don't even want to eat a tuna sandwich. Didn't Rosa say something like 'exhausting idealism'? I need to move on and I've found a way. It's the prison so-called population—that's where I need to be. *With them.* Actual deeds will be possible there.

Lois's misremembered quote aside, this was unlikely to be an argument that Rosie would find persuasive. Although well-versed in a rote kind of way in her mother's ideology, Rosie had never really grasped the underlying emotional commitment—Lois's need to be *with them*, to live out devotion, to make the world a better place. Indeed, Rosie was quite impervious to that appeal, seeking, in so far as she was able, to distance herself from them through her determined consumerism. Lois loved her daughter none the less for this failing. And in closing the letter, she told her so.

The moment had come and now all at once Lois was a laggard. She felt heavy, unwilling to leave the kitchen table. She turned her letter to Rosie over and over in her hands as if she could impart to it something of the physicality of her motherhood. Finally, she forced herself up and looked in the refrigerator. There was the jug of wine she had bought and the eggs and bacon, pound cake, and milk for their coffee. He used to like pound cake for breakfast, she had remembered, and coffee very light. She went upstairs and pulled the bedspread up and opened the window to the sharp air and looked at herself in the mirror over the dresser. I don't look very good, she mused, but before too long I'm probably going to look a whole lot worse.

With this grim thought to energize her she went out to the car and drove to the telephone booth she had scouted for this purpose. She dialed Ernie Blyda's number. Moments later Special Agent Randall "Rip" Parks was on the telephone. She would give herself up to him. To him. Again. She returned to the farm house to wait—steady in her faith and feeling strong once more.

• • •

Though the motel's Wagon Wheel Lounge was a room entirely lacking in allure, it was for Frieda all the more romantic for that. She reveled in the decor, about which there was such an unmistakable sense of other people's reality—the littered red carpet, black vinyl upholstery, wet tables and unlit hurricane lamps. Off to one side, a young man at an electronic piano entertained them with songs of love; the small dance floor was empty. Frieda studied the other patrons—their lives shone through them—the room surged with the intensity of their presence, and this swell, along with the drink and the music, swept her up in its current. Frieda and Paul had never had such a good time together.

The drive had been a high point for Frieda. Even Rosie's endless carping from the backseat could not ruin it for her. Paul had promised places of interest and, to her astonished delight, the places had been of interest. What were the chances of that happening, she wondered, a bit giddy to think that she and Paul were building a shared history of such quality. President Garfield's assassination had come as a shock. The President's own park ranger had shown them the white rose wreath Queen Victoria had sent for the state funeral. Mrs. Garfield had had it dipped in wax and there it was. Frieda gaped at this tender gesture of remembrance. She contemplated her own anxious restraint, the very absence of tenderness in her hasty moves. Perhaps this unfortunate, ungenerous lack of ease could yet be rectified.

As they drove, Frieda began to see Paul in a more nuanced light and Paul began to see himself in something of his old light. Frieda touched his hand on the steering wheel. His hand looks good on the steering wheel, she thought. "Do you happen to know how they attach the tires on those big eighteen-wheelers?" she asked him.

"Very, very tightly." Paul took her hand. Frieda looked out the window overwhelmed with the awareness of how precisely his action matched his words. My hand is rough and dry was Frieda's thought but she did not pull her hand away.

"That's worth knowing," Frieda told him happily; indeed, she thought, with a mental nod to Dr. O.H., it was worth quite a lot.

The barmaid set their drinks down on the glistening table. There was a nervy excitement in the air; it stoked them, heightened their color, turned them giddy or deadly earnest on a whim.

"Bujumbura," Paul said with a tender look Africa alone could not account for.

"Snohomish, Puyallup, Enumclaw," Frieda volleyed to his delight. And she did pause here to credit Kevin-for-crying-out-loud; Kevin who had developed his love of stamps during a Washington state childhood.

While not material with which the curious barmaid could do much, their conversation seemed to both of them stimulating, deeply satisfying discourse, leading them just where they wanted to go. Paul realized suddenly that he was very much himself, and that Frieda was coming near to him, becoming very dear to him. As for Frieda, there were amid these fragmentary exchanges, instants of highly charged reality, treasured moments when she felt, yes! this is what life is—this.

There was, too, something present this evening which emboldened them to think that love's promise might yet hold all that the young piano man would have them believe. Just after midnight, Frieda and Paul stepped onto the dance floor for the first time. They swayed to a melody equally familiar to them both, clasped together closely, hanging on to each other for dear life.

Made in the USA
Las Vegas, NV
17 September 2022

55369297R00152